Realm
of the
Forgotten

Emma Shelford

This is a work of fiction. Names, characters, places, and incidents either are the product of the author's imagination or are used factitiously, and any resemblance to any persons, living or dead, business establishments, events, or locales is entirely coincidental.

REALM OF THE FORGOTTEN

www.emmashelford.com

First edition: May 2018
ISBN: 978-1986646260

For Ronya,
for the gift of time

Chapter 1

The moon burned with a cold and pale intensity, mirrored in a frozen puddle. Bare linden trees sent twisted shadows across a narrow, paved road through a small wood. A badger snuffled nearby, but silence reigned with its departure.

A soft ripping sound emerged in the nighttime stillness. It would have sounded like the finest gossamer fabric being rent in two, had anyone been around to hear it. A hole in the fabric of the world appeared in the shadows of a tall linden. Long strips of existence hung from the opening. There were more trees on the other side, trees that were dense and covered in a thick layer of snow, which only accentuated the darkness of their massive trunks.

A breeze wafted through the still night. The torn strips fluttered, attracting a passing cat. The cat stopped, and its hackles rose. When it detected no threat, it paced forward and batted at the ragged pieces. A moment's indecision, and then the cat leaped nimbly through the hole.

Silence fell once more. A car passed on a distant road.

Moments stretched into minutes in the darkness.

A howl pierced the night through the opening. Seconds later, the cat shot out of the hole. It hissed and spat as it barreled down the road and out of sight. Another howl disturbed the darkness.

***

Queen Isolde of the Velvet Woods sat on a velvet-covered stool before her gilded vanity and sighed in contentment.

"The dancing was divine tonight. Lord Connell has such grace and poise—we're fortunate he chose to join us for the solstice festivities." She pulled off her earrings, then leaned her head forward to expose her neck. "Unclasp my necklace, please, darling."

"Of course." Corann, Isolde's advisor and consort, stood from his seat on the bed and fiddled with the clasp. The necklace of garnets slithered down Isolde's throat and landed in her waiting hands. Corann stroked the back of Isolde's neck lightly, and she smiled into the mirror at the dark-haired man behind her.

Corann looked more closely at Isolde. She was thinner than usual, her high cheekbones even more distinct, but perhaps it was a trick of the candlelight.

"Has the kitchen completed their plans for the confectionary? I gave them my instructions yesterday, but they must decide upon details." She pulled three long hairpins of polished bone out of her hair, and black locks cascaded down her back. The white strands at her temple flowed thicker than ever. "I have a vision of merengue swans floating down an icy waterfall of spun sugar."

"I'm sure it will be stunning," said Corann. He lay his hands on her shoulders. Under the silk of her plum-colored gown, her body trembled.

"Why are you shaking?" he asked. "Do you feel poorly?"

"I'm fine, my love." She looked up at him and smiled. "Never better."

Corann frowned but let the matter slide.

"Shall we have an outing tomorrow at the winter pavilion?" Isolde said. "If we tell the servants now, there will be enough time to prepare overnight. The pavilion is so dazzling in the snow, with a roaring fire in the hearth and boughs of winter ivy strung throughout."

"Perhaps." Corann traced Isolde's collarbone with one finger. This was no trick of the light—Isolde's bone stood out sharply from the sunken flesh surrounding it.

"Have you given any more thought to replacing the restoration spell's magic?" he asked.

"That's a weighty topic before bed." Isolde picked up a boar-bristle brush and pulled it through her hair.

"We must discuss it sometime. The spell powers the realm entirely. But it won't last forever, and we need an alternative defense for the realm."

"Yes, yes." Isolde looked annoyed. "It must be dealt with one day. But it's not necessary to implement that sort of upheaval now, not when the realm is functioning so smoothly."

Corann's voice held a bite of impatience.

"That day will come sooner than you think. What about having a reserve army, as the Wintertree realm does?"

"And what will I give this army? Faolan has far more resources than I do."

"What about the eternal song of the Whitecliff realm? Their magical defense is powered by the continuous singing of a rotation of their realm's inhabitants."

"And they train their children from birth to sing sweetly enough for the magic to properly coalesce. No, singing won't do."

"What about—" Corann started, but Isolde cut him off.

"We won't resolve this tonight. Let the restoration spell do its work, and I'll worry about the next steps when I need to."

"But—"

"Leave it, Corann." Isolde's voice was firm but kindly. "Don't trouble yourself over difficulties that do not exist yet." She put down her hair brush. "Did you see Lady Alanna's gown? I thought the color very fine, although the cut did nothing for her figure."

Corann turned his face away from the mirror to hide his expression of mutinous frustration. When he had mastered his emotions, he turned back with a forced smile.

"Indeed. If you'll excuse me, my lady, there is something I must attend to."

He bowed stiffly at Isolde's back and fled the room before Isolde could respond. She turned and stared, openmouthed, after Corann.

***

Gwen Cooper leaned back into the tweed couch with a sigh and slid off the hair elastic that fastened the end of her long braid, colorful blue strands nestled in the black tresses. Her father Alan settled comfortably beside her.

"It was a long flight, but food did wonders," he said. "Thanks for the delicious dinner, Aunty Ada. You outdid yourself."

Gwen's great-aunt, seated in a wingback chair beside the crackling fire, clucked at her nephew. She looked over her gold-rimmed glasses and arched a penciled eyebrow from under tight iron-gray curls.

"Hardly. You flew halfway around the world to visit me. The least I could do was toss a roast in the oven." She smiled to soften her words.

"Yes, thanks, Aunty Ada," Gwen said. "Tasting your food reminds me of how limited my own cooking skills are. Now that I've moved out of the house, my menu is pretty boring."

"That's no good. I'll give you a few lessons while you're here for the holidays," Ada said kindly. "Although, I do admit it's difficult to bother cooking for one. Ever since Gerald died in September, well..." Her normally strong voice trailed off, until she said firmly, "I can't cook for a husband anymore, but cooking for company is even more pleasurable. You're more complimentary, for one. The old sod loved to gripe about my scrambled eggs."

Alan chuckled.

"I'm happy to eat anything and everything you cook. I'm glad we could reconnect, even if it took a funeral to finally make Christmas plans."

"Hey, Aunty Ada and I had a nice visit in May, remember?" Gwen said in protest. "I'm far more social than you, apparently."

"So you did, so you did," Alan said. "You're more social than your grandmother, at any rate."

"Now, now, no need to point fingers at those who can't be here to defend themselves. My sister, bless her soul, was no great shakes at correspondence, but then neither was I." Ada leaned forward to place a new log on the fire. "No point in regretting the past. But Gwen, dear, you were here in August as well, do you recall? What was that for, again?"

"Umm." Gwen glanced at her dad. The real reason for her summer visit had been because her Breenan friend Bran had magically pulled her to England from her home in Vancouver. "I was helping my boyfriend Aidan pack. He moved to Vancouver in September for school."

"That's right." Ada settled back in her chair. "He must be a hopeless romantic, to move across the globe for love."

Gwen laughed at this description of Aidan. She couldn't envision him writing soppy love poems for her, despite how tight-knit they had become. This past term had been blissful with Aidan so close—she really knew him now, and could only laugh at her past self, so nervous about their relationship's future.

"He came for the music program. It wasn't just for me. He's doing really well—I went to a recital and was really impressed."

"Hmm," said Ada in a knowing tone, but she left it at that. "And do you and your father have any plans to sightsee while you're here? The weather is terrible, unfortunately, so you'll have to make the best of it. The university's drama school is putting on their annual Christmas panto in a few days—you might want to take it in."

"That's a good idea," Alan said with a yawn. "Not too much tomorrow for me. Maybe a walk, Gwennie?"

"Sounds nice. Let's do it in the afternoon—I said I'd meet up with Aidan in the morning."

"That's right, you mentioned his mother lives near here," said Ada. "What was her name again?"

"Deirdre Lynch. She's a nurse."

"Hmm. I don't believe I've met her." Ada sat up straight in her chair and pierced Gwen and Alan with her hazel eyes over narrow glasses. "Take care on your walk, you two. There have been reports of wild animals lurking in back gardens. Really nasty ones. The word wolf has been bandied about, but it's far more likely that some large dogs have gone feral than wolves have recovered from extinction. All the same, keep a sharp eye."

"Thanks for the warning," said Alan, his jaw cracking in another huge yawn. "A mauling is not what I want for Christmas. Boy, I'm beat. I think I'll turn in now."

"I'll retire also," said Ada. "Your beds should be made."

"Thanks, Aunty Ada. Coming, Gwen?"

"If it's all right, I might watch some TV before I turn in."

***

Gwen was a strange mix of exhausted and wired, as if her limp brain had been pulsed with a jolt of electricity. She stared at the remote for a minute, then pushed buttons at random until the television flickered on. A talking head in a navy-blue suit monologued in a soothing British accent about local politics. Gwen switched the channel and fiddled with a locket around her neck absently. She had asked her Breenan mother, Isolde, to give her the locket after learning that Isolde could use the magic within it to create portals and kidnap humans. She had taken to wearing it ever since her last visit to the Otherworld in August—its small weight on her chest somehow felt right. Aidan had laughed in disbelief at that, and she couldn't explain it. Flick, flick, she needed something brainless, not news nor some complicated drama series, flick, flick...

A reality game show flickered onto the television. Gwen stopped pressing buttons and settled into the cushions. It was a dance competition show—Gwen remembered vaguely that it was called Dance Till You Drop, or at least the American version was—and the contestants were garbed in excessively bright costumes, gamely stepping to the beat. Gwen figured it must be season eleven by now.

Gwen's eyes glazed over, and she let the colors assault her brain in a blur. Hopefully this would calm her body enough to sleep.

After a few minutes of flailing limbs and pounding feet, the show cut to a backstage shot. The contestants were in a large dance studio practicing moves under the watchful eye of their instructor. He was a slight man with sharp features, in his late thirties, and his hair was as dark as Gwen's own. He was dressed in tight-fitting pants and a sleeveless top that exposed toned biceps and much of his shoulders. The man turned to comment on a pair of dancers near him, and Gwen blinked in surprise. She sat up.

On the man's left shoulder, in precisely the same spot as on Gwen's own, a green tattoo sprawled. She stared for a moment to make sure she wasn't mistaken, then she fumbled for her phone.

"Aidan!" she said when he answered. "Turn on the TV. Channel 16. Quick!"

"Uh, all right." Gwen heard him scrambling in the background, then the sound of the television. "It's on. What was so urgent about watching Dance Till You Drop? If you're a closet super-fan, we might have to reconsider our relationship."

"No, of course not. Look at the black-haired instructor. Do you see? On his shoulder?"

Aidan waited until the man turned. His shoulder was clearly visible for a moment, and Aidan drew in his breath sharply.

"You saw it, right?" Gwen said. Her heart pounded fiercely. So much for calming down before sleep.

"Yeah," Aidan breathed. "He's a Breenan."

They watched the man in silence for a few more moments. A commercial broke their trance.

"Do you know what episode this is?" Aidan asked.

"Not a clue."

"All right, hold on a minute."

Gwen heard the click-tapping of a computer keyboard. She frowned, and her tired brain tried to process this information. There were more Breenan living in the human world? Was this man full Breenan or half? How many tattoos lay hidden under shirt collars and long sleeves?

"I have it." Aidan said with repressed excitement. "I

have his name. It's Finn Sayward."

"What? That was quick." Gwen shifted on the couch. "Now what?"

"Hold on." More tapping, then Aidan said, "I have his home address. It's in the outskirts of London. Are you busy tomorrow?"

"What? You want to just turn up on his doorstep?"

"Why not? He's the first Breenan we've seen here. Aren't you curious what his story is?"

"Well, sure, but…"

"Come on, Gwen. Let's do it. I'll pick you up tomorrow morning?"

The show was running once more, and Gwen stared at the face of the unknown Breenan man. Who was he? A wave of curiosity threatened to overwhelm her. She gripped the phone tightly.

"Okay. I'll be ready at ten."

***

Gwen peered out of the windshield, then again at her phone.

"The map says we're close," she said. "Hey, if you turn left here, I think it's a shortcut."

"All right." Aidan started to turn, then swerved sharply forward again. "One way. We'll have to take the long way."

"What are we going to say to him?" Gwen tapped her fingers nervously on the armrest. "Do we come about it roundabout? Or ask straight up?"

"Nice to meet you. Lovely day. Are you from another

14

world?" Aidan leaned his head on the headrest contemplatively. "I don't see how else to do it."

"What if we ask him if he believes in…" Gwen trailed off. Believe in what? Magic? Faeries? Parallel universes?

"We'll have to play it by ear. Where do I turn?"

"Just up here."

Gwen wrung her hands together as Aidan slowed to a stop outside a row of townhouses. Steps led up to black doors, each with a tarnished number in the center.

"Number forty-five, there it is," Gwen said quietly. They sat in silence for a minute. Aidan broke the stillness.

"Come on, he won't bite." A frown crossed his features. "I don't know, perhaps he will. He could be a raving lunatic, for all we know. Bodies in the basement."

Gwen swatted his arm.

"Now you're just bugging me. Let's get this over with."

Gwen opened the car door and stood, enjoying the stretch in her cramped legs. Short steps led to the front door, which loomed above her. She mentally shook herself and marched toward the stairs.

Halfway up, Aidan grabbed her arm.

"Look, a neighbor," he hissed, then raised his voice. "Good morning."

A man holding a paper bag of groceries on the next-door steps turned their way. A small boy wearing a green knitted hat peered out from behind his legs.

"Morning." He shifted the groceries to one arm.

"We're looking for Finn Sayward. Do you know if this is the right address?"

"That's the one. Finn's lived there for ages, since before we moved in, and we've been here for almost five years." The neighbor nodded.

Gwen wasn't sure if she felt relieved or anxious that this was the right place.

"Know him well?" Aidan asked.

"Can't say that I do. Are you friends of his?" The neighbor looked momentarily suspicious.

"Distant relations," Gwen said after a pause. The man relaxed.

"Well, I don't know if anyone really knows him well. Never seen any family, nor friends neither. He's a nice enough bloke but keeps himself to himself. Not what you'd call chatty." He ruffled the boy's hair absentmindedly when the boy plucked at his coat.

"I'm glad we came, then," said Aidan. "It sounds as if he could use some Christmas cheer."

"I reckon he could. If he's not at home, try the White Hart, the pub on the next street." He pointed down the road. "He's often there. They serve a nice meat pie, if you're hungry. Happy Christmas to you."

"And to you," said Aidan. The man nodded and slid his key into the lock. The boy stared at them through the doorway as the door closed.

Aidan lifted his fist to the door.

"Ready?" he asked Gwen, who nodded. Aidan rapped smartly on the black paint.

A silent minute passed. Aidan knocked again, louder this time. Nothing stirred.

"Well," said Aidan at last. "Time for a pint?"

***

It was lunchtime, and the warm pub was full and buzzing pleasantly with contented people anticipating the holidays. Exposed beams hung low over patrons' heads, and a warm glow shone through numerous stained-glass lamps over tables. Gwen shifted from foot to foot as she scanned the crowd.

"I can't tell if he's here," she said.

"Let's walk around. There are more rooms over here." Aidan led the way, then stopped. "Do you suppose we'd recognize him? What if he had makeup on for the telly?"

Gwen grabbed Aidan's arm.

"Look, at the bar," she whispered loudly to be heard over the din. "That man with black hair. He's alone."

"It could be," said Aidan doubtfully. "We'll have to get closer to truly know." He strode toward two empty bar stools beside the man.

"Aidan!" Gwen squeaked, but she scurried after him.

They slid into the seats, and Gwen sneaked a glance at the man's profile. A sharp nose and a narrow, almost gaunt face convinced her immediately that they had found Finn Sayward. He stared morosely into his pint, his plate of chips largely untouched before him. His quiet melancholy was a striking contrast to the happy crowd behind him.

Aidan glanced at Gwen, and she nodded once. He turned to Finn.

"Hello, mate."

Finn glanced up briefly with disinterest.

"Hello."

"What's good on the menu? We're passing through."

Finn waved at his plate.

"The chips are good." He picked one up and took a

resolute bite, perhaps more to stop the conversation than because he was hungry. Aidan glanced at Gwen in mute appeal.

"I think I saw you on Dance Till You Drop," Gwen blurted out. "You're Finn Sayward, right?"

"That's me." He took a swig of his pint with a practiced grace. Gwen wondered how many he'd had already. "Fans, are you?"

"Oh, yes, big fans," Gwen said. She dithered for a moment, then said, "I noticed your tattoo last episode. I really liked it. Where did you have it done?"

"Nowhere nearby."

"Can I see it?"

"What, now?" Finn said. When Gwen nodded, he shrugged. "Whatever, all right."

He started to unbutton his shirt. The bartender bustled over.

"Oi! No shirt, no service. Do I have to cut you off, Sayward?"

Finn waved him away and rebuttoned his shirt. A frown crossed his face.

"Why did you want to see it?"

Gwen looked him in the eye.

"Because I have one just like it."

Chapter 2

Gwen watched as the meaning of her words slowly sunk into Finn's drink-befuddled brain. First, confusion; then, suspicion; finally, a blossoming of disbelieving hope, like the sun peeking through a rent in storm clouds. He looked at Aidan.

"You too?" he asked hoarsely. Aidan nodded. Finn stood abruptly, grabbed his coat, and pulled Aidan's arm up roughly. "Come. Let's find somewhere quiet."

Gwen trotted after Finn, who walked to the back of the pub with purposeful strides. A snug tucked into a corner had a cozy group of four on inset benches, drinking happily amid wood paneled walls hung with prints of hunting scenes.

"Snug's reserved now," Finn said abruptly. The other patrons looked affronted, and one of the men stood up and opened his mouth. Finn raised a hand and waved him off. Every one of the four took on a dazed expression and toddled out of the snug.

Gwen slid onto the bench. Finn was already seated and staring at them.

"Well?" he demanded. "What's your story?"

Gwen glanced at Aidan, who nodded at her.

"I have a Breenan mother, who left me on my human father's doorstep as a baby. Aidan's father is Breenan. We fell into the Otherworld last spring, by accident." Gwen pulled at the collar of her shirt to expose the edge of her tattoo. "That's where we got our marks."

"Let's see." Finn gestured to Aidan, who glanced around before he pulled off his sweater. Finn leaned in to examine the mark under his shirt, then sat back with an exhalation of amazement.

"Declan's son. What do you know? I'm the reason you exist, Aidan. I'm the half-blood who dragged Declan on my forays to the human world."

Aidan looked windblown by this pronouncement. He shrugged on his sweater. Finn took a long drink from the nearest glass.

"You're not full Breenan?" Gwen said. "Did you grow up here or in the Otherworld?"

"Otherworld. Human father whom I've never met. I tried to find him while I was here, of course, but a picture with no name isn't much to go on. I grew up with the forest people, although my mother was a queen. She visited occasionally." He took another drink, then gestured to Gwen. "Let's see yours."

Gwen pulled the collar of her shirt over her shoulder, stretching the fabric enough for Finn to see the mark. Finn leaned forward to look.

"Will wonders never cease," he said at last. He peered at Gwen's face for long enough that Gwen wriggled in discomfort. She let her collar spring back into place.

"What?"

"Well met, niece of mine." He took a drink while Gwen sat in stunned confusion. "Your grandmother, bless her flinty, overbearing, hypocritical heart, was my mother. Your mother Isolde is my sister. Not that I've ever met her, but there it is." He began to laugh, and even though there was little happiness in the sound, he suited a smile.

"That's crazy," Gwen said. She stared at her new-found uncle. Isolde had mentioned a half-human brother, but Gwen hadn't given him much thought. She could hardly think of what question to ask first. "Why did your mother keep you in the Otherworld and visit you? She made Isolde send me to my dad here."

"As I said, hypocritical." Finn stared moodily into his almost-empty drink.

"Why are you here?" said Aidan. "In the human world, I mean? If you grew up in the Otherworld?"

"Not by choice, that's for certain. Years ago, I came through on a lark, then my mother died unexpectedly and now I'm stuck here. You know, I left behind a beautiful wife, and a baby daughter too." He stared at his drink, and his eyes were moist. Gwen put a hand to her mouth.

"I'm so sorry."

"She's ten years old today. I should be there, in our little cottage in the valley of the Forbidden Lands. My wife Nialla would make apple tarts and Ione—well, I don't even know what she would like to do, I don't know her."

He looked so morose and heartbroken that Gwen cast about for a change of topic to distract him.

"What are the Forbidden Lands like?" All Gwen knew was that they were where the tribeless ones went, those

21

who received unusual marks in the Breenan coming-of-age ceremony.

"It's pretty there," he said vaguely. "Very pastoral."

Something seemed to click then, and Finn's eyes sharpened. He glanced between the two of them.

"You're both human-world born, right?"

"Yes."

"I'm not thinking straight. Too much drink. I assumed you were stuck here, but you're in the human world by choice." Finn shook his head in wonderment with a hopeful glint in his eyes. His hands gripped the edge of the table. "Your anchors, are they still alive? Isolde, Declan?"

"Yes," Gwen said. "I was going to ask if you'd like to go back. I know how to make portals."

Finn's breathing grew fast.

"Yes," he croaked. "Yes, yes, a thousand times yes." He slid along the bench until he sat next to Gwen. "Make it here, right now. It's the snug, no one will see."

"You want to leave right now?" Gwen glanced at Aidan, who shrugged. "Don't you need anything at your house?"

"The only things I care about are in the Otherworld. The rest can burn, as far as I'm concerned." He gripped Gwen's hand tightly. "Please, don't make me wait. Nine years is long enough."

"Okay, okay. Of course. But not here. And at least take some food. Aidan, go get the quickest food the kitchen has."

"Here." Finn passed Aidan his wallet. "Get a cold meat pie. And meet us behind the pub. Thanks, mate."

Aidan left, and Finn stood unsteadily.

"Are you sure you should go in this state?" Gwen said.

"The Otherworld is my home." He graced Gwen with a serene, blissful smile. "I'm going home."

Gwen smiled back and gave Finn her arm. She took his coat and pressed it into his hand.

"Here, you'll need this. It's snowing on the other side." Gwen frowned in thought. "If you have a daughter, could you have used her as an anchor? Does it work that way?"

"It might," said Finn. "I did try, but she lives in the Forbidden Lands, which is a place without magic. Nothing came of my attempts."

Aidan met them behind the pub. Gwen looked at Finn.

"It was nice to meet you, Uncle Finn." She grinned at the familiar title. Finn laughed.

"And you, niece of mine. You are always welcome at my home, but you'll have to visit me—I will never venture to the human world again." He took her hand with a sober expression. "Always travel together. I would hate to think of you stranded in a world you don't wish to be in."

Gwen nodded fervently.

"We will."

She squeezed his hand, then withdrew her own to hold it out in front of her. Her core warmed, and magic poured up her arm. The air fluttered as if in a breeze, then ripped. A large portal appeared before her.

"I hope you find your family," Gwen said. Finn stepped through the portal and turned with a hand raised.

"Thank you, Gwen and Aidan. And farewell."

Finn disappeared but the portal remained. Gwen frowned, then grabbed the edges of the world-fabric and pulled. The ragged edges slowly wove themselves together over the course of a minute, far slower than usual.

"I didn't think you'd have a family reunion today," Aidan said at last.

"No. Relatives keep popping out of the woodwork. I can't believe he's been away from his wife and daughter for so long. I'm glad I saw that TV show."

"I, for one, feel pretty good about our act of Christmas charity. Fancy trying that meat pie before we leave?"

"Lead the way."

***

Gwen carried her coat into the living room, where her father and Ada sat with cups of tea in their laps.

"Ready for that walk, Dad?"

"Sure. Let me grab my coat. Thanks for the tea, Aunty Ada."

"You're welcome, love. You two be careful out there. I don't suppose you've seen the news. Terrible weather blowing up suddenly, more so than usual. And don't forget those animals." Ada twisted her floral-patterned teacup in its saucer absentmindedly.

"Oh, yes, the wolves. Probably a big dog," Alan said with a chuckle. "Don't worry about us. We're from Canada. We can manage animals and weather."

"Look, I'll bring my toque," said Gwen, brandishing her knitted hat at Ada. "We're prepared. Come on, Dad."

They followed a path near Ada's house that led across a partially flooded field. They crossed a paved bicycle trail and then walked between two stiff-branched hedges. Beside the path in the middle of the next field was a cluster of white tents and tall lighting on poles with police tape draped around the whole collection. A hum of voices came from the tents, but no one was in sight. Gwen exchanged raised eyebrows with her father. When they walked closer, a security guard emerged from behind the closest tent. He held coffee in a Styrofoam cup and looked bored.

"Afternoon," said Alan. "What's the occasion? The weather's a bit grim for a campout."

"Don't I know it," he said glumly. "The sodding weather will be the death of me."

"It's nice out now," said Gwen. The sun shone over green fields from low in the sky.

"Yeah, it is now." The guard put emphasis on the last word. "From one minute to the next, I don't know if it will be snowing or hailing or raining."

"Sounds rough," Alan agreed. "What needs to be guarded so well in a cold December field?"

"Some sort of disturbance in the air. The experts called it a localized weather event—I call it bloody odd." The guard sniffed loudly and tucked his free hand under his arm. "It might be unsafe, so I'm here to stop people wandering into it by accident."

Gwen frowned, then her eyes widened. Disturbance in the air? Could it be a portal? She dismissed the idea almost immediately. Just because her thoughts jumped to otherworldly portals didn't mean that natural phenomenon weren't more likely.

"This disturbance," she said. "Does it come and go?"

"Might be a little smaller than when it was first discovered. It's going nowhere fast, though."

"Stay warm on your vigil," said Alan. He raised a hand with a cheery wave and they continued down the path. At the edge of the field, Gwen ducked behind the hedgerow. The chance of the disturbance being a portal was slim at best, but Gwen couldn't rest until she had ruled the possibility out.

"Make sure no one's coming, Dad," Gwen said. She brought her magic out from her core, envisioning Isolde as she did so. "I want to check if it's a portal in that tent."

"You're going through right now?" Alan said, staring at the portal with wariness and fascination.

"I'll just be a minute."

Before he could protest further, Gwen ducked through the waist-high opening and entered the Otherworld.

It was bitingly cold in the snowy woods, and Gwen pulled the zipper of her coat higher. The crunch of snow under her feet was muffled by the drifts piled high beside each tree trunk.

Gwen peered behind her through the silent forest. A strange glimmer shifted in the distance. Gwen looked around quickly. Nothing stirred, so she pushed through the snow toward the glimmer.

Her feet were wet and cold by the time she reached the portal. There was no mistaking that strange tear in the fabric of the world. The white canvas of the police tent was visible through the opening. A voice spoke from the other side and Gwen froze.

"Come on, it's time for a cuppa. This thing isn't going anywhere fast."

Gwen danced away from the portal until she heard footsteps, then the swish of the tent flap closing behind someone. She waited for a few moments, but when only silence greeted her ears she risked a peek. From what she could see, the tent was empty.

Gwen reached out to the edge of the portal with a frown. Shreds of material, ragged and frayed, fluttered between her fingers. Why wasn't the portal closing? They scarcely lasted ten seconds for Gwen. Except for the one she had opened for Finn Sayward...

How would one go about closing a portal? Gwen held up the ragged strips and brought out some of her core's magic. She thought of a mending spell she and Aidan had invented last month and applied it, to no avail. Nothing happened when she concentrated on her father or Isolde, except a slight widening of the opening.

Gwen stepped back, flummoxed. This was beyond her abilities. She trudged back through the woods, following her own footsteps. When they stopped abruptly beside a large oak, she peered around the other side.

Her father's face appeared in the still-open portal, wearing an expression of strained relief. He held out an arm and Gwen steadied herself as she climbed through.

"Well?" Alan said. "What did you find?"

"Definitely a portal. I have no idea why it's not closing. I tried a few things, but no luck. I just don't know enough."

"Gwen. You don't think—" Alan frowned. "Those wolves on the news."

Gwen gasped.

"Oh, no. That's exactly what happened. They came through that portal."

"Or another one." Alan bent down behind Gwen. "Is

27

this still supposed to be open?"

Gwen whirled around. The edges of her portal shimmered innocently at her. Instead of waist-height, it was only up to her knees, but it was still there.

"It should have closed fully by now. What is going on?" She touched the edges of the portal and tried to pull them together. Magic poured through her hands as she desperately tried to close the opening.

Slowly, reluctantly, the hole in the fabric of the world shrank until nothing was left but air and a view of the hedgerow behind. She exchanged a worried glance with her father.

"That's not typical, I take it?" he said.

"No. And I have no idea what to do about it."

"Presumably the inhabitants of the Otherworld are onto it. After all, magic is their bag." Alan pulled his gloves on tighter, then put his arm around Gwen. "Come on, let's get back to Ada's and warm up."

Gwen let herself be steered away, but her mind roiled uneasily. As far as she understood, freely open portals hadn't existed for hundreds of years. Would the Breenan want them shut again? The wild man Loniel had closed the portals initially. Was he behind their reopening? Gwen resolved to text Aidan when they arrived back at Ada's.

***

Once Gwen and Alan passed through the willow gate leading to Ada's snug cottage, Gwen stopped.

"Aren't you coming in for lunch?" Alan asked.

"Give me ten minutes? I want to try something, portal-wise." Gwen waved to the corner of the cottage, where a path led out of sight. "I'll be in the back garden—it's more private there."

Alan sighed.

"You really feel the need to delve into this mystery?"

"I just want to have another quick look. I'll be careful, I promise." Gwen gave her father a reassuring smile, which he countered with a raised eyebrow. "Ten minutes."

"All right, you know your business. I'll have lunch ready when you're done. Don't let any wolves through, hey?"

Gwen spontaneously kissed her father on the cheek. He grumbled incoherently but gave her shoulder a squeeze on his way to the front door.

Gwen hurried around the cottage, past lavenders and heathers carefully trimmed for winter. The garden behind the house was tiny but surrounded by bare-branched trees and brilliant green hedges that provided ample privacy. Gwen tucked herself in the back corner behind a holly bush out of sight of the cottage's windows and held out her arm.

A portal tore open and presented the same snowy vision of her mother's forest as had the previous portal. Gwen squeezed through the opening, which she had purposefully made as small as possible so that it would have less trouble closing. As it was, the portal stayed bewilderingly open after she passed through.

The forest was still bitingly cold, and Gwen regretted not changing her damp shoes before venturing through once again. Icicles weighed down tree branches, and the occasional brown leaf was trapped in an icy embrace.

Nothing broke the monotony of cold white except a dead mouse lying at the base of a tree, too frozen to be an appetizing morsel for an owl.

She turned back to look at the portal from this side. It was a fraction smaller than before but was closing too slowly for Gwen to see the motion.

Gwen ran her fingers around the edge of the opening. Only the faintest sensation tingled her fingers, like cool water trickling over the tips. She tried to pull the edges shut again, with every combination of spell and magic she could muster. Admittedly, there wasn't much to muster. Not for the first time, she wished that she'd had the same sort of magical schooling that their Breenan friend Bran had enjoyed, instead of the wild guessing and conjecturing that she and Aidan currently employed.

The portal stubbornly refused to close any more quickly than before. Gwen stepped back and looked around. She needed to speak to someone who knew about portals, someone with magic. She could look for Isolde, but she shrank from that idea. Meeting Isolde rarely ended well.

Loniel was a better choice. If anyone knew more about portals than he did, she would be surprised. But how to contact him?

"Hello?" she called out, feeling foolish. Loniel spent his days wandering Isolde's forest realm with his pack of revelers and had no fixed abode. The only times that Gwen had met him were when he had found her. Gwen cast her mind around for magical ways of contact, but she knew so little. She had no tracker ring for Loniel, no physical link that would connect them.

Loniel was different, though. He was old, far older than

any human or Breenan, and he was connected to the forest in ways that Gwen didn't understand. She thought of the night she and Aidan had met him, when he had led them to his bonfire...

Gwen rustled in the undergrowth and extracted a few damp branches. She banged the snow off and broke the branches into manageable pieces, then lay them in a rough pile. With her hand over the wood, she brought out the magic from her core.

The next moment, a fire burned merrily in the silent woods. Gwen sat back on her heels and enjoyed the warmth for a minute. Then she brought out some more magic through her hands, which glowed with a dazzling white light. She shaped a spell in her mind, cobbled together from modified summoning and naming spells that she and Aidan had been playing with this autumn. With Loniel's face firmly recollected, she sent her magic into the fire.

"Loniel, if you can hear me, there's something wrong with the portals," she said clearly into the silent woods. "They don't close anymore. I—thought you should know." She sighed and released her magic. It retreated to her core and left the woods dark and forbidding. The fire burned, unchanged, and Gwen's shoulders slumped in disappointment.

With a crack, the flames vanished.

Gwen jumped, then held her hand over the blackened wood. The branches were cold. Heartened by the response to her spell, Gwen stood and looked for her way out of the Otherworld.

Her portal was smaller, but still large enough for Gwen

to squeeze through. She took one last look at the snowy Otherworld then turned toward the cottage. The portal shrank slowly, so slowly, until at last it winked out of existence.

***

The tail of Crevan's horse flicked off the accumulating snowflakes. Bran sniffed and rubbed his nose.

"I swear this is the coldest winter we've had in years. I don't know why we're bothering to patrol—no one in their right mind is out in this weather."

The other two riders in their patrol, a man and a woman, both nodded in agreement, but Crevan shook his head.

"What about those not in their right minds? Or creatures who don't feel the cold like we do? Or—"

"All right, all right, I hear you." Bran shrugged deeper into the thick fur collar of his cape. "You're always so responsible. Could you admit for one moment that you'd rather be back in your bed?"

Crevan grinned briefly, and the resemblance between the two brothers emerged.

"I won't deny that. And my little Ella took her first steps last week, before we left. I want to see how she's coming along."

"Wait, look." Bran pointed to their right. At some distance away, a flash of bright color spilled through the trees. Bran slipped off his horse without delay, threw the reins carelessly over the saddle, and darted toward the light.

"Bran!" Crevan called out in exasperation. "This isn't a pleasure hunt. You're on patrol now, and you must follow the directions of the patrol leader. Me, in case you've forgotten."

"I've never been very good at following directions," Bran said, his feet carrying him forward.

"Don't I know it. Don't make me make you get back here."

"Honestly, Crevan, what's the point of patrolling if we don't explore strange things on our path? Relax your protocol for one moment and come have a look."

With that, Bran disappeared behind a large holly bush and out of sight. Crevan threw himself off his horse with a scowl and tossed his reins to his companions.

"We won't be long. Mind the horses."

Before long, Crevan caught up to Bran, who had stopped before the bright patch in the dim gray twilight of a winter's afternoon. Bran was uncharacteristically silent.

"What is it?" Crevan said at last. Bran turned to him with shining eyes.

"I think it's a portal. A way into the human world."

They both turned back and gazed at the portal. It was an opening wider than the width of their shoulders. The edges were ragged, and strips of the fabric between worlds lay shredded around the opening. Beyond lay a quiet woodland glade, bright and free of snow. The air from the portal wafted across their faces, still cool but much warmer than their side. Bran's brow furrowed.

"I don't know why it's still open. When Gwen opened a portal, it always closed after a few moments."

"Perhaps whoever made this one was much more

33

powerful." Crevan gingerly lifted a torn strip of material and examined it. "Do all portals look this rough?"

"No," said Bran. He looked thoughtful. "They're usually much tidier."

Crevan stared at the portal for a few moments. Bran grinned.

"Go on, you know you want to."

"Want to what?"

"Go through. Step into the human world."

"And get stuck on the other side? No, thank you. How would you like to explain to Ella why she has no father?"

"It must be terrible being you. Look!" Bran waved his hand through the portal. "Everything is fine."

"No, nothing is fine. Portals should not be appearing in the forest." Crevan waved Bran in the direction of their horses. "I'm cutting this patrol short. Father needs to know."

***

Once they were in the stables after a few hours' ride, the building warm and smelling of horse and hay, Crevan swung off his mount and beckoned to a stable hand.

"Where I can find the king?"

"I believe he's in the great hall," the stable hand said. He took the reins of Crevan's horse and Crevan waved to Bran.

"Come on, Bran. We need to report to Father."

"You don't need me for that. You're the patrol leader."

Crevan shook his head in exasperation.

"You should learn what happens in the kingdom, even

if you don't care. It affects you, whether you realize it or not." He turned and strode toward the inside doors, carved with rearing horses. "Hurry up."

Bran trotted after his eldest brother. A frown of annoyance flashed only briefly on his face before his eyes brightened with interest.

"Why do you think there's a portal in the woods? Why is it such a big deal?"

"Use your brain, Bran. All the portals were closed hundreds of years ago. To have them start opening again—there must have been a huge act of magic to allow it."

"But I used the locket to open a portal."

"That was a small piece of localized magic, and from what you said, the portal closed again almost immediately. This portal that we found was open and stayed that way. Who knows how long it has been there?" Crevan reached out his hands and pushed the double doors open wide. "Let's see what Father thinks."

Faolan sat facing them against a wall of translucent windows that ran from floor to cavernous ceiling. The light that filtered through the glass glinted on copper and gray strands of his hair. His chair was carved with an ornate likeness of a deciduous tree, barren of leaves, and was strewn with silver fox furs to stave off the chill of winter. Despite the cold, Faolan wore only a shirt and a fur-trimmed leather vest over his lean figure. In his hands was a pine branch wrapped with sprigs of holly and mistletoe.

Faolan glanced up from his examination of the branch. The frown of concentration on his stern face turned to one of questioning at the sight of his two sons.

"You're early. What news?"

"Bran discovered a portal to the human world near the Fairweather bridge crossing, on the borders of the Longshore realm."

Faolan sat up straight. He stared at Bran.

"You're certain it was a portal?"

"They're not like anything else, are they?" Bran said. "Rather hard to miss. It looked just like the one I made, but with ragged edges."

"And it wouldn't close," said Crevan. He and Faolan exchanged a meaningful look.

"I fail to see how this is bad news," Bran said. "A portal to the human world! Open all the time! Finally, Queen Kiera's foolishness put to rights. I can't wait to explore."

"You'll do no such thing," said Faolan sharply. "I allow you plenty of lenience, but I must insist on this. It's far too dangerous."

"The human world isn't so bad," said Bran. "I was fine last time."

"And what if the portal closed suddenly and you were trapped there forevermore? If you won't listen to the pleadings of your father, then obey the command of your king. Stay away from the portal, Bran."

Bran sighed but said, "All right. No portal."

"Good." Faolan turned to Crevan. "This is not the first report I've received, but it confirms my theory that the disturbances the patrols report are indeed portals." He held out the pine branch to Crevan, who took it. When Crevan interpreted the twists of foliage that contained the message in Breenan plant-writing, his face settled in grim lines.

"So many," he said. "What could have caused it?"

Faolan shook his head.

"I have wild theories, nothing more."

"But what does it mean?" Bran said. "What's happening?"

Faolan gazed at his youngest son.

"The fabric of the world is tearing itself apart. What will be the result, I do not know. Nor do I know how to reverse the damage."

Bran looked at his father, one of the most powerful Breenan in the nine realms. The worry on Faolan's face made Bran shiver.

***

Tristan, Aidan's Breenan half-brother, knocked firmly on the door of a small thatched cottage. Evergreen ivy crawled upon the wooden walls in a welcoming pattern, and Tristan smiled.

The door creaked open and his sister Rhiannon looked out. Her unbound blond hair fell in soft waves over her shoulders but did nothing to soften Rhiannon's sharp gaze.

"You're dressed for patrol. What's going on?"

"And hello to you, too," Tristan said. "I'm very well, thank you. And yourself?"

"Come in, come in. I thought you and I had no need for formalities."

"You're practically a stranger since you moved out of father's house," said Tristan. He stepped over the threshold. A large blond man sat at a small table made of an oiled slab of driftwood atop sturdy oak legs. He nodded to Tristan with a friendly smile.

"Tristan, good morning."

"Morning, Angus. Still eating breakfast, at this hour?"

"Help yourself, please." Angus waved at a plate of eggs and seaweed-flecked biscuits. Tristan plucked a biscuit off the plate.

"What do you mean, a stranger?" said Rhiannon. "I've seen you practically every day since I married Angus. You're as sticky as fish scales."

"I like to watch your transformation from feared hunter of the woods to novice biscuit maker of the domestic sphere." Tristan looked at the remaining half of his biscuit. "The seaweed was an interesting choice."

"It's how my mother used to make them." Rhiannon narrowed her eyes. "And if that was an invitation to come hunting with you, name your day. We'll see then who's lost their edge."

"I'd love to, but I'm here to tell you to prepare yourself. The king has called for emergency patrols, starting now."

"What for?" Angus asked. Rhiannon pursed her lips but walked to the bedroom door without speaking.

"The instructions were rather thin on details, but we are looking for 'disturbances in the air.' It said we would know them when we see them."

"That's it?" Angus frowned. "How will you find something that you don't know anything about?"

"We've been given tracking tools to sense the disturbances."

"The king must be worried if he's calling for extra patrols. Rhiannon wasn't due to leave for another week."

"No, I've never heard of an emergency patrol." Tristan

38

shrugged.

Rhiannon appeared, dressed in clothes for riding and with her hair in a tight braid. A soft leather bag was slung over her shoulder.

"Out you go. I'll be right behind you." Rhiannon made a shooing motion with her hands. Tristan grinned widely.

"Ah, young love. Say goodbye to your man—make sure he misses you while you're gone. Goodbye, Angus."

"Safe travels, Tristan," said Angus.

Tristan ducked out of the cottage and waited by the horses until Rhiannon emerged, her cheeks pink and her braid slightly askew. She swung into the saddle of her waiting horse.

"Come on, Tristan. Let's see what all the fuss is about."

***

Loniel appeared in the silence of the wintry woods, as quiet as the falling snow. He ran a hand over the rough bark of a nearby tree, the peppered silver fur of his cape sliding off to reveal his patchwork green-sleeved arm. His golden eyes raked over the spectacle before him, and his eyebrows contracted.

A portal was open before him. It was not in one of the ancient ways, the places where portals used to open and close before Loniel shut them all permanently, hundreds of years ago. Nor was it the clearly-wrought, ephemeral portal of a half-blood, open for seconds at the most. Loniel ran his hands along the ragged edge of the irregular hole. This portal was like none Loniel had ever seen before, large and unkempt. It appeared as mangled as though a huge beast had mauled its way across the worlds.

Loniel's fingers glowed as he touched the portal. With blues and reds, sparks and shimmers, Loniel attempted spell after spell to close the gap. The portal remained unchanged. He gazed at the hole in consideration for a long moment. Then he ducked through and entered the human world.

The light of a chill winter's sun winked at Loniel off the metal slide of a playground. The portal itself was partially obscured by large laurels in the garden adjacent to the park. Loniel gave only a cursory glance at his surroundings before he turned to examine the portal from the human side.

A quiet whine interrupted Loniel's thoughts. He tensed and grew still. Another whine floated through the opening from the Otherworld. Loniel peered through the hole, and his eyes narrowed. Two wolves slunk his way, their magnificent cinnamon-tinted coats contrasting sharply with the gleaming snow. The leader saw Loniel, and its jaw opened in a grin filled with sharp fangs.

The joyful laugh of a young child traveled clearly from the playground. Loniel's head twitched briefly to look at the little boy on the slide, dressed for school but enjoying the park on his way. The ears of the two wolves twitched in response, and the leader stepped forward.

Loniel turned without warning, his face transfigured in a snarl that ripped from his throat. He launched himself through the portal and landed before the two wolves. Brilliant green light shone from his outstretched hands, too bright to look at. The wolves backed away and fled into the forest.

Loniel pressed his hands to the cold earth and a wild hedge of boxwood covered the portal. He glanced once at his work, then paced quietly into the snowy trees.

***

Isolde sat on her throne in the ballroom, the chair carved with woodland animals and a multitude of vines. Only one dance, and she was already flushed and sweaty. She patted her black hair into place, the white strands at her temple swept back in an elegant chignon. She beckoned to a nearby servant.

"Bank the fire," she said to him. "It's clearly too warm in here."

The servant's brow creased in confusion, but he bowed and left to do her bidding. Isolde rested her arms on the armrests and gazed around the ballroom with an expression of contentment. The hall glittered with candles that glistened through forever-frozen icicles hanging from chandeliers. Huge garlands of ivy, frosted with snow, draped gracefully around the room. The dancers were stunning in her mandated color scheme. Silks of the purest white, clear diamonds, and snowy feathers swung in glittering arcs around the room in elegant formations that resembled frost blooming on a window. Isolde smiled serenely at the spectacle.

The huge double doors that led outside were flung open with a crash. The orchestra stopped, and Isolde stood in indignation at the vulgar disturbance.

It was Corann, flanked by ten of her finest guards. Isolde pursed her lips in annoyance. To make such a scene, and then to not even wear the requisite white? Corann's burgundy blouse stood out like spilled wine on a white tablecloth.

"Why do you disturb the festivities, Corann?" Isolde raised her voice, so it carried across the ballroom, but Corann made no answer. Instead, he jerked his head and the accompanying guards swiftly crossed the ballroom. The dancers parted like breaking ice on a river.

"What are you doing?" Isolde demanded. "Is there urgent news? You may request a private audience, there is no need to halt the dance." She waved at the orchestra, but none of the musicians picked up the instruments from their laps.

The guards reached her. They should have stopped, bowed, and asked permission to speak. Instead, their tall boots thumped softly onto her dais and surrounded her. Two at her side took her forearms in firm hands.

Outrage flashed across Isolde's face. She flung her arms toward her body to dislodge the hands, but they clung remorselessly. She looked at each guard in turn. They stared forward and would not meet her gaze.

"Unhand me at once! How do you expect to get away with this? Your punishment will be grave, indeed."

"They act on my orders." Corann had followed the guards slowly, and now paced to the foot of the dais. He gazed at Isolde evenly with calm green eyes. "There will be no punishment."

Isolde's eyes flashed with anger, and she balled her fists. Sparks ran along her arms and the guards flinched but held firm. Isolde stared in shock at the hands still encircling her arms. Her magic had failed. Corann's expression grew sad.

"I've been trying to tell you for months. The restoration spell was never meant to last. As the spell fades, the defenses weaken. As do you."

"Nothing is wrong with me." Isolde raised her chin in defiance, the effect rather dampened by her captive state. A bead of sweat slid down her forehead.

"And yet you could not prevent the guards from seizing you. A few months ago, they would have been obliterated for their impudence." He stepped up on the dais a few paces from her and the guards let go of her arms.

"I should have no need to protect myself from my own guards." Isolde raised her voice and addressed the crowd. "What say you, my people? Will you allow this indignity to your queen?"

The silence was absolute. No one stirred, no dresses rustled, no feathers trembled. Instead, a sea of pitying faces gazed upon Isolde's.

"No one will speak," said Corann gently. "Everyone can see what you are blind to—that your rule is failing." He grabbed both her hands in a firm grip and looked in her eyes. His were filled with tender pity, love, and firm resolve. "I can't bear to see you fall into sickness and ruin, not again. You almost died before the restoration spell was cast."

"I'm not dying now," Isolde said firmly, but she glanced at her trembling limbs.

"It's only a matter of time. And you can't even protect yourself—how can you safeguard the realm?" Corann's face crumpled in worry. "You're fading away, I can't watch you destroy yourself and this realm we've worked so hard to preserve. I love you too much to stand by and watch without acting."

"What are you saying?" Isolde whispered. Her hands were cold in Corann's warm ones.

"I will take your burden, my love," he said gently. "You needn't worry any longer about the cares and responsibilities of the realm. I will rule in your stead."

Isolde's face was frozen in shock for a long moment. Then she threw her arms down to release them from Corann's grip. He did not resist, but a resigned expression swept across his features. She stepped back, and the guards wrapped their strong fingers around her forearms once more. Her eyes blazed.

"Release me at once," she shouted, attempting to imbue her words with as much authority as she could muster. Corann nodded at the guards and they let go. Isolde stepped closer to Corann.

"Betrayer," she hissed, long and low. Corann paled. She swept past him and down the dais, her white skirts swishing behind her. The dancers parted like frothy waves on a pale sea and silently watched her passage. She met none of their eyes and stared only at the open ballroom door to the snow-clad forest beyond.

No one stopped her, no one spoke. The castle behind her appeared as a ruinous edifice of crumbling stone and moss. The forest was silent and the snow dull, with the bright illusions held in place by the restoration spell broken now that Corann had taken over. Before long, Isolde stood on the path out of sight of the castle. She was queen no longer. Her breath came faster and faster, and she swallowed.

"Queen Isolde," a voice said from behind her. She whirled in a windstorm of white silk skirts. Loniel stood before her, the green man swathed in silver furs above his usual green attire. The fur and his glossy brown hair covered the tattoos that crept up his hidden throat. He gazed at her. "Or perhaps not a queen, given your state of dress outside. Did Corann finally carry out his plan?"

Isolde's eyes flashed.

"Everyone knew but me, it would seem. The betrayer did a cowardly action."

"You brought this upon yourself, Isolde. Deep down, you know this. You relied on the restoration spell. It could never last, and yet you did nothing to change. I applaud that you gave up the locket that was used to power the realm, but to not provide an alternative?" He shook his head. "As I said, you are the designer of your own doom."

"Did you have any other purpose in confronting me besides your reprimands? I neither need nor care about your judgement."

"Just this: the decay of the restoration spell weakened more than yourself. The fabric between the worlds is growing thin and tearing away entirely in places." Loniel's face grew grim. "It will do neither Breenan nor human any good to have free passage between the worlds, and I fear that the tearing will not stop." Loniel waved at the frozen trees. "Even though the spell no longer powers the realm's illusions, the ill-effects continue to wreak havoc."

"You closed the portals centuries ago, didn't you?" Isolde tossed her head. "Why don't you do so again, if it worries you?"

"It should worry everyone here," Loniel said sharply.

"The destruction this may cause... you cannot begin to imagine. The world you know will cease to be. I have tried to close the portals, but it is far beyond my abilities."

"No spell should have an effect this far-reaching."

"I can only guess at the cause. It is obvious that the queens who designed the restoration spell used some forest-folk magic to create permanency in their spells. But I fear that the restoration spell was not meant to be performed by half-humans. Somehow, their spell involved both worlds, and now that it is decaying..." Loniel grimaced.

"And what do you expect me to do about it?" Isolde snapped. "As you so bluntly pointed out, I am no longer queen here."

"The realm must be whole again. Until it is whole, it cannot heal itself against the power of the decaying spell. You must seek out the only one who can remedy your mistake." Loniel looked forlorn. "These tidings will not be to her liking, but the fate of both our worlds may depend on her. There is an open portal through the nearest old way. Good luck." And with that, Loniel melted into the forest, leaving no trace of his passage.

Isolde stared after Loniel with a thoughtful expression. Then she nodded decisively and paced along the snowy path. Her whispering skirts carved a wide swath through the drifts. Onward she strode, heedless of the cold, until her steps brought her before a crumbling archway. The stones were rough and covered in moss and a blanket of snow. The view through the archway was not of snow-covered forest, but instead showed soggy fields of shorn grasses. Isolde smiled faintly and stepped out of her world.

Chapter 3

Aidan pushed the back door of his mother's house open with his foot. Cold air poured into the kitchen, and he slammed the door shut with his hip.

"It's a cold winter this year," said Aidan. "I swear it dropped ten degrees while I was out there."

"Did you find the decorations?" his mother Deirdre called from the living room.

"Yeah, they're all here. Even that musty little elf I made you in nursery school." Aidan kicked off his boots and moved to the living room, where Deirdre was stringing colored lights on a short Christmas tree.

"Oh, that lovely little elf. That's essential holiday décor. You were so proud when you gave it to me."

"What time is Aunty Lucy coming on Christmas day?" asked Aidan. He opened the box and passed Deirdre a roll of tinsel.

"Mid-morning, I believe. She'll stay for the day. I hope she remembers the pudding—she said she'd bring it, but you know how scatterbrained she can be."

"Call her." Aidan hung a snowflake ornament on an

upper branch. The tree wobbled.

"You know, I might." Deirdre held the tinsel in her lap and regarded her son. "Will you play us some Christmas carols this year? I'd love to hear how you're progressing."

"Sure," said Aidan. He looked confused but gratified. Deirdre grabbed his hand.

"You know how proud I am of you, don't you?" She squeezed his fingers. "No matter what you do. Especially because of what you do."

"Yeah, I know." Aidan gave a little shrug. Deirdre patted his hand, then released it and stood.

"I made Grandma's old recipe for eggnog. Would you like some?"

"Would I ever," said Aidan. "Christmas doesn't come often enough."

Deirdre walked to the kitchen. The sound of rustling from the fridge floated toward Aidan, then a loud tutting.

"Someone's let their dog sneak into the back garden. It's huge. Some sort of husky? It had better not damage my roses."

Aidan followed his mother to the kitchen, where he found her peering through the window over the kitchen sink. His eyes followed hers, and they widened.

"I don't think that's a dog, Mum. It looks like—a wolf."

"Don't be absurd. There haven't been wolves in Britain for centuries."

They stared at the pacing animal, whose gray fur was dusted with snow. There was none on the ground.

"How did it get in here?" Aidan said slowly. "The gate is closed. And I've never seen a dog in here before." He pulled out his phone and searched for something while Deirdre kept an eye on the animal. He shoved the phone in front of his mother's face. "Look, Mum. Tell me that isn't what's outside."

Aidan had found a photo of a European wolf online. Deirdre's eyes flickered back and forth between the photo and the animal.

"This is mad," she breathed. "Did it escape from a zoo? I'll call the police, see if they can send someone to capture it."

Deirdre rushed over to the phone. Aidan watched the wolf with an expression of growing comprehension. He ran upstairs, taking the steps two at a time. In his mother's bedroom, he wrenched up the window sash. A cold blast of air greeted his face. He grabbed a tissue box and lobbed it at the unsuspecting wolf. His aim was true, and the box hit the animal with a thwack. The wolf yelped.

"What are you doing?" Deirdre yelled. "Don't antagonize the creature!"

"Just making sure it's…" Aidan's voice trailed off, and he spoke quietly to himself. "Real. Not magic."

The wolf looked up at him with a long gaze that held no fear. Aidan held his breath. Finally, the wolf turned its head with supreme indifference and sauntered behind an apple tree in the center of the garden. The trunk of the tree was no wider than Aidan, yet the wolf did not appear on the other side of the tree. Aidan swallowed.

"There's a portal," he whispered.

Back downstairs, Deirdre craned her neck to look through the window. Aidan clattered into the kitchen.

"Where did it go?" Deirdre said.

"Must've escaped the way it came," said Aidan. He waited a moment, then said, "I forgot to bring the lights in. I'll run and grab them."

"You can't go out now!" Deirdre clutched Aidan's arm. "There's a wolf in our garden."

"I threw the tissues at it—must've scared it off. It'll be long gone now. I'll be quick, I promise."

"Aidan!" Deirdre said with exasperation, but Aidan darted past her and out the door.

"Won't be a minute. Christmas must go on," he called out over his shoulder.

Aidan's eyes raked the apple tree as he approached. Sure enough, a ragged hole in the world's fabric opened to a snowy forest, out of place in Deirdre's rain-soaked garden. Aidan watched it for a moment, frowning, but the portal did not shrink at all. Aidan continued to the shed for appearance's sake and rummaged within for a string of lights. A minute's searching yielded a string that he knew didn't work, but it would do for an excuse. He turned and stepped out of the shed.

A deep growl made him freeze. The hairs on his neck lifted and his eyes took in the scene before him. The wolf was back. And this time, it wasn't alone.

Aidan's eyes darted between the three wolves. The central one bared its teeth in a throaty snarl, and they all took slow steps toward Aidan. A sharp rapping on the kitchen window revealed Deirdre's terrified face shouting soundlessly and waving at Aidan to back into the shed. When he didn't move, she burst out of the door with a carving knife held aloft.

"Get in the shed, Aidan!" she screamed.

"Mum, stay back!" Aidan shouted. The wolves had turned at the sound of the door and now stared at Deirdre. Aidan raised his hands, squared his shoulders, and narrowed his eyes. Blue flames poured from his outstretched fingers in a fiery jet. The wolf closest to Deirdre was thrown off its feet with a high-pitched yelp. Its fur danced with blue fire. Still yelping, it tore off through the portal.

The other two animals faced Aidan with a snarl. He raised his hands. Blue fire danced around his fingers. The wolves lowered their lips and backed away, then scampered after their burning fellow.

"And stay out!" Aidan yelled after them. The flames died from his hands and he ran his fingers through his hair in relief. He sighed explosively, then glanced at his mother with wariness.

Deirdre was staring at him, hand over her mouth, an unreadable expression on her face. Aidan shifted from one foot to the other.

"You—you're still doing that?" Deirdre said finally.

"Yeah." Aidan set his jaw. "I'm still doing that."

"That was—" Deirdre shook her head slowly and Aidan held his breath. "Incredible."

"Incredible?" Aidan blinked. "What does that mean?"

"The fire—and the way the wolves simply ran—I suppose I never realized what your abilities could do. Just incredible, love."

As if remembering the peril they had both faced, she ran toward Aidan and hugged him fiercely.

"Come back inside. My brave, brave boy." She caught a glimpse of the portal and her jaw dropped. "What is that?"

Aidan studied his mother for a moment. Then his expression cleared, and he put an arm around her to steer her into the house.

"I have something to tell you, Mum. About how I met Gwen. About somewhere I went last May."

***

Alan placed his fork and knife on his plate and sighed in contentment.

"Delicious dinner, Aunty Ada. You've outdone yourself again. I haven't been so well fed in years."

"I hope you've left enough room for my shortbread. The recipe was from my grandmother on my father's side—that would be your great-great-grandmother." Ada nodded to Gwen.

"There's always room for dessert," Gwen said, and bit into one of the crumbly, buttery cookies. "Yum, these are great," she said after she swallowed her mouthful. "Shortbread cookies and Christmas almost make the early sunsets worthwhile." She gestured at the window, whose curtains were drawn against the black evening sky.

"Bearable, at least," said Ada.

Before Gwen could finish her cookie, they were interrupted by a knock on the front door, which echoed from the sparsely furnished hallway.

"That's odd. I'm not expecting anyone." Ada made to get up, but Gwen stood and pressed her gently back down.

"I'll get it, Aunty Ada. You finish your tea."

"Thank you, dear." Ada settled back in her seat. "I

52

wonder why our visitor didn't ring the bell. If it's someone selling something, send him on his way as quick as you can."

Gwen nodded and ambled to the hall. She was pleasantly full and sleepy after dinner and felt no rush. The door unlocked with a simple deadbolt and swung open with Gwen's pull.

A woman stood shivering on the stoop, her white silk gown not nearly enough protection against the chill wind that rustled her long skirts. Her dark hair, pinned back in a chignon that highlighted the white stripe at her temple, was falling out of its trappings in messy wisps that danced in the breeze. Relief washed across her face at the sight of Gwen.

"Gwendolyn," Isolde said quietly.

Gwen stood frozen and let shock pour cold waves over her. Her Breenan mother Isolde, here in the human world. The human world of her existence and the newly discovered Otherworld of her heritage were completely separate in Gwen's mind, and she hadn't realized how much she relied on keeping them apart. It felt bizarre and abnormal for Isolde to trespass on Gwen's life here. Every previous encounter with Isolde had resulted in dangerous adventuring, and Gwen preferred to keep Isolde at a distance.

It was a few moments before Gwen realized that Isolde waited for an answer. What was Gwen supposed to say? All capacity for speech had fled her like heat through the open door. She clutched at her shirt, where the locket Isolde had given her lay against her chest. She had brought it on this trip, for no reason she could understand herself.

Had it drawn Isolde here?

"Gwen? Who is it?" Ada's sharp voice shook Gwen from her stunned state. Anger flooded her, anger at Isolde for meddling in Gwen's life in the human world where her mother didn't belong.

"You shouldn't be here," Gwen hissed. "Go back to the Otherworld. Leave me alone."

Isolde closed her eyes with slow, sorrowful resignation, as if she had both expected and feared Gwen's response. Her shoulders trembled with shivers from the cold.

"Gwen?" Alan's voice drifted from the living room, and footsteps thumped across the floor.

"Quick! You have to leave." Gwen started to shut the door in Isolde's crestfallen face before her father could see, but when Isolde's eyes flickered to look past her shoulder, she knew she was too late.

"Alan," Isolde breathed in a throaty voice. Her hands trembled.

Gwen sighed and, bowing to the inevitable, opened the door wide. She looked at her father, who gazed at the mother of his only child for the first time in twenty years. Gwen didn't know how to interpret his look. Certainly, he knew who Isolde was. There was recognition, and some confusion—why was Isolde here, anyway?—and perhaps some old feelings being stirred. Gwen didn't want to think about that.

"Dad," she said loudly enough to break the long gazes. "This is Isolde. If you remember."

"I remember." Alan frowned and looked at Gwen. "Why is she here? Now?"

Gwen shrugged. Alan waved Isolde inside.

"Come out of the cold, at least," he said. "No point heating the great outdoors."

Isolde's skirts swished over the threshold and her face was awash with relief. Gwen pursed her lips. She didn't know where this was going, but she didn't like it, not one bit.

After the door closed, Gwen asked, "Why are you here, Isolde?"

Isolde pressed shaking hands over her skirts to smooth them, but before she could speak, Ada entered the hallway.

"Who is this?" she asked. Her sharp eyes raked over Isolde and took in every detail of her outlandish ballgown and disheveled appearance. Gwen looked at her father in panic.

Alan visibly gathered his thoughts, then tore his eyes off Isolde and turned to Ada.

"This is Gwen's biological mother," he said firmly. Ada's penciled eyebrows rose toward the hairline of her tightly curled gray hair. Alan continued, "They were recently acquainted, through unusual circumstances. We didn't tell you, because it's still a rather delicate matter."

Ada nodded crisply.

"Of course. Quite. It's late for an old woman like me, and I have a new book that is calling my name. I shall retire early. Please help yourself to tea." With a regal nod to Isolde, a pat on Alan's arm, and a half-smile for Gwen, Ada climbed the stairs.

No one spoke until Ada had vanished from sight and the door to her bedroom clicked shut. Gwen gave a despairing look at her father, who waved to the living room.

"I think we all need to sit down," he said faintly, the fortitude he'd shown in front of Ada fading. Isolde nodded and swept ahead of them as if she were in her castle. Gwen rolled her eyes.

Alan gave Gwen a swift, one-armed hug before he followed Isolde into the living room. Isolde picked up a figurine of a china statue of a shepherd from the side table but put it down without much interest. She sat and arranged her skirts in a fussy way that didn't completely hide her discomfort. It was an odd look on one who was always so confident.

Gwen sat across from her in an armchair by the fireplace. Alan hesitated, then sat gingerly on the other end of the couch from Isolde.

"You still haven't answered my question, Isolde," Gwen said. Isolde's intrusion into her life had her rattled and in no mood to be nice, especially not now that Isolde was on Gwen's territory. Gwen found that she liked the power it gave her—or, at least, the lack of fear that she felt in Isolde's realm. "Why are you here?"

"Gwen," Alan said. "Give her a minute."

"No, she's right," Isolde said with a brief glance at Alan. She looked quickly away again and focused on the china shepherd. "This visit is most—unexpected."

"More like impossible," Gwen said. "Or should be. How did you get through? Do you have another locket you've been hiding? Or did you come through a broken portal, you and the wolves?"

"A ragged portal was open in the archway. The old ways are open once more. I promise, I have no other way to pass between the worlds." In her earnestness, Isolde finally looked up and met Gwen's eyes. Something had disappeared from them, some fire or light that used to drive Isolde had evaporated and left her looking tired and old. She let out a breath that was not quite a laugh. "Would you believe this is the first time I've been in the human world since—" Isolde paused, and her eyes flickered to Alan. "For twenty years."

"Yes, I believe it," said Gwen. "You always sent Corann to do your dirty work here."

At the sound of Corann's name, Isolde flinched, and a spasm crossed her face.

"He is the reason I'm here," she said, with the first scrap of passion she had shown this evening. "He betrayed me."

Gwen frowned in puzzlement.

"I thought—you two seemed like a thing, that's all." At Isolde's questioning look, Gwen clarified. "An item? Together?" She refused to say the word "lovers," not to describe her mother, and not in front of her dad. Isolde's face darkened.

"Yes, he was my paramour." She cast another furtive glance at Alan, who sat silently with his fingers steepled. "I trusted him with the deepest secrets of the realm. He repaid me with usurpation of my throne. I am—" She swallowed. "No longer queen of the Velvet Woods."

"Oh." Gwen sat back in her armchair and digested this news. Isolde was no longer the queen. What did that mean for the realm? Gwen didn't trust Corann as far as she could throw him, even before his coup d'état. Would he reinstate the kidnappings that Isolde used to rely on? Gwen wouldn't put it past him. She focused on Isolde's anguished face. "How did he take over? Did you just let him? Don't you have any guards?"

Isolde's mouth grew thin in a furious line.

"He went behind my back, spoke to all my courtiers, swayed them to his arguments. Not one stood up for me at the crucial juncture."

"And what were his arguments?"

"He wanted to set up the defenses of the realm to avoid relying on the restoration spell." Isolde tossed her head. "He thought that my health was compromised because of it, and that the spell wouldn't last much longer."

"Is it true?" Gwen asked. "The restoration spell was only supposed to be a temporary fix, as far as I understand."

Isolde waved her hand in a dismissive gesture.

"I was forming plans to replace it, but there was no rush. No rush at all. My health has never been better." Isolde clasped her hands in her lap tightly, which did not entirely hide their trembling, nor did the dim light mask the pallor of her cheeks. "It doesn't matter now. That meddling green man Loniel had the gall to confront me after I left the castle. Blamed me for allowing the usurpation while the realm was under the restoration spell." Isolde looked away from Gwen and her fingers twisted in her lap in an oddly nervous fidget. "He said the barrier between the worlds is falling apart because of it."

Even though Gwen didn't know what Loniel had meant, her stomach still dropped. The portal in the field crossed her mind. Aidan had also called yesterday to describe his encounter with Otherworld wolves. What was happening? Why were Gwen's worlds colliding?

Isolde straightened.

"None of this would have happened without Corann's betrayal. I suppose I could have adjusted the defenses earlier, but there was really no rush."

This was the most admission of guilt that Gwen expected from Isolde.

"And," Isolde continued. "He should know better. His taking power is against the natural order. Corann was not my heir."

"Come on, Isolde." Gwen sighed in exasperation. It felt safer talking to Isolde this way when Gwen was in her own world. "I know the Breenan function under absolute monarchies, but there are lots of other ways to set up a government."

Isolde frowned.

"You clearly do not understand the nature of my rule. I am connected to the realm with ties of magic, as have been those in my family for generations. We have grown with the realm, and the realm has flourished under us. Now, my lineage is the only one capable of governing the Velvet Woods in its current form. The form of magic my family wields, through long use and association, is now the only form capable." Isolde smoothed her skirts with deliberation. "Not only that, but an heir must be declared by magical means."

Alan spoke then, after silently regarding their conversation.

"You still haven't answered Gwen's question," he said mildly. "Why are you here?"

"And who's this 'heir?'" Gwen said. "Why aren't they stepping up? If you're so powerless, get them to put

Corann in his place. Surely your court would back your true heir."

Both Isolde and Alan stared at Gwen, her father with dawning comprehension and horror, Isolde with a look of consideration. There was silence for a moment. Isolde spoke next.

"You are my heir, Gwendolyn."

Chapter 4

Gwen stared at Isolde. What did she mean, Gwen was her heir? It was an absurd statement.

"What are you talking about?" Gwen said in a repressive tone, hoping to inject some common sense into the conversation. "Of course I'm not your heir. I'm half-human, for pity's sake. And you haven't even acknowledged that I exist to any Breenan."

"And yet, I performed the magic that bound you to the role," Isolde said quietly. "After I found out that you had magic. When I gave you the locket, do you remember the incantation? You are my daughter, after all. My only child."

"Daughter by blood only," Gwen snapped.

"But that is the important link, in this matter. In your veins runs the magic that will allow you to bind to the realm and bend it to your will—tree, earth, person, animal. The portals are opening due to the miscast restoration spell, but with your ascension, a new regime will begin and the worlds will heal." Isolde nodded as if the matter were already decided. "Once you are queen and assume the throne of the realm, you may choose the line of defense you think is best. I would be happy to reside in the castle and guide you in this role."

Gwen had only let Isolde speak for so long because she was speechless. Isolde's certainty prodded her into speech.

"Why the hell would I become queen of the Velvet Woods?" Gwen shook her head and looked to her father. He looked as flabbergasted as she felt.

Isolde looked confused.

"It is no small thing to be queen. While the role comes with responsibilities, it is true, there are many benefits. As the head of the realm, you have the pick of the finest dresses, the most sumptuous furs, food to envy—"

"Stop right there." Gwen put up her hand. "I don't care about any of that. I don't want to live in the Otherworld. I have a life I love right here, among my people."

"The Breenan are your people, too," Isolde said gently. "And without an appropriately appointed ruler of the correct bloodline, those people will suffer greatly once the realm falls apart."

"This is insane," Alan said with heat. He perched on the edge of the couch and leaned toward Isolde to emphasize his point. "Gwen has no need to be bound to a responsibility like that, in a world where she doesn't belong."

"It's already done," Isolde said flatly.

"You have no idea who Gwen is." Alan stood, his voice raised. Gwen had never seen her mild-mannered father so impassioned, so heated. His fury radiated off him. "You have no idea what it's like to have a daughter. And that was your choice, if you remember. You gave up your claim nineteen years ago. You have no right to ask anything of Gwen."

Isolde visibly deflated. Even through her shock and anger, Gwen was astonished at the sight. Isolde put her head in her hands.

"I know," she said quietly to the floor. "Oh, I know. I wouldn't ask this if there were any other way." She looked up at Gwen, unshed tears gathered in her eyes. "But I have no other children, although not for lack of trying. My people will suffer if I don't provide for them, by drought, famine, war. In a way, I am a mother to them all, and I must take care of them."

The hard knot in Gwen's stomach only tightened with Isolde's words.

"Pretty words. But you could have taken better care of your people by changing your defenses after the restoration spell." Gwen's voice rose. "Why is it that I have to fix your problem? Who's the mother here?"

Isolde flinched, but did not answer. Gwen stood and strode to the window, where she flicked the curtains open. A lone streetlight lit the quiet street before her, and trees swayed in the gathering wind.

Gwen didn't know what to think. Her first instinct was to open a portal and push Isolde through it, back to the Otherworld, but the memory of the forest people of Isolde's realm stayed her hand. She had met them on her last foray into the Otherworld. They had dealt with famine and displacement then, too, and Gwen's heart contracted with the memory of the orphaned children she had given bread to, and the young refugee family they had met on the road. With a start, she recalled Loniel's words to her as she left the Otherworld in the summer: "Some would say that you are a natural choice for the succession." Should she have been expecting this thunderbolt from Isolde? Whenever the Otherworld was involved, Gwen's life grew more complicated.

She stared out of the diamond shapes of the leaded glass window, not truly seeing the dim street before her eyes. The room was silent behind her, but she didn't spare any attention for her parents. Her thoughts were disjointed, unfocused—they were like frenzied butterflies in a cage. She felt trapped, locked in a room with no escape. Once again, the weight of responsibility pressed down on her, mercilessly crushing her shoulders to the ground. Her mind scrambled for solutions, but nothing presented itself, nothing except the terrible option Isolde had brought with her.

"Gwen." Alan's voice broke the silence and jarred her mind back to the current situation. "I'd like to speak with you in private, please. Kitchen."

Gwen turned and nodded, then followed her father out of the room. Isolde stared at the china shepherd.

"I know what you're thinking," he said without preamble once they had reached the sanctity of the kitchen, with its copper pans hanging above the stove and a large wooden clock ticking quietly above the fridge. "I can see it in your face. You want to fix this."

"I don't *want* to do anything. But sometimes we can't do what we want."

Her father held her shoulders firmly.

"Listen to me, Gwen. You have no obligation to help Isolde, no responsibility, nothing. This is entirely on her.

You don't have to do anything for her, nothing at all."

"But that's just it," Gwen said with a frown. "She's got herself in such a mess that it's not about her anymore. Trust me, I have no desire to be Isolde's heir, live in the Otherworld, whatever she's going on about." Gwen put her hands gently on her father's wrists. "But how could I live with myself if a whole realm's worth of people suffered, maybe died, and I could have done something to save them?"

Her father's face contorted in anguish, but he said nothing in reply. Gwen managed to tweak her mouth into a convincing half-smile before she spoke.

"Nothing has to be decided tonight. Let's sleep on it. I bet there's a way around all this that we can't see yet."

Gwen didn't believe her own words in the slightest, but she had to say something to her father. To her relief, he brightened marginally.

"You're right, nothing is done yet, nothing is written in stone. We will figure this out." Alan gave a great sigh and removed his hands to scrub his face. Gwen's shoulders missed their solid weight. "I know you want to help these people. But I'll be damned if I see my daughter trapped in a life she doesn't want. Whatever I can do, however I can help, I will."

Gwen hugged him fiercely, and he squeezed her back. Gwen finally straightened.

"What do we do with *her*?" She jerked her head toward the living room.

"I guess she'll have to stay here. It doesn't sound like she has anywhere to go in the Otherworld."

"And no money to pay for a hotel room."

Alan chuckled weakly.

"I'll ask Ada."

"She can have my bed, if Aunty Ada doesn't mind me sleeping on the couch," said Gwen. "I don't want her put to any trouble, and since I'm the reason Isolde's here…"

"Gwen—"

"I know, I know, it's not my fault."

Alan smiled wanly and ushered her into the living room while he moved toward the hallway.

Isolde's hands were in her lap and she stared at them blankly. At Gwen's approaching footsteps she stiffened but did not look up.

"Have you made your decision, Gwendolyn?" Isolde said quietly.

"No," said Gwen. "Dad's asking if you can stay for the night."

"Thank you." The relief in Isolde's voice was only partially masked by her usual collected tone. She hesitated a moment, then said, "I don't understand your hesitation, Gwendolyn. Many would give away their magic for a chance to be queen of the Velvet Woods."

"So, let them."

"You know I cannot. It really is an exalted life—I'm sure you would enjoy it. I cannot fathom your dolorous mood at the news."

"I wouldn't expect you to."

Isolde had chosen her role over her lover, her child—of course she wouldn't understand Gwen's reluctance to leave the people she loved to dwell in a land of strangers. Isolde looked as if she wanted to say more, but Gwen's tight face must have convinced her otherwise. They remained in awkward silence, Isolde on the couch and Gwen standing at the door, until Alan stepped in beside Gwen with Ada behind him in a plush violet dressing gown.

"Good evening, Isolde," Ada said with dignity. "My name is Ada Smith. I am Gwen's great-aunt."

Isolde gave her a regal nod.

"I am pleased to make your acquaintance."

"Gwen." Ada leaned toward Gwen and whispered in her ear. "Shall I say she can stay? What's your preference? I don't wish to distress you."

"Thanks, Aunty Ada," Gwen said. "I don't mind. Thank you for having her. I know it's a lot to ask."

Ada waved Gwen's comment away, then addressed Isolde.

"I hear you're in need of a bed tonight. I can accommodate you. If you'll follow me."

"I thank you," said Isolde formally to Ada. She tried to catch Gwen's eye, but Gwen looked away. Instead, she put a tentative hand on Alan's arm.

"Thank you for your help," she said.

Alan nodded stiffly and moved his arm away.

"You're welcome."

Isolde quickly followed Ada, her skirts swishing on the floor behind her. Gwen heaved a huge sigh when she was gone.

"Time for bed?" Alan said. "Perhaps when we wake up we'll find that this whole evening was a terrible dream."

"Here's hoping." Gwen rubbed her eyes. "I'll call Aidan first. Get him thinking of solutions. Three heads are better than two, right?"

***

Bran stared at the wooden slats of the barn roof with an expression of mindless contentment. The hayloft was dusty and cold, but there was comfortable hay under his back and he wore a toasty fur cloak. Motes of dust drifted across an errant sunbeam. Bran bit into an autumn apple. It didn't crunch, exactly—it was too old and wrinkled for that—but what it lacked in crispness it made up in sweetness.

"Have you tamed that new colt yet, Snowleaf's foal?" he asked his companions with idle interest. Two stable hands lounged on their own hay piles, finishing the apples Bran had passed around.

"Almost," one said. "He's a fiery one. Shouldn't be too much longer, though. Who's he destined for?"

"He's such a beauty," said the other. "Definitely meant for a great lord. Not you, then, Bran."

Bran flicked his apple core at the stable hand, who laughed when it hit him in the chest.

"Bran?" An annoyed voice drifted up to the hayloft. Bran said nothing. A moment later, the blond head of Bran's brother Owen appeared through an opening in the floor.

"I thought I'd find you here." He vaulted up the last rungs and dusted off his trousers. "It's where you come when you're shirking your duties. As usual."

"And why are you looking?" Bran idly twirled his fingers, and Owen's ponytail began to twist and swirl, dancing to unheard music. The stable hands unsuccessfully hid their snickers behind their hands.

When Owen realized what Bran was doing, he clamped one hand on his wildly swinging hair and the other he threw forward in a defensive gesture. A wave of power slammed against Bran, and Owen's hair calmed.

Bran grinned, unruffled.

"You warded me? Where's the fun in that? Surely even you can do better."

Owen ignored Bran's comment.

"Father's summoned us. Something about the extra patrols, I think. Come on, they're all waiting for us."

In the main hall, bright winter light streamed through translucent windows onto Bran's waiting brothers.

"I am here," Bran announced. "You may begin."

A few laughed, and a couple of sparks flew Bran's way. He dodged them with a grin.

A door opened along the back of the hall and Faolan paced out. His usually immaculate silver-flecked hair was ruffled, and his sleeves were rolled to the elbows. Lanterns flickered behind Faolan before the door closed firmly.

Faolan strode to the center of the empty hall, to where his sons were assembled. His face was creased in concern.

"Are more patrols needed, Father?" asked Owen.

"Hmm? No, not as such." Faolan's lips drew into a thin line. "I've sensed disturbances for the past few days. Irregularities in the earth paths. They all come from the Velvet Woods."

"Velvet Woods again?" said Kelan, the youngest brother next to Bran. His short blond hair glinted in the pale light. "I thought they were sorted out."

"So did I," said Faolan.

"Any ideas what's happening?" said Crevan.

"Unfortunately, no. That is why I called you here. I need spies I trust to investigate. The patrols report that defenses in the Velvet Woods are crumbling, so there should be few organized impediments. Crevan, Delwyn, and Lir will travel as official visitors and approach from the north. Owen and Turi, you will journey by stealth from the west."

"I'll join the stealth group," Bran said quickly.

Faolan narrowed his eyes at Bran.

"I think not. You gave me your word that you wouldn't travel through a portal, but temptation is a difficult beast to master. You will stay here and help me further examine the signals coming from the room of enchantments. Kelan, you too. Three will give us more power." Faolan ignored Bran's crestfallen face and waved at his other sons. "Go, now. Find answers as swiftly as you can."

***

A chill wind tousled Gwen's hair below her knitted winter hat, but she was glad they were in the garden. Aidan's mum was lovely, but Gwen needed to talk to Aidan alone. Suddenly, she ached for Vancouver and time alone with Aidan. She hugged herself.

Aidan swiped at a frigid-looking rhododendron with uncharacteristic fury.

"I can't *believe* Isolde would make you her heir. Without telling you." He glanced at the sky as if thinking. "Oh, wait, yes I can. Bloody typical."

Gwen was quiet. What was there to say? It was all true.

Gwen had been shocked to her core at Isolde's announcement, but when the initial amazement had worn off, she hadn't been surprised at Isolde's thoughtless actions.

"And to say that 'people are suffering,'" Aidan continued. "It's manipulation, is what it is. She knows you'll want to help. She's using your humanity against you. It worked in the summer, didn't it? Bloody scheming woman." He kicked a loose pebble with enough force that it ricocheted off the garden fence.

"I don't think it's like that. She gave me that locket back in the spring, the one that let Corann make portals to capture humans. That was before the realm fell apart. Fell apart the first time, that is. I don't think she planned to need help again in this way." After the words left her mouth, Gwen wondered why she was defending Isolde's actions.

"Even so, all of this is Isolde's fault. She is completely irresponsible. She should have figured out the succession long before a chance encounter with you. She should have sorted out the realm after the restoration spell. It's insane. Why can't she get her own house in order? Why does she expect you to clean up her messes?"

Gwen shook her head and brought her hand to her eyes. It was insane. Her life had been a room full of open doors. Now all had slammed shut except for one.

"It doesn't matter now whose fault it is, does it? There's only one way to stop chaos, and I'm the only one who can do it."

Aidan stared at her for a few long moments.

"Are you seriously considering this? Being queen of the

Velvet Woods? In the Otherworld?" His breath escaped him in a puff of disbelief. Gwen turned her head to look at the top of a swaying apple tree. She couldn't meet his beautiful green eyes any longer, full of love and hurt.

"I don't want to talk about this." She swallowed. "I can't think about it." How could she leave everything behind? Her life was only beginning. There was so much more to see, to do—she had only been with Aidan for a few months. What of their future? There had to be another way. She couldn't live in the Otherworld.

Aidan paused, then enveloped her in a warm embrace that she only resisted for a moment before folding gratefully into him.

They rocked together for a minute. Gwen's cheek pressed into the soft knit of Aidan's sweater, and she tried not to think of the future. Aidan tensed.

"Gwen. What if we talk to Faolan?"

Gwen looked up at Aidan's face. His eyes were bright with hope.

"Bran said Faolan was one of the most powerfully magic Breenan," said Aidan. "Perhaps he'll know how to fix the realm without you needing to stay."

Gwen nodded slowly. Her chest tightened with fearful hope. Might there be a way out of this mess? Would Bran's father have the answers they needed?

"Yes," she breathed. "Maybe he'll know how to change the realm's succession, or fix the restoration spell…"

"Let's go see him." Aidan's fingers gripped her waist in his determination. "We'll get some answers."

"One more trip to the Otherworld." Every time Gwen left the Breenan world, she thought it would be the last time. And yet, here they were again, ready to pass through a portal once more. "I'm not looking forward to walking through the woods for days. Surely there's a better way to get to the Wintertree realm."

"I have an idea for that." Aidan's smile was the first she'd seen on him that day.

***

Aidan placed his backpack on the floor beside his shoes. Deirdre looked around at Ada's front hallway, bare but for a long Persian rug and a watercolor of orange hills behind a placid lake. Gwen gestured at the living room.

"I'll just be a few minutes. There's not much to pack, thanks to your mum," Gwen smiled at Deirdre. "We have plenty of food."

"I'll break my back," Aidan said, making a show of stretching. "The jar of blackcurrant jam was excessive."

"You'll be thankful for it before long, I have no doubt," Deirdre said. She chivvied Aidan into the living room. "We'll wait for you here, Gwen. I'd like to meet your father and hear the plan."

Gwen raced up the steps and knocked firmly on the guestroom door.

"You may enter," said Isolde faintly from inside. Gwen swung the door open and gave her mother only a cursory glance before she turned to the dresser for clothes. Isolde lay on Gwen's bed, dressed incongruously in a spare pair of Gwen's jeans and a loose cardigan of Ada's. The white ballgown hung over a chair, ripped and stained beyond redemption. Isolde stared at the ceiling, her face pale and her long black locks strewn across the pillow.

Gwen threw spare underwear and shirts into a backpack borrowed from Deirdre. She had shoved her toothbrush in the front pouch before Isolde spoke again.

"You are preparing for a journey," she stated without inflection. "Where will you go?"

"The Otherworld, obviously, to fix your mess." Gwen didn't bother to hide her irritation. Hadn't Isolde guessed what Gwen would do? Isn't that why Isolde had made her the heir, had come here to foist the weight of responsibility directly on her shoulders? Because she knew Gwen would take it on? Gwen ground her teeth and shoved her hairbrush deep into the backpack.

Isolde said nothing else, and Gwen shut the door behind her with more force than necessary. She trotted downstairs and heard her father's voice.

"Ah, Gwen," Alan said when she entered the living room. "I was just chatting with Aidan and his mother Deirdre." He looked searchingly at her. "What's happening?"

"Dad." She swallowed, then forged ahead. "Aidan and I are going to the Otherworld for a little while. I need to figure out what to do about the succession."

"Gwen, you don't need to do anything." Her father clenched his fists and glanced toward the stairs with frustration. "Anything that happens now is entirely on Isolde's head. She had no right to put anything on you."

Gwen took his hands in hers and smoothed out the tight fingers.

"Dad, I know," she said gently. "I don't have to do anything. It's all Isolde's fault. But she's out of commission, and the worlds are ripping apart. I might be able to help. How can I say no?"

Alan gazed at her.

"How was I blessed with such a strong, beautiful daughter?" he whispered. "I don't want you to throw your life away in the Otherworld."

Gwen exhaled sharply in a little laugh.

"I have no intention of taking Isolde's throne, not unless it's the very last option. No, Aidan and I are going to see Faolan. Maybe he can figure out how to remove the succession magic or fix the portal rips. If anyone knows, he will."

Alan nodded slowly, but the worried expression did not leave his face.

"I still don't like you going back there again. I know you've done it before, but you've risked it so many times—surely you're pushing your luck."

"If I might interrupt," Deirdre said softly. Alan turned to look at her and she put her hands up. "I know, I don't like the idea of these two traipsing off to another world either. Especially since yesterday was the first I'd ever heard of it." She threw a glance at Aidan, who looked abashed. "I saw Aidan fend off three massive wolves. Wolves, of all things! If their—magic," her mouth was clearly uncomfortable with the word. "Can achieve that, my fears are appeased. Slightly."

Alan's mouth was tight, but he eventually nodded.

"It's powerful, but the others are more powerful still. I'll come with you this time. I may not have magic, but I can help protect you all the same."

"You can't," Gwen said at once. "If you're in the

Otherworld, I can't make a portal to get back. Then we're relying on Aidan's connection. If anything happened to Deirdre, we would be stuck there, just like my uncle was." This wasn't entirely true, as she could escape the Otherworld through the torn portals that were cropping up with greater and greater frequency. But the thought of her father in the Otherworld frightened her. There was too much overlap between her worlds as it was, and she needed to know that he would be there, waiting for her to return.

Alan sighed and rubbed his face.

"If you must go, keep your head down. And," he put his hand on Gwen's shoulder. "None of this disappear-for-a-week nonsense. You make a portal and call me every day. Understand?"

Gwen gave him a reassuring smile.

"Good idea. This is a planned trip, we can be prepared."

"And we won't be traveling through the Otherworld this time," Aidan added. "At least, not as much. I think Faolan's palace is in Bury St. Edmunds, or close by. We can take the train right there and walk the remainder."

"Look for the Crescent Lake," said a voice from the hallway. Gwen turned sharply to see Isolde leaning against the doorway, her face pale.

"That's Gwen's mum," Aidan whispered to Deirdre. "From the Otherworld." Deirdre nodded, her wide eyes raking over Isolde with intense curiosity.

"If one is to believe the stories," Isolde said. "The Crescent Lake is one of the few obvious landmarks that are unchanged between the two worlds, along with the shoreline of the Whitecliff realm, and a few others. The Crescent Lake is to the east of the Wintertree capital."

"That sounds like Ampton Water, in Great Livermere," Deirdre said. "Does it have a tiny lake at the north end?"

Isolde nodded.

"Then you can take the train to Bury St. Edmunds, and take a cab to Great Livermere," said Deirdre. "You'll practically land on top of it."

Gwen looked at Aidan, who raised an eyebrow.

"Ready for a meet and greet with your favorite Breenan king?"

"I guess I'll have to be," she replied. "I packed that ridiculous tiara, so we can ask him what he meant by giving it to me."

"What's this?" Deirdre asked. Gwen rustled in her backpack and extracted a leather-wrapped bundle, which she carefully unfolded to reveal the tiara. It was rose gold, with an intricate working of blue sapphires and emeralds in the form of flowers and leaves. It looked impossibly expensive.

"A gift from Faolan after we saved his son Bran. Aidan hid it at your house, so I wouldn't have to explain it at customs. Faolan accompanied it with some cryptic words about me needing it."

"He knew I had no other potential heirs," Isolde said. "He would have guessed that you would be the only choice."

Her knees buckled then, and she caught herself on the door frame. Alan leaped up and helped her to the couch. Gwen shuffled over to make some distance between herself and Isolde. Even weak and defenseless, Isolde still felt dangerous to Gwen.

"I was going to ask why Isolde couldn't go see this Faolan," said Alan as he perched on the coffee table. "But I guess we have our answer."

"Corann was right." Isolde put her head in her hands. "My magic was drained out of me, and my strength with it. My recovery will be slow."

Gwen ignored her. She had no patience for Isolde's moaning or her self-reflections. She was surprised to see her father's hand touch Isolde's shoulder tentatively, and turned to Aidan to avoid the uncomfortable sight.

"Ready to go? How often do the trains run?"

"Every hour, I believe," Deirdre said.

"No time like the present." Aidan shouldered his pack. "Let's find the Crescent Lake, also known as Ampton Water."

***

Alan shut the door behind Aidan, Deirdre, and his daughter with a soft click. He leaned his forehead against the closed door briefly with eyes tightly shut. Then he heaved a great sigh and slowly walked to the living room.

Isolde stood beside the dying fire, facing the hallway. Gwen's borrowed jeans rode above the ankle on her longer legs, and Ada's oversized cardigan hung askew on her shoulders. She looked awkward, diminished, a far cry from the raven-haired beauty Alan had first met on the hill so many years ago, or even the confident queen Gwen had described from the Otherworld. Alan looked at her for a long minute, then sighed again.

78

"Tea, Isolde? Or perhaps something stronger—I think Ada has some sherry tucked away."

"Thank you," Isolde murmured. "You may decide."

Alan took two fussy crystal glasses and a dusty bottle of sherry from the sideboard cupboard and poured two large portions. He offered one to Isolde. She took it, careful not to touch Alan's hand this time. Alan sat heavily on the couch and gulped half of his sherry in one go. Isolde perched on the edge of the couch and sipped.

"Is it bad?" Alan asked. "The loss of your magic, I mean."

Isolde nodded.

"I feel empty. I find it difficult to stop trembling from the drain, the loss. I—I don't know who I am without it." She took another sip. "The condition should be temporary. Once I have a chance to recover, without the strain of maintaining the realm—I have hope. Without the connection, my fate is no longer tied to the realm's." Isolde's face darkened. "If Corann had not usurped my throne—how could he betray me so?"

Alan took a contemplative sip before he answered.

"Your symptoms, when did they start?"

"A few weeks ago, I suppose."

"And Corann took over yesterday." Alan nodded. "The restoration spell, it was meant to be a temporary fix, is that right?"

"Well, yes, but it was working—"

"Who oversees defenses of the realm?" Alan asked mildly. Isolde stared at him.

"Me, of course."

"And yet, the temporary restoration spell was still the

main defense, to the detriment of your health."

Isolde looked at the floor. Her eyes filled with tears.

"You're saying it's all my fault. My illness, the realm disintegrating, all of it."

Alan said nothing. Isolde dashed away tears with the back of her hand.

"But Corann's betrayal. How could he do that?" Her voice grew quiet. "I thought he loved me."

Alan shifted closer to Isolde, who sniffed. He held out a wrinkled tissue for her.

"You say he loves you. Well, when you love someone, you don't want to see them get hurt. It hurts you when they hurt. You'll do anything to take their pain away."

Isolde met Alan's clear gaze with tear-filled eyes. He watched her, detached yet with a mote of pity.

"You're saying Corann took over the realm because he couldn't bear to see me ill. You think he was right to take control."

"I don't know about that. But his actions are understandable in that light."

Isolde stared into the amber liquid swirling at the bottom of her glass for a long moment. Then she put it down on the side table and stood.

"Thank you for the drink, Alan. I shall rest now."

Alan nodded, and Isolde walked out of the room, her too-large cardigan brushing the couch as she left. Alan finished the remainder of his drink in one swallow.

***

Corann leaned against the back of the wooden throne in

the ballroom. The grand room was uncharacteristically empty—no dancers spun on the gleaming parquet floor and no music drifted between the stone pillars. Corann's fingers ran over carved deer on the armrest, then he shifted as the carvings dug into his back. He squinted at a branch of holly in his lap covered with carefully placed berries and deciphered the message they contained.

A door that led into the castle swung open to discharge three courtiers, two male and one female, in no-nonsense attire. Their slim-fitting trousers, leather coats, and light boots were a sharp contrast to the finery the ballroom was used to hosting. Their apparel was made of fine materials and was clearly expensive, indicating their positions at court.

"My lord," the woman said, bending her knee in the modified bow used by female Breenan when not in skirts. The men behind her bowed as well. "We have gathered all the eligible warriors of the realm for your army, as you ordered."

Corann leaned forward.

"How many?"

The man's brow wrinkled.

"More than we expected, but most are woefully undertrained."

"It's been so many generations since we've had a proper fighting force, it's no wonder." Corann waved his hand in dismissal of the courtier's concerns. "Numbers are the crucial thing. Fighting can be taught. Start training drills this afternoon. And organize them into fighting groups of three—I want patrols to start within a week. Wintertree has the right idea."

"But King Faolan combines his patrols with defensive magic garnered from the Wintertree," said one man.

"And once I've tapped into the magic of our realm, we will supplement also," Corann said with easy assurance. The man opened his mouth to speak, but the bang of a door silenced him. A maid ran toward the group and threw herself into a hasty curtsey.

"My lord, I'm so sorry to interrupt."

"You may speak," Corann said with authority.

"It's in the kitchens. I don't know what—it's like nothing I've seen before. No one knows what to do."

"I don't understand," said Corann. "Is it an animal?"

"No! Rather a great hole from nothing, to…" The maid spread her hands helplessly.

Corann's eyes narrowed in thought.

"Take me there."

The maid led Corann and the three courtiers through the castle door and into a wide hall lined with alternating lengthy mirrors and deep purple curtains made of thick velvet. The maid held open a curtain in the center of the right wall to reveal a stout wooden door hidden behind it. She clattered down a plain wooden staircase unadorned except by a glowing lantern.

The stairs led to a cavernous kitchen, dimly lit by more lanterns and roaring fires in twelve hearths inset in the walls. Cooks and maids bustled about long wooden tables, preparing the next meal.

"It's in the storeroom," said the maid they followed. "We're almost there."

Another set of stairs led down through a small archway, their stone treads worn smooth by countless feet. The storeroom was packed with crates, barrels of oil, racks of wine, hooks with dried meat, and every other food needed to prepare meals for all the castle inhabitants.

Corann and the courtiers didn't spare a glance to this vision of plenty. Instead, their gazes were fixed on the portal before them.

Torn fragments of the fabric of the world shimmered around a hole large enough to walk through with ease. The other side, the human world, displayed a packed wall of soil. During the long silence while they stared, a thick worm wriggled out of the dirt and fell to the stone floor. It squirmed.

"It's a portal," Corann said at last. "A portal to the human world."

"It appeared overnight," said the maid in hushed tones. "No one went down there, cook is certain. And it grows bigger."

A faint ripping punctuated her words when a strip peeled away from the side of the hole. The maid stepped back and covered her mouth, and the courtiers glanced at each other in alarm. Corann narrowed his eyes, then turned to face the maid.

"You needn't worry. It's perfectly harmless. Simply leave it be and continue on with your work."

The maid curtsied then backed away hastily to the stairs. Corann looked at the gaping courtiers.

"You're certain it's safe?" the female courtier ventured before Corann could speak.

"Perfectly." Corann waved at the portal. "It's blocked on the human side, so nothing can pass between the worlds."

"I suppose you would know. You traveled there for Isolde, did you not?"

"I did."

"Why is it here? Who made it?" The courtier looked worried.

"I expect it's the consequences of the failing restoration spell," Corann said. "Isolde put her confidence in the wrong things: first, the portal-making abilities of her half-breed daughter, and second, the spell that the same half-breed wrought for her. It was foolish, and we pay the price." Corann smoothed his shirt. "Thankfully, with your support, I can now set the realm to rights."

The other three looked reassured.

"Defense with trained soldiers is an excellent start but the people of this realm deserve more," Corann said. "It's time I mastered the room of enchantments."

"Do you think it will work for you?" said the woman doubtfully. "It's intimately connected to the ruling family. They gathered the windfalls from every type of tree within the realm—"

"Even the tools for carving were crafted from stone from the land," one of the men added.

"And when they made the room, they infused their own magic in it," the woman continued. "They, and only they, connect to the realm in deep ways through the power of the room. How do you plan to master it?"

Corann smiled.

"Don't be concerned. My ancestor was the younger brother of Isolde's great-grandmother. The room will recognize my right, I'm sure. Go, now, organize the training, and I will bring you good news this evening."

The others smiled and nodded, then turned to file up the stone steps. When the last disappeared through the doorway, Corann's confident smile fell from his face and worry creased his brow. With halting steps, he walked back upstairs.

Once in the empty ballroom, Corann moved slowly to a small but imposing wooden door in the wall behind the dais, carved with a medley of woodland animals and curling vines. He stared at the door for a long moment, then reached out and firmly pulled the handle.

The door did not budge. Corann frowned and pulled harder. Nothing happened. It wasn't until Corann put a foot on the wall and threw his weight back that it finally swung open.

Corann tumbled to the floor then sprang up and looked around. The ballroom was devoid of witnesses, so he strode forward into the room of enchantments. The door slammed shut behind him of its own accord.

The room was the black of a starless night. Corann lifted his arm, and a dim light glowed from lanterns mounted on the walls. They flickered with pale yellow fire.

Corann looked around, a wary expression on his face. He was surrounded on every side by the carvings of countless animals, rendered lifelike by the fluttering light. Lions glowered, wolves sneered, and even deer looked askance at the usurper. The walls pressed close and the wooden ceiling lay low over Corann's head. A movement caught his eye and he whirled around, but nothing was there. He glared at the carvings, then squared his shoulders and raised his hands. They glowed with molten yellow light that dripped to the massive carved daisy covering the floor.

"I am Corann, descendent of Donovan the Hunter. I am the ruler of the Velvet Woods and I claim my right to use this room of enchantments for the defense of the realm."

The already dim lanterns darkened to a menacing red and pulsed. Corann looked unnerved but tightened his jaw. More yellow light of his magic poured out of his hands and spread over the petals of the daisy.

The air rippled subtly. Corann narrowed his eyes and sent his magic to the carved walls, where it spread to cover vines and animals alike.

But the room had had enough. The huge daisy heaved and buckled. Corann fell on his side, and three massive petals rose high. Corann rolled uncontrollably toward the door, which swung open to allow his passage. He landed in a heap on the threshold and the door closed with a heavy finality.

Corann leaped to his feet with his hair mussed and his shirt untucked. His fist rose to pound on the door but paused when he noticed the wondering gazes of two fighters passing through the ballroom.

"I'm testing the limits of the room of enchantments," he called out. "It's very powerful. I'm pleased—our defenses will be strong."

The fighters nodded and continued walking. When they disappeared, Corann yanked at the handle. The door didn't budge. He rested his head on it in despair.

***

Loniel gazed at the scene before him and smiled. The fire burned bright and hot, and drums throbbed in the cold night air. His people leaped and danced around the fire, barefooted despite the snow, their gleaming faces happy, or blissful, or serene. One woman twirled away from the dance and picked up a goblet from a tray. She moved gracefully to his side.

"Won't you drink and dance with us, Loniel? It is unlike you to be so restrained."

Loniel took the goblet from her and drank deeply.

"No, it is not. Events are unfolding that cloud my mind."

"You must heed your own advice." She took his hand and pulled him playfully forward. "The bonfire is for those who wish to forget their past cares. Leave your worries and woes, for at the bonfire there is only this moment."

Loniel laughed.

"Quite right. I forget myself." He drained the goblet and tossed it to one side, then let himself be led to the dancers.

A crashing noise from deep in the forest caused everyone to freeze. They all looked at Loniel with anticipation. Loniel held up his hand, and it hung there, motionless. The crashing grew louder, then there was a shout.

"Hello! Can you help me? Help!"

Loniel bought his hand down in a swift motion. The fire died instantly, dark and cold in a pile of blackened logs. Loniel's people snatched up trays and drums with practiced silence and slipped away through the trees. Loniel led them as they ran noiselessly after, until they reached another clearing. Drums were hastily placed to the side and dancers arranged themselves in a circle. When Loniel was certain they were ready, he pointed his hand at the center of the circle.

A fire burst to life, roaring and hot as if it had been burning for hours. The drums pounded, and the dancers moved with wild grace.

Crashing in the distance cut through the drums. At a distant shout, the dancers looked to Loniel with mischievous smiles. He raised his hand once more but before he could quench the fire, a shout from a different direction gave him pause. There was another one, and another.

"Hi! Over here!"

"Where are we?"

"Please help me!"

Loniel brought his hand down and the fire died, but his smile had been replaced by a frown. He led his people along a winding track to a different opening in the forest. Another fire was lit, another dance begun, but still the shouts pursued. Loniel sighed.

"Let the humans come. The pleasure is diminished when the sport is too easy."

His people shrugged and continued to dance around the fire. Some revelers picked up jugs of wine and prepared to greet the humans.

Five of them burst into the clearing, disheveled and wild-eyed.

"We're lost," said one woman, her parka zipped up tightly against the cold. "Please, where are we?"

"Right where you should be, right here, right now,"

said Loniel calmly. He spread his arms. "Come, warm yourselves by the fire. Eat, drink, rest after your toils. You are welcome here."

Some looked suspicious, others merely relieved. Wine bearers quickly poured goblets of dark liquid and pressed them into the humans' hands. As they drank, a blissful expression stole across each face. As one, they dropped to the ground, unconscious.

Loniel gestured to his people. Five men came forward and picked the humans up as they slumbered.

"Come, to the nearest portal. I am weary of this game tonight."

The men followed Loniel through the forest to a wild boxwood. Loniel passed his hand over it and branches retreated to show a ragged portal. He jumped nimbly through, and the others followed more slowly with their loads.

"Leave them here," he said. Once the sleeping bodies were deposited in a pile of limbs, Loniel waved his hand and a glowing green dome descended upon the group.

"That will warm them until morning." Loniel clapped a hand on the shoulder of the nearest man. "Back to the bonfire with you all. Enjoy it in my absence."

"Where do you go?" asked one as he stepped through the portal.

"There are too many portals, too many humans in our world." Loniel touched the boxwood and it grew back into place over the portal. "I must find out more."

***

Aidan pointed down the train platform.

"This way, Gwen. Have your bag? Good."

Gwen jogged after him and slipped her hand in his. He glanced at her with a smile.

"This is nice," said Gwen. "I feel like we're taking a holiday together."

"Ha. The transportation will be a little unorthodox from now on. And Faolan is a terrible concierge."

They pushed through the people lined up for tickets and grouped in clusters in the waiting room until they exited the glass outer doors. Aidan looked around to get his bearings.

"It's only a few miles. Do you want to make a portal and walk from here? I don't want to miss Faolan's city."

Gwen glanced around until she spotted a solid cement partition leading to a loading bay.

"Let's make the portal over there. It looks empty."

They sauntered over, then ducked behind the partition when nobody was looking. Gwen spread her hand toward Aidan.

"It's all yours. Go for it."

"You don't want to?"

"Isolde's in the human world," said Gwen with a shrug. It still felt wrong for Isolde to be here. "I can't make a portal without my anchor, remember? There's no one on the other side for me to visit."

"Oh, right." Aidan rolled his shoulders and held out an arm.

"Not too big," Gwen said. "Who knows how long it will take to close."

"Right," Aidan said again. His eyes closed, and a

moment later a portal appeared in midair, no larger than the width of Aidan's shoulders.

"Nice. Ready to go back?"

"Let's do it," said Aidan.

A ripping noise interrupted his words. Aidan's perfectly round portal was now oblong, with a strip dangling from the base of the circle. Gwen gasped.

"Oh, no. That can't be good."

"Will it close?" Aidan gingerly lifted the strip and attempted to press the pieces together, to no avail. When he dropped the strip, it ripped further.

"Let's get to Faolan, and quickly," Gwen said. "We need answers."

"What if someone stumbles across this portal?" Aidan looked around, then dragged an empty wooden crate to partially obscure a view of the portal from the road.

"That will have to do," Gwen said. She put a hand on the crate to steady herself, then climbed through the portal. Aidan clambered in after her.

Chapter 5

Bran threw open the door of Wintertree realm's room of enchantments with an expression of relief. His brother Kelan followed and shut the door carefully behind him. Bran collapsed onto a nearby bench and wiped his brow with his sleeve.

"Father's a tyrant," he said. "Working us to the bone like that."

"You do like to complain," said Kelan, but his forehead glistened under his blond hair and he looked tired. "Father's still in there, and twice our age."

"That's an unfair comparison. You know he's a maniac."

"At least we've pinpointed the exact location of every new portal in the realm," said Kelan.

"Except new ones keep cropping up," said Bran with an uncharacteristic frown on his face. "You can tell Father's concerned."

"Well, look at you, worrying about things." Kelan ruffled Bran's hair. "Acting like an adult for once. Did your elder mark finally sink in?"

Bran swatted Kelan's hand away with a grin.

"I'm sure it won't last long, don't worry." A thoughtful expression crossed his face, and he pressed a hand against his chest.

"What's wrong?" Kelan asked.

"Something—I think someone is summoning me." Bran stared at Kelan with dawning excitement. "It feels like the ring I gave Gwen, my half-human friend. That must mean she's in our world."

"How strong is the summoning?"

Bran closed his eyes briefly.

"She's close."

Kelan glanced at the door of the room of enchantments.

"He'll be in there for hours on that particular spell, and it's a solitary one. Shall we find this Gwen of yours?"

Bran leaped up and clapped Kelan on the back.

"Grab our cloaks and weapons. I'll meet you in the stables."

***

Dead grasses rustled against Gwen's calves, grasses that covered a meadow in the clutches of winter. There was no snow, but a biting wind tore through her jacket. It caused her to shiver and Aidan to tighten the drawstring of his hood. Gwen rubbed a copper ring on her thumb absentmindedly. They passed through shallow rolling hills for almost two hours before they reached their destination. The Crescent Lake lay at their feet, its quiet waters still against the shore. It was only a small waterway, but peaceful with ducks floating serenely on the surface.

There were no signs of habitation, let alone the capital of the Wintertree realm. Gwen's shoulders slumped in disappointment. She had hoped that Isolde's directions would lead them directly to the city gates. She wrapped her arms around herself.

"Where's Faolan's palace?" said Aidan. "The lake is familiar, but nothing else is."

"At least we're closer than last time. Supposedly. Assuming we have the right spot."

Gwen adjusted her backpack and followed Aidan across the meadow interspersed with clumps of high bushes. She was thankful for her warm coat and sturdy walking shoes, neither of which she had worn on her previous trips to the Otherworld.

Conversation between Gwen and Aidan eventually drifted away into the gray air. The oppressive silence of the wintery landscape lowered Gwen's spirits until all she could think about was the wooden throne of the Velvet Woods. It loomed in her mind, relentlessly reminding her of what the future would hold if Faolan had no answers. Assuming they could find Faolan, of course.

If I become queen, Gwen thought. *The first thing that will change is the name of the Velvet Woods*. Then she shook herself. Was she seriously thinking of ruling as a possibility? She quickened her footsteps to draw level with Aidan.

"Any sign of the Wintertree capital?" she asked him. They had found a dirt track, muddy in places, that meandered toward the Crescent Lake. It had led them out of a frozen forest ten minutes ago.

"Only this road we're following," said Aidan. He

glanced at it with narrowed eyes. "Hardly worthy of the name."

"Deer track, more like." Gwen put her thumbs through her backpack straps. "I hope the capital turns up soon. I didn't bargain on walking all afternoon."

"Did you hear that?" Aidan said sharply. He put a hand on her arm to stop her. Gwen strained her ears. Was that the snorting of a horse in the distance? They looked at each other, their eyes wide. Gwen swallowed. She was never certain if they would encounter friend or foe in the Otherworld.

Footsteps thundered nearby before a holly bush exploded beside Gwen. She shrieked and clutched Aidan. Who was attacking them? What would they do now? Any defensive spells she had practiced with Aidan flew out of her mind in the panic. Their attacker, with hair as copper as Aidan's own, opened his arms to surround them. That face…

"Bran?" Gwen gasped when she found herself in a tight embrace with Aidan and Bran. Bran pulled back and grinned widely.

"You summoned me with your ring!"

"Did I?" Gwen was perplexed. Had she done a spell? "I must have done it without realizing."

"Handy, though," said Aidan. "Your subconscious has a great sense of timing."

"This is excellent!" said Bran. "What are you doing here? Where are you going?"

"The Wintertree capital, actually," Gwen said when she had caught her breath.

"Then why are you on this road? It's the wrong way,

certainly. You would have missed Winterwood—it's past the peak, but on the east, not the west." Bran waved at his brother. "Gwen, Aidan, this is my brother Kelan. The youngest besides me. Not as much of a worrier as Crevan, not as joyless as Owen…"

"Hardly a difficult proposition," said Kelan.

"True enough," said Bran. He threw an arm around each of Gwen's and Aidan's shoulders, knocking his black fur cloak off his arms. "I brought spare mounts—it's quite a walk otherwise."

"Great, horses," Gwen said without enthusiasm. The memory of her sore bottom when she had last ridden a horse resurfaced.

Aidan looked resigned, but he said, "Thanks, Bran. The sooner we get to Winterwood, the better."

"Why did you come? Was it to visit me?" Bran said as he helped Gwen into her saddle. Gwen laughed.

"Just a wonderful bonus." She was quiet for a moment while her horse followed Kelan's, wondering where to start.

"Is it something to do with the errant portals being created?" asked Kelan. Gwen lifted her eyebrows.

"Yes, actually. We thought your father might have some answers about that, and a related issue."

"Save the explanation for him, then," Kelan said. "Father will want the full account."

There was a moment's silence, which Bran broke.

"It's lucky I found you. You and your portals—you have no idea what the terrain looks like in our world when you're in the human world. You could be anywhere— Wintertree, Velvet Woods, imagine if you went to the

Forbidden Lands!" He clearly had not been dwelling on the mystery of Gwen and Aidan's reasons for visiting the Otherworld.

"Bran, what do you know about the Forbidden Lands?" Before Gwen had sent her uncle Finn back through a portal, he had said he was from the Forbidden Lands, but his description had been vague. She was curious to know more. "I found out that—"

"I always forget how much you two don't know!" Bran interrupted. "The Forbidden Lands are where escaped tribeless ones gather, those who didn't get their proper mark. No one goes there. I have no idea what it's like. It's a refuge for them, though."

"It's surrounded by a powerful magic that neutralizes their powers," said Kelan. He helped Gwen onto her horse. "Honestly, Bran, it's astonishing what you don't know. The tribeless ones can't control their magic, so they are sent to the Forbidden Lands where they can be safe, for themselves and everyone else. Their magic is volatile and unpredictable, and the mountains around the Forbidden Lands contain them."

"That's why?" Bran stroked the mane of his horse. "I thought they were hunted down after the marking ceremony."

Kelan shook his head, then nudged his horse into a trot. Gwen digested the slew of information while they rode. After a quarter hour's gentle ride, their horses climbed a grassy rise and slowed at the crest. Nestled in a valley below them was a cluster of roofs liberally covered with barren and evergreen vines. In the center rose a large wooden mansion.

"There's Winterwood," said Bran.

***

Bran burst through the massive double doors, past the shivering guards into the hall beyond. The eyes of the stuffed animal heads lining the walls from floor to ceiling stared beadily at him. He took no notice.

"We're here!" he said unnecessarily to the others. He shrugged off his thick fur cloak and handed it to a servant who had hurried toward him. "Coats off, then let's have some fun."

"Your father first," Aidan reminded him.

"Oh, right." Bran looked crestfallen for a moment, then brightened. "After?"

"Hopefully," Gwen said. Kelan rolled his eyes.

"He's in the great hall. This way."

Kelan led them down the wide corridor to another set of double doors.

"Do you think he'll have finished the locator spell yet?" Bran asked.

"Probably only just. He still had to do the directional spell without us." Kelan paused at the doors and held a hand to his forehead with a wince.

"Headache?" said Bran. "Where's your healing charm?"

"I thought I would try without it for a while." Kelan pulled a plain silver bracelet from his pocket and pushed it on his wrist. Immediately, his face cleared with relief. "A bad idea, apparently."

"Does that bracelet take away your headache?" asked

Gwen with interest.

"It lessens the symptoms, makes them more manageable. I'm prone to headaches, and the charm reduces the pain. Come on, best not to keep Father waiting." He pushed the doors open with more care than Bran had shown earlier.

Gwen looked around the hall. The semi-transparent glass windows that rose from floor to tall ceiling let the dim light of a winter's afternoon filter over the empty room. Empty, except for one lone figure sitting on a bench beside a small wooden door. Faolan's eyes were closed and his slumped shoulders spoke of his fatigue. His eyes sprang open sharply and his back straightened when he heard their footsteps.

"Bran, Kelan, you're back. Good. I want to try the cluster spell." His eyes raked over Aidan and rested on Gwen's face. "Your companions seem familiar..."

"You remember Gwen and Aidan, Father," said Bran. "They saved my life a few months ago."

A look of comprehension passed over Faolan's face, and he stood up.

"Of course. My apologies. Declan's son and Isolde's daughter. Half-humans. Wait." He looked abruptly at Kelan. "Does this mean your brothers are back? What news from the Velvet Woods?"

"No," said Kelan. "They arrived separately." He looked at Aidan. "By way of the Velvet Woods?"

"In a manner of speaking," said Gwen. "Do you know what happened in Isolde's realm?"

"I have sent spies to gather information, but there is no news yet," said Faolan. "Something is amiss, this I know—I can sense it in my connection to the realm."

"Amiss. Yeah, you could call it that," said Gwen. "Isolde's second-in-command, Corann, took over rule of the realm. Isolde escaped to the human world to find me. Says I'm her heir and I have to take the throne to bring stability to the realm. Is that why you gave me this?" She pulled the tiara out of Aidan's backpack, brandished it at Faolan, then set it down on the bench. "Oh, and the decaying restoration spell is creating portals everywhere, according to Loniel."

Faolan listened to Gwen's monologue in silence, his face growing stony. There was a hush when Gwen finished.

"I dislike critiquing my fellow rulers, but Isolde is worthy of castigation," he said at last. "She should have known better than to rely on the restoration spell for so long. And to require it in the first place..." He paced toward the center of the hall and then turned. "And now Wintertree is paying the price. The other realms, too, if my observations are correct." He waved impatiently at the room of enchantments. "Portals are opening frequently, with no signs of closing. The greatest number are within the Velvet Woods and spread from there into other realms."

A chill crossed Gwen's shoulders.

"How many portals?" she asked quietly.

"Dozens, with more every day." Faolan looked tired.

"Everyone is so gloomy about this," Bran said, looking around at them all. "Maybe these portals opening is a wonderful opportunity to join the worlds together! I know humans don't have the best reputation here," Bran glanced at Gwen and Aidan. "But they really are fun. I'm sure we could learn a lot from each other."

Bran's declaration garnered an uncharacteristic twitch of Faolan's mouth that Gwen was tempted to interpret as an indulgent smile. Then he sighed.

"As admirable as your sentiments may be, Bran, it's unfortunately an impossibility. If the Gwerud, Loniel, is correct—and with his experience, I suspect he is—then the portals will keep opening until the worlds rip apart. Our inclement weather is only the first sign of the catastrophes to come, I fear."

"Now what?" said Kelan. "We have to instate Gwen on the throne to close the portals, of course. But how?"

"War," said Faolan. "The usurper must be removed by force. Mainly because I doubt he will step down without sufficient motivation, but also to send a message to other potential usurpers. It's an excellent opportunity to remind our people of who rules them and why."

"The last thing I want is to be queen of the Velvet Woods," said Gwen, her heart hammering at Faolan's blasé acceptance of her rule. "That's why we came here—to ask you if there is any way to change the succession. Everyone always says you have the most powerful magic, so we hoped you would have an answer."

Faolan stared at her for a moment and looked thoughtful.

"Most desire the throne, so there is not much precedent to inspect. If you'll allow me to examine you, I can verify your status as heir. It would be prudent to confirm the validity of your claim before we go to war, in any event."

Faolan walked to the wooden door set into the only

wall without windows. He opened it and gestured to Gwen.

"This way."

***

Gwen walked slowly into the room after a hesitant glance at Bran, who nodded. Faolan entered after and closed the door with a deliberate thud. It was as dark as a moonless night for a few moments, long enough for Gwen's heart to begin hammering in her chest.

Then, a gentle glow emerged from seven orange flames ensconced in glass-fronted lanterns on the walls. It illuminated Faolan's room of enchantments, which was far different from Isolde's.

The room was round and lined with wood, but there the similarities ended. The walls were carved roughly with no discernable pattern or pictures, and splintery wood hung in disintegrating strips. Nothing was polished or oiled except the floor, which gleamed with smooth perfection.

"It's like we're in a tree," said Gwen aloud.

"Very perceptive," said Faolan. Gwen wasn't sure if he was serious or mocking her. "The Wintertree, in fact. This palace was built around the remains of the great oak of the realm's beginnings. The Wintertree's roots run deep, further still when strengthened by generations of my ancestors' magic."

"Why was it called the Wintertree?" said Gwen, interested.

"Legend has it that the tree had no leaves, as if in a perpetual winter, yet continued to grow and flourish.

Perhaps it was powered by a deeper magic than we now know. Much is lost to time, but the tree remains a powerful link to the land, even in its current state." Faolan's voice turned brisk. "Stand in the center of the room and hold your arms out before you."

Gwen walked forward to the midpoint, her interest in the Wintertree withering in the face of the unknown tests Faolan would do on her. She stood on the inset circle of pale polished wood in the smooth floor and swallowed.

"How much control do you have over your magic?" he asked with narrowed eyes.

"I've been practicing. I can do a few things. Move things around, small stuff. Portals."

"Of course. Good, that will make this process easier." Faolan rolled up his sleeves. "I could perform the tests either way, but it simplifies the procedure. Bring your magic out of your essence into your hands and hold it there for as long as you can."

"My essence?"

"In here," he patted his chest. "Where the magic resides."

"Oh, right." Gwen quickly closed her eyes and reached into the warm core of magic in her chest, then brought it into her hands.

Faolan stepped in front of her and carefully examined the glowing white light pooled in her palms, first with his eyes, then with fingertips glowing with his own orange light. Occasionally, he sent tendrils of magic to prod her own. His eyes were intense with concentration and reflected the white and orange glows.

It was harder than Gwen had imagined keeping her

magic in her hands. It wanted to escape, to work on a spell, and when Gwen didn't let it, it tried to retreat up her arms. Faolan's prodding, while not unpleasant, was not comfortable either.

"Do you have the object of succession?" Faolan said finally. When Gwen looked confused, he clarified. "Did she spill her blood on something?"

"Oh, the locket." Gwen let her magic retreat and reached into her shirt to draw out the necklace. "It's right here."

She lifted it over her head and placed it in Faolan's waiting hand. He waved her away.

"Off the center, please. I must conduct a test with the locket."

Gwen hopped away from the center and Faolan placed the locket on the polished floor. He kneeled and placed one hand on the floor with fingers spread. The other he held over the locket.

Faolan's magic poured visibly out of both hands and his eyes closed in concentration. Gwen stepped back and held her breath. The room with its crumbling wooden walls wavered in Gwen's vision as the flames in the lanterns dimmed and throbbed.

A few moments passed, then Faolan's eyes popped open with a frown. He pulled a short dagger out of a sheath on his belt.

"I need your blood," he said without preamble, and held out his hand.

"My blood?" said Gwen. She swallowed.

"Don't entertain foolish notions, girl. A pinprick will do. Give me your hand."

Gwen held it out and tried not to wince when Faolan quickly but lightly jabbed her index finger with the tip of his dagger. He brought the dagger tip to lie beside the locket while Gwen sucked the metallic blood from her injured digit.

Faolan spent a few minutes prodding at the two objects with his magic. A few indistinct murmurs escaped his lips. Gwen stayed quiet on the side of the room and wondered what Faolan was doing. Was it a good sign that he was taking so long? Would he find out how to change the succession? Gwen wished he would say something—Faolan was nowhere near as forthcoming as his son Bran.

Finally, he stood up stiffly with a grimace and sheathed his dagger. He waved his hand at the locket.

"You may take the necklace back." When Gwen stooped to pick it up, he continued. "You are the chosen heir, of that there is no doubt. It was not a simple matter to confirm your status—my spells had to be modified to accommodate your half-human nature—but the results were clear. And with Isolde bearing no other children, the only option is you."

Chapter 6

Gwen's heart sank, and she felt nauseous. It would have been so much easier if Isolde had made a mistake.

"What about transferring the succession to someone else?" Gwen asked, clinging to this last hope.

"I have never heard of that occurring, but that does not mean it has not happened." Faolan strode to the other side of the circular room and opened a door that Gwen could have sworn wasn't there before. It swung open silently, and Gwen followed Faolan outside.

They were in a vast garden, surrounded by low walls and covered by a ceiling of uniform gray clouds. The plants varied greatly—some were trimmed neatly while others were wild, some were barren while others had green leaves fluttering on frozen stems—and a multitude of paths crossed the garden beds. Faolan strode ahead, and Gwen trotted to catch up.

"What is this place?"

"The history garden of the realm of Wintertree," Faolan said absently. "The accounts are more succinct in the winter, due to a lack of foliage, but the information we need will be there."

"What are we looking for?" Gwen glanced around the garden and marveled at how anyone could make sense of the twisted profusion of branches and leaves. Was there really a whole library's worth of history books within the stone walls of the garden?

Faolan stopped in front of the gnarled stems of a hawthorn tree. His eyes raked over the branches for a few moments, then he knelt before a small heather bush covered in tiny white flowers.

"By chance, the full account is in bloom and able to be studied," Faolan murmured.

"What is it? What does it say?" Gwen peeked over Faolan's shoulder, but the heather meant nothing to her. Faolan touched the petals gently with one finger.

"It is an account of the ruling family of Silverwood. The tale that concerns us took place many centuries ago, long before the closing of the portals. Cameron, a distant cousin of the ailing king, felt he had a more reasonable claim to the throne than the king's three-year old daughter. The king died, and the stories are unclear whether his death was a natural one or was hastened by Cameron, but that very month Cameron assumed the throne."

Faolan stroked the petals once more, and the branches shifted to expose new flowers.

"What happened then?" Gwen asked.

"Multiple accounts all describe strange portents in the winds and the rains, the sun dimming in the sky, the earth shaking. And the portals, the known paths to the human lands, the reports state that they shifted and shimmered in unforeseen ways." Faolan stood up and dusted off his knees.

"How did they stop it?" Gwen asked and held her breath.

"They removed the usurper and put the little daughter on her rightful throne," said Faolan in a matter-of-fact tone, then he looked at Gwen's downcast face and his eyes softened marginally. "I'm sorry. I know it is not what you wanted to hear. If it is any consolation, I believe you will make a fine queen, despite your reduced magic and half-blood status. You've shown deep loyalty, fortitude, and wisdom during your quest to heal my son last summer, all of which will hold you in good stead during your rule."

He nodded at her, then beckoned her to follow him. Gwen's footsteps were as heavy as her heart, and she blinked back tears. Faolan's magic and knowledge had been her only hope at escaping the fate Isolde had placed on her. With that faint hope now vanquished, Gwen could only see one path ahead.

***

She followed Faolan in a daze through the garden and back through the room of enchantments. Bran, Kelan, and Aidan were waiting on the bench in the great hall, but Aidan jumped up when the door opened. Gwen's face must have reflected her turmoil within, because Aidan groaned and covered his eyes with one hand, his fingers digging into his temples with white-knuckled ferocity.

Bran looked from Gwen to Aidan, then at his father.

"Well? What's the news?"

"Rather more ominous than I'd feared," said Faolan. He

unrolled his sleeves and smoothed them into place. "Usurpation has taken place before, and the records show that our current weather problems and portal rips will only worsen with time. A true heir must be placed on the throne of the Velvet Woods, and Gwen is the only candidate." He clapped a hand on Kelan's shoulder. "She will need our help taking her rightful place. But this is a problem that involves all the realms. Call for a conclave."

Kelan hurried from the room. Aidan looked ready to burst.

"So, that's it?" He clenched his fists at his sides. "Gwen has to be queen, and that's the end of it?"

"Precisely," said Faolan. He gazed at Aidan from under stern eyebrows. "She is the only one who can right this wrong. The fate of your world is also at stake, do not forget."

"There has to be something," Aidan said wildly. "Wait! What about Isolde? Kick Corann out and put her back. Then—she can have another baby or something."

"I rather think Isolde is past her child-bearing years," Faolan said. "And since she gave birth to no other children, we can assume that she was unable to do so. The succession is of the utmost importance, and Isolde would not have left it to chance. And while your notion of reinstating Isolde is a sensible one, the realm's room of enchantments would never allow someone to rule who was not powerful or capable enough to keep her crown. It would reject her, and we would be no further ahead. A new ruler is needed, with a new way to power the realm that does not involve temporary restoration spells."

Aidan's shoulders slumped, and his jaw worked. Gwen

walked over and put her arms around him.

"I can't believe this is happening," he murmured as he clutched her. "How could our lives be turned upside down in a heartbeat? Are you really going to live in the Otherworld forever?"

Forever. It was such a final word. The thought of never seeing her father, Aidan, and Ellie again overwhelmed her until she forced herself to shut the feelings away. She stepped back from Aidan as a thought occurred to her.

"How am I supposed to power the realm? I know hardly anything about magic, not really. If it's so difficult that Isolde can't manage it, what chance do I have?" Maybe if she wasn't magical enough to rule, she would be off the hook.

"There are many ways to power a realm," said Faolan. "The continuous song of the Whitecliff realm, the tidal magic of the Longshore realm, these are different ways to harness your power and connect it with the realm. And these decisions do not have to be made all at once. You can set up a physical defense with fighters and patrols, and eventually develop your magic once you explore your realm and find its strengths."

Gwen sighed, overwhelmed. She was not prepared for any of this.

"Gwen, Aidan," said Faolan. "You will need to take word to Isolde. She will be indispensable in our battle planning, since she knows her realm intimately. Leave at first light tomorrow and bring her back here with all haste."

"Father, you should send along an official Wintertree envoy to make sure they collect Isolde appropriately," said

110

Bran. He bounced on his heels.

"Quite right, Bran," said Faolan. "When Kelan comes back, we'll tell him to prepare for his journey to the human world tomorrow morning."

"Father!"

Faolan cracked the first true smile Gwen had ever seen on him.

"Yes, Bran, you may be my envoy."

***

Corann tapped his foot on the wooden floor of the room of enchantments and looked at the human man with annoyance.

"Think harder, will you? Everyone knows that humans are creative instead of magical, but I haven't seen much out of you yet."

"Please," said the man, his forehead sweating under stringy brown hair. He looked no older than twenty. "I don't know anything, I took a shortcut through the woods after the pub and ended up here."

"Yes, I'm quite aware of your story. And I didn't capture you for your knowledge—although that would have been a nice surprise—but for your innate abilities as a human to think creatively, to solve problems. My race has magic, but yours excels in solving problems."

"Are you an alien?" The man looked as if he wanted to laugh at the absurdity of the situation but didn't dare. Corann waved him off.

"It doesn't matter what I am. What matters is the problem. Here it is, again: this room will only respond positively to the heir of the throne, which I am not. The heir must be a relative of the ruling family, to which I am distantly connected. I need a way to make the room of enchantments accept my rule. I've already explained the properties of the magic room to you. Now, what is your suggestion?"

The man gazed blankly at Corann. When he realized that Corann was waiting for an answer, he blanched.

"Have you tried asking nicely?" The man winced at the expected reprimand for his sarcastic answer, but Corann looked thoughtful.

"An interesting notion. The room has exhibited a certain—personality, so the idea of appealing to it as a sentient creature has some merit." He waved the man off the center of the daisy and the man jumped sideways as if shocked. "Velvet Woods," Corann said clearly. "I beseech you to hear me. I am Corann, descended from Donovan the Hunter, and I now rule the realm. I vow to restore and improve it in all aspects. Isolde was failing you, but I swear to bring the realm back to the glory of old."

Nothing happened for a long moment. Corann waited, a look of cautious triumph growing on his face.

The flames shrunk until only the man's eyes were visible, shining whitely in his terror. Then the central floral disc of the daisy shot upward to send Corann flying.

The flames returned to their normal height and Corann scrambled to his feet, his face livid. The human cowered on the edge of the room while Corann stomped onto the daisy once more.

"Isolde is gone!" he shouted and sent the pale yellow light of his magic pouring from his hands onto the floor.

"And Gwendolyn is not of this world. You must accept me or suffer the consequences!"

Corann closed his eyes with a furrowed brow, straining with concentration. The room groaned. Flames from the lanterns shot up to the ceiling and the human yelped. The floor began to rock back and forth, slowly at first but with increasing intensity. Faintly, howls, squeaks, barks, and roars began to sound from the carved walls of the chamber. Wooden eyes flashed with eerie life, and limbs began to move.

Corann opened his eyes at the sounds and stopped his magic with an open mouth. He backed away toward the door, and the human stumbled after him. There was a knock from outside and they fell over the threshold. Corann slammed the door shut behind him.

A courtier stood with a questioning look.

"My lord, is something wrong? How goes your work in the room of enchantments?"

Corann attempted to control his breathing.

"I'm getting a strong response. It certainly recognized my claim. Not much longer, I think, until it is fully functional under my rule."

The courtier looked satisfied. The human gave Corann an incredulous stare but was cowed enough to stay silent. Corann snapped his fingers with a few purple sparks, and a servant hurried out of a nearby archway.

"Take the human to the cells," Corann said to the servant, who bowed in response. "I'll retrieve him later for more testing."

The courtier waited until the servant had led the protesting human out of the ballroom before speaking.

113

"A summons has arrived." The courtier held open a wide, shallow box lined with burgundy velvet. Inside were placed nine pendants. One pendant, carved from a dense brown wood with the insignia of a barren tree in silver on the face, glowed red.

"The message pendants of the nine realms," breathed Corann. "I had forgotten. You are the keeper?"

"I am, my lord. And as soon as the pendant lit, I came to you." The courtier shifted the pendant gently so Corann could see the insignia better. "It's from Wintertree with a summons for a conclave."

"Really? There hasn't been a conclave for many years. In fact, I can't recall the last time all the leaders of the nine realms gathered for a conclave. Ah, yes, it was when Queen Brenna ascended to the throne of the Riverside realm." Corann gazed at the ring with anticipation. "Perhaps this conclave is in honor of my ascension?"

"It is likely," said the courtier with a smile. "We were right to trust you, my lord. Even the other rulers acknowledge your claim. On behalf of the realm, I thank you for your courage to take the difficult steps so necessary in these troubled times."

Corann patted the courtier on his shoulder in a genial fashion.

"It was my duty, and my privilege. Come, I must leave at once. Notify the stable hands, if you will, and I'll see to it that the servants pack our clothes and supplies."

"Mine, too?" The courtier looked surprised.

"Of course. It would not be fitting for me to travel without a retinue of respected nobles."

The courtier bowed and hurried to the outer door.

Corann threw the closed door of the room of enchantments a baleful glance.

"And as for you," he muttered. "I'll deal with you upon my return."

The door shuddered in response.

***

Gwen examined the schedule board while Aidan pulled out money for the ticket seller at the train station.

"Your mum was right—the trains run every hour until eight at night." She checked her watch. "Ten minutes until the next one, thank goodness. I'm ready to sit after that walk in from the countryside. Winterwood is not on the right side of the peak."

Bran grinned.

"Good, time to explore. What's this, Gwen?" He pointed down the platform.

"That's a garbage can. And that," Gwen said before Bran could ask what he was pointing at. "Is an umbrella. It keeps you dry in the rain."

"That's brilliant," said Bran loudly. "What a wonderful idea! Humans are so inventive. Perhaps we can buy a brumbella to take back."

"Shh," Gwen said. A few of the waiting passengers were looking askance at Bran. A young woman with pink-tipped hair stared with narrowed eyes at his fur cloak. "Not so loud. People are looking."

"Do you think they'll hunt me down, or lock me up?" Bran peered with interest at the staring passengers, who then cleared throats, shuffled feet, and flicked newspapers.

"No, just—they might start asking questions," Gwen said.

Aidan joined them with three train tickets in hand, his backpack hanging off one shoulder.

"We should be near Amberlaine in forty minutes," he said.

"Is that short?" Bran said.

"Reasonably."

"Trains are brilliant. Perhaps I can get Father to put some in at home. Do you know how to build one?"

Aidan chuckled.

"Sorry, I'm not taking railway engineering at uni."

A stiff wind caught them by surprise. Aidan only barely clutched their tickets as the breeze whipped fiercely across the platform. Hats and newspapers went sailing across the tracks to a chorus of shouts. The wind continued to buffet them, and they huddled against the schedule board.

"This weather." Aidan glanced at the forbidding gray clouds above. "It's the worst I remember seeing it this time of year, and that's saying something here. And mainly in Cambridgeshire, according to my phone. Although the rest of the country is feeling the brunt of winter."

"I hope it's better when we get back to the Otherworld." Gwen pulled the hood of her jacket over her head.

"I doubt it," Bran said. He still looked around with interest, totally unperturbed by the inclement weather. "It was stormy when we left, with no sign of stopping."

A loud clattering noise and the sound of an engine interrupted them. Bran gazed, open-mouthed, at the passenger train that slid to a stop at their platform.

116

"This is amazing," he shouted over the squeal of brakes. "We're really getting on this? I'll never ride a horse again if this is an option."

Aidan ushered them up the steps. He had to drag Bran across the threshold when Bran stopped to examine the rubber on the door seal. Gwen pushed him down into the first available seat, but he leaped up again immediately for a better view out the window.

"He's like a kid at Christmas," said Aidan with a grin.

"Yeah, and Santa was very good to him," said Gwen.

The train shuddered and rolled down the track, slowly at first but accelerating rapidly. Bran whooped loudly, and the other passengers tutted.

"Come on, Bran." Gwen pulled at his shirt. "Sit down."

They flew through the countryside, farms and hedgerows whipping past their window. The rain was ceaseless, and the sky grew steadily darker. Soon it was difficult to see out of the rain-glazed window. Every subsequent group of passengers that boarded the train was wetter than the previous. Wind rocked the carriage sideways on its tracks.

After twenty minutes, the train slowed to a stop with no station in sight. The overhead speaker system crackled to life and Bran clutched Gwen's arm.

"This is your driver speaking. There is a tree down across the tracks from the storm. Crews are clearing it, but we have an estimated ten-minute wait here, so find yourself a comfortable seat."

"That's unusual," said Aidan. He and Gwen looked at each other, then Gwen turned her gaze to the sleet now driving against the window. In the distance, lightning cracked.

"It's getting worse," said Gwen.

"Look at this." Aidan passed a folded newspaper across the aisle to Gwen. The headline he pointed at said, "Unprecedented earthquake rocks Bedford." Gwen scanned the story then passed the paper back.

"I thought England didn't get earthquakes. That's why you have so many brick buildings over here."

"We don't."

"Does all this feel unusual to you?" Gwen said, staring out the window. "Too coincidental?"

"What, the weather? Or the earthquake?"

"Both."

"You think they're connected?" Aidan looked skeptical. "Surely not."

"It's because of the extra portals, remember?" Bran said without turning from his examination of the window latch. "Father said it would make the worlds unstable. Rip them apart, eventually. What does this do?" He pointed at the latch. Gwen exchanged a horrified glance with Aidan.

"What does 'rip apart' mean? Faolan wasn't clear about the consequences of all this earlier."

"Who knows? It's never happened, has it?" Bran leaned back in his seat. "But all signs point to the destruction of both our lands if this continues. Perhaps they will rip apart entirely and drift away to become wastelands, perhaps they will fuse together and create a whole new world—after severe chaos, of course."

"Of course," Aidan muttered. Gwen reached across and grabbed his hand.

"We'll figure something out. I don't want England to

118

turn into a wasteland either."

"But the alternative…" He squeezed her hand tightly.

Gwen sighed. The train jolted forward, and Gwen welcomed the change of topic.

"Looks like we're moving again."

"What happens when we arrive?" said Bran. "Where is Isolde? Can we walk there?"

"Too far, especially in this weather," Aidan said. "We'll catch the bus."

"Really?" Bran's eyes shone with excitement. "What an amazing day."

***

Gwen rang the doorbell of Ada's cottage. She shivered despite her warm coat. Above, lightning cracked in the darkening sky from which rain flowed with ever-increasing ferocity. Aidan's shoulders were hunched under his rain jacket, and Bran held his cloak over his head. He watched Gwen press the doorbell with curiosity.

"This trifling rain doesn't dampen your spirits, does it, Bran?" Aidan said.

"Did you see that button Gwen pressed? It made a noise."

Aidan was spared from answering by the front door opening. Ada peered out at them over her reading glasses. Her eyes widened when she spotted Gwen.

"You must be soaked. Come in, come in—no, don't mind the rug. It's only a bit of water. Close the door—I'd rather not lose our heat."

Gwen waited introductions until they had shrugged off

coats and slid out of boots.

"Aunty Ada, this is our friend Bran. He lives—north of here."

"Nice to meet you." Bran stuck out his hand with the fingers splayed slightly. Gwen stifled a giggle. Ada grasped Bran's hand with dignity.

"And yourself. I expect you've had a long trip from not too far away." She gave Bran an uncharacteristic wink and Bran laughed. He kissed Ada's hand.

"Just so."

Gwen exchanged a startled glance with Aidan.

"Aunty Ada, what did you mean?"

Ada patted Gwen's shoulder with a smile.

"I may be old, but I can put two and two together all the same. I've often wondered about Alan's disappearance and your mysterious birth. Along with my grandmother's bedtime tales and your mother's recent appearance from thin air, I have a pretty good notion of what it all means. But I won't intrude, my dear. I'll be in my sewing room if you should need me."

Gwen could only shake her head in amazement at Ada's pronouncement before her father clattered down the stairs and Ada walked to a back room out of earshot.

"Gwen!" He gave her a swift hug. "You're back. Thank goodness. What's the news? Let's go into the living room. And who's this?" He nodded to Bran.

"Aidan, can you do intros? I'd better get Isolde before we explain everything."

Aidan nodded, and her father pointed up the stairs.

"She's in the guest room."

Gwen ran up the stairs and banged on the bedroom

door.

"Enter," Isolde's low voice responded. Gwen didn't wait for a second invitation and barged into the room. Isolde lay on top of the quilt, her white-streaked raven hair disheveled on the pillow.

"Hi," Gwen said. "I saw Faolan. He's calling a conclave and you need to be there."

Isolde sat up straight immediately. Her eyes pierced Gwen's.

"Conclave? Of course. The situation calls for it, certainly. And he will need a representative from the Velvet Woods. Yes."

She swung her legs off the bed and stood. Her pale skin flushed with color. A frown creased her brow.

"But what shall I wear? I have nothing. Nothing!" She held out her cardigan with dismay. "I cannot possibly show myself like this at Faolan's court, let alone at conclave. Where is your nearest seamstress? Send for her right away, there is no time to lose."

Gwen shook her head in exasperation. Of course, Isolde would focus on her looks. She hadn't asked about whether Faolan had an answer to Gwen's conundrum. Her vanity took precedence.

"You can wear your white dress for now. Aunty Ada kindly cleaned it for you the best she could. Then ask Faolan for clothes to borrow. Bran lent me a dress last time I was there."

"Never!" Isolde rushed to the mirror and ran her fingers through her tangled hair with a look of consternation. "I cannot ask for charity, from Faolan of all people. Not as the queen of the Velvet Woods."

"But you're not queen anymore, are you?" Gwen said. Isolde visibly wilted, and Gwen regretted her harsh words. Isolde's fretfulness had little to do with the state of her clothes, and everything to do with her loss of the only life she'd ever known. Pride was masking fear. Gwen sighed. "Change into your white dress once we get to the Otherworld, and we can figure something out there. Okay?"

Isolde nodded mutely. There was a knock at the door, and Gwen went to open it. Ada stood outside.

"Apologies for the intrusion," said Ada. She held out a bundle of fabric. "It's cold out there. I thought this shawl might coordinate with Isolde's dress better than a coat."

Gwen took the shawl.

"Thanks, Aunty Ada. That's great." She passed the shawl to Isolde, who held it out to examine it.

"It will do," said Isolde. At a meaningful glance from Gwen, she added, "Very nicely. My appreciation."

Ada raised an eyebrow but nodded and withdrew.

"Since, as you say, I am no longer queen," Isolde said quietly. "Who will take my place at conclave?"

"Corann, as far as I know. Faolan sent the summons."

"Faolan summoned the usurper." Isolde's tone was bitter. "So, he acknowledges Corann's claim. His fictional claim. I expected better of Faolan."

Gwen decided not to comment on this.

"Let's go downstairs. I need to tell Dad what's going on, then we have to leave."

Gwen left the room before Isolde could protest and clattered down the stairs. The others were in the living room. Alan and Aidan sat on the couch, Alan warily watching Bran circumnavigate the room. Bran was enthusiastic in his explorations.

"You say this thing tells you where the sun is? You don't need to look outside?" He peered at a ticking clock on the mantlepiece and tapped its face.

"Close enough." Aidan caught Gwen's eye and grinned. "And the lights turn on with that switch over there."

Bran leaped across the room and pushed the switch up. An overhead light flickered on. Bran's face opened in euphoric awe.

"Humans are so wonderful." He flicked the light off and on rapidly. In the strobe effect, her father's face showed alarm at Bran's flightiness. Gwen could almost hear his inner protests over Gwen leaving with Bran. Before he could voice his concerns aloud, Gwen spoke.

"Stop the lights, Bran. I need to tell Dad what's happening." Bran took his finger off the light switch and put his fidgeting hands behind his back. Gwen turned to her father, whose hopeful expression drained away at the look on Gwen's face.

"I'll keep it quick," she said. "Faolan doesn't know any way to cancel or move the succession without another suitable heir." Alan's shoulders slumped, and his face crumpled. Gwen forged ahead. "He confirmed that I'm the chosen heir, magically speaking. And the only way to stop the worlds from tearing themselves apart is to put me on the throne." Gwen found she couldn't look at her father's stricken face any more, and instead addressed her comments to the floor. "Obviously, Faolan wants to stop the destruction, so he's called a meeting of the rulers of nearby realms to get them to help attack Corann and force him off the throne."

"War," Alan said flatly. "He's declaring war. This is insane. This whole thing is insane. Pack your bag, Gwen. We're heading to the airport today and taking the first flight home."

"I can't do that, Dad," Gwen said gently. "You know I can't. The destruction has only just begun. The worlds will keep ripping apart, the Otherworld and England both, until—who knows what will be left?" She scrubbed her face and risked a glance at Aidan, who looked as mutinous as Alan. "Let's take it one step at a time, okay? Maybe the other rulers have another idea about the succession."

"I can't convince you otherwise, can I?" Alan looked at the ceiling. "How did it come to this? How did my Gwennie end up on a battlefield in another world?"

"There's no battlefield yet, and definitely not for me," Gwen said. "And nothing has been decided yet. I'll call you every day, and every time I hear something new. Okay?"

Alan looked at her and nodded mutely. Gwen bit her lip, but then nodded.

"Aidan, Bran, Isolde. Let's go."

Chapter 7

Isolde pulled her borrowed cardigan tightly around herself and gazed through the train window at the gray skies drizzling rain. A large carpet bag containing her dress and Ada's shawl rested against her on the adjacent seat. Bran leaned toward Gwen.

"What's the fastest this train thing goes? How does it work? What do you feed it?"

"Umm…" Gwen glanced at Aidan, who shrugged.

"I'm in music, not engineering. Petrol? Electricity? We've moved on from coal, I presume."

"Astounding," said Bran with a glint in his eyes. "I'd love to stay here. Father would probably lock me in the dungeons if he heard me say that, but it's true."

"How long until our arrival?"

Gwen jumped at the sound of Isolde's voice. She had been quiet for the whole trip until this moment.

"We're slowing down now," Aidan said. He peered out of the window. "Yeah, we've arrived."

The train pulled into the station and Bran leaped up, then staggered when the train jolted to a stop.

"Whew. Let's go!"

"We need a cab," said Aidan when they had exited the station. "I don't fancy the walk again."

"What's a cab?" said Bran. In answer, Aidan waved at the line of black cars. Bran grinned.

"Where to?" said the driver once they had settled into the cab, Aidan in the front and the other three squeezed into the back. Aidan checked his phone.

"A half-mile before Great Livermere. There's a big oak tree beside the road."

The driver stared at him.

"You don't have an address for me? Why do you want to be dropped off there?"

"We have reasons," said Aidan. When he said nothing more, the driver shrugged.

"As long as you're ready to walk."

Their path led through the outskirts of Bury St. Edmunds, and past a sign to Great Livermere. The driver pulled onto a narrow track through a field and stopped. A massive oak waved barren limbs above their heads.

"Here we are. Better you than me." The driver closed his fist around the pound notes Aidan placed in his hand. He jerked his head. "Out you go. I've a long drive until I find another fare."

They all climbed out. Bran gave the cab a fond pat on its roof before it backed out of the lane and roared away to Bury St. Edmunds. The four were silent in its wake.

"I shall need to change clothes," Isolde said finally. "I cannot enter my world dressed in *this*." She gestured to her borrowed jeans and cardigan. Gwen looked around.

"There's a bush over there. You can change behind it."

Isolde stared at the bush for a long moment and tears gathered in her eyes. She said nothing, however, but picked up the carpet bag and slowly walked to the bush. Aidan glanced around until he spotted the remnants of their previous portal.

"Here it is. I'll open this one a little more, so we can get through." He stared at it for a moment. "I shouldn't expect them to close anymore, should I?"

Gwen shook her head.

"Not until we figure out how to fix things." She turned to Bran. "What's going to happen at this conclave?"

"The last one happened when I was too young to attend." Bran shrugged. "But from what I heard, it's part boring meeting, part excellent party. The delegates from each realm dress in their realm's traditional clothing and bring their own cooks to make traditional dishes from their realm for the feast."

"And there'll be dancing, no doubt," Aidan whispered in Gwen's ear. She stifled a snort.

Isolde emerged from behind the bush. Her white dress hardly showed the dirt stains, and Ada's beaded shawl distracted from the imperfections. Isolde had braided and pinned up her hair in a simple but elegant knot at the nape of her neck.

"Good," said Gwen. "Let's go face the music."

Aidan held out his arm with a theatrical flourish. The portal opened wider with a delicate swishing sound of ripping gossamer fabric.

"After you," Aidan started to say, but Isolde had already swept through without a backward glance. Gwen rolled her eyes and put her arm around Bran's shoulders.

"Come on, let's get you home."

Bran looked longingly around the road and fields but followed Gwen's gentle pressure through the portal. Aidan followed quickly, but the portal did not close behind him.

Gwen looked around at her surroundings in the Otherworld. They were standing in a horse stall in the stables of Faolan's palace, the same place they had left from in the morning. The smell of warm horse permeated the air, and motes of hay dust drifted before Gwen's eyes. The portal to the windy human roadside was an aberration in this warm refuge. A horse in the next stall whickered and Isolde pursed her lips in distaste.

"I had forgotten how enamored Faolan is with these odiferous beasts." She lifted her skirts out of the straw. Aidan leaned into Gwen.

"You come by your dislike for horses honestly, looks like."

Gwen grinned. Bran pushed the stall door, but it was latched from the outside. The door was no deterrent to Bran, who shimmied up and over it before Gwen could say anything. It creaked open and Bran waved them forward. He was flanked by two sheepish-looking guards.

"We didn't hear you come through the portal, Prince Bran," said one. "I'll alert the king at once."

"No need. We'll go ourselves. This way, everyone." Bran strode with swift footsteps to the doors leading into the palace.

Gwen snuck her hand into Aidan's, and he gave it a squeeze. They left Isolde to trail behind them, doing her best to appear regal and dignified. The guards whispered in her wake.

Bran swept them through a narrow corridor into the hall covered with stuffed animal heads. Gwen tried not to examine them too closely, and Isolde sniffed behind her. The double doors of the great hall loomed ahead, and Bran swing them open as if he owned them.

"Father! We're back, and the mission was successful." He waved at Isolde, who drew herself up and let the shawl drape gracefully over her arms. She inclined her head.

"King Faolan. I bring you respectful greetings from the Velv—from myself." Isolde flushed slightly, and her hands trembled as she arranged her shawl, but her chin went up in defiance.

"Gwen, Aidan, Isolde. You were prompt, which is just as well, as we have no time to lose. Already the delegation from Whitecliff has arrived, with the rest expected tonight."

From Isolde's indignant expression, it was clear that she was insulted by Faolan's less-than-deferential greeting. She said nothing, however, perhaps realizing she would receive no sympathy from the Wintertree ruler.

"Conclave will begin promptly at sunrise in this hall," Faolan continued. "Bran will acquaint you with your rooms."

"Thank you for your hospitality, Faolan," Isolde said with her chin held high. "I am happy to represent my realm at conclave."

"The only reason you are here," said Faolan without emotion. "Is for your knowledge of the Velvet Woods, nothing more. Do not deceive yourself. You are no longer a queen. You may go now." Faolan turned back to a bundle of branches on the table he had been studying when they arrived. Isolde's eyes were wide with indignation, then they cast downward to her stained dress and filled with tears. Gwen grabbed Bran's arm.

"Bran," she whispered. "Do you have any clothes for Isolde? She has nothing, but she'll never ask."

"Of course!" Bran patted her hand. "Come on, I'll show you around. You can have supper in my chambers tonight—less formal and stuffy than the hall."

***

Gwen stood with Aidan in the corridor outside of Isolde's room. She fidgeted with her sleeve. The gold embroidery at the cuff gleamed in the torchlight.

"What is she doing?" Gwen said. "It's almost sunrise. I don't want to be late."

"Lucky it's winter and sunrise is nice and late. I can't imagine midsummer conclaves." Aidan stretched his long arms over his head, and Gwen smiled at him.

"I'm so glad you're here with me." She suddenly hugged him around the midriff. His arms descended to drape across her shoulders.

"Where else would I be?" he murmured in her ear, then he straightened at the sound of a door opening.

Isolde was framed against the dim light of predawn that filtered through the room's windows. She was resplendent in an emerald-green ballgown of crushed velvet with accents of gold. Gwen pursed her lips and looked down at her own dress. It wasn't a ballgown, more of a slim-fitting tunic with slender brown trousers, certainly a more functional choice of clothing. Gwen was relieved, for she never felt comfortable dressed in the fanciful gowns that Breenan women seemed to favor. The neckline of her dress almost entirely hid the green tattoo that wrapped from her shoulder blade to collarbone, and the tunic was also green velvet with gold. Gwen hoped it wasn't a misguided attempt at a matching mother-daughter outfit, because she was not interested in celebrating her relationship.

Aidan must have noticed too. He looked from one to another, then down at his own outfit. He wore brown pants with a white shirt and a mid-length gray leather coat with bright detailing on the sleeves.

"I didn't get the velvet memo. Was there a dress code I missed?"

"It is the traditional dress of the Velvet Woods," said Isolde. "And yours is of Wintertree, with a nod to your Silverwood origins. See, there, the embroidered cuffs."

"Perhaps I should wear my jeans to show my human origins," said Aidan. "Come on, let's go downstairs. It's almost sunrise."

Gwen followed Aidan silently down the wide stairs that swept into the front hall. The double doors to the great hall were wide open and a throng of people waited quietly beyond in a large circle.

"I think we're late," Aidan muttered to Gwen. She grasped his hand tightly, then squared her shoulders. They strode into the conclave.

Chapter 8

Gwen's heart stuttered with relief when Bran stepped forward from beside the doorway. Behind him, the tall windows cast long beams of dull light over the gathered crowd. Everyone stood in a wide circle in the hall, roughly clustered into eight groups.

"Good morning! We're about to start. I'll show you to your places." Bran winked at Gwen then trotted off around the outside of the ring of people and gestured to an empty spot. Gwen slid into place with sweaty hands and a pattering heart. She avoided eye contact with the intimidating Breenan and especially ignored Corann's gaze from across the circle. Aidan stood close beside her, but Isolde didn't join them for many moments. When she finally glided into place, Gwen realized she had been making an entrance. Gwen suppressed an eyeroll.

Bran quickly moved toward his brothers, who stood behind Faolan. All were dressed in brown pants and gray leather coats but trimmed with fur instead of embroidered cuffs. Faolan wore a tightly woven circlet of barren branches on his head. Once Isolde had finally settled in place, Faolan gazed around the circle.

"Thank you, all, for answering the summons so promptly." His voice rang out sonorously in the stillness. "I assure you, only a matter of the gravest importance would have compelled me to call an urgent conclave.

"But first, a reckoning. The summoning realm shall begin. Present, King Faolan of Wintertree, thirty-second of his line, and protector of the Silverwood realm." He gestured at the next in the circle.

"Present, Queen Brenna of Riverside, sixteenth of her line." A tall woman with glossy brown hair wearing a fitted gown of deep blue and a tiara of sparkling diamonds inclined her head.

Corann stared at Isolde, trying to make eye contact, but Isolde gazed at the windows to avoid his regard. An older man with streaks of white in his dark brown hair stepped forward. He wore a leather band around his forehead and a thick fur cape that made him look like a bear.

"Present, King Weylin of Midvale, twelfth of his line."

"Present, Queen Ula of Longshore, twentieth of her line," said the next ruler, a tall and graceful blonde with a sleek gown of shiny silver that reminded Gwen irresistibly of fish scales. Her headpiece was a fine silver netting adorned with pearls of every shade.

Corann was next, dressed similarly to Gwen and Isolde in green velvet and gold braid, and he squared his shoulders before speaking.

"King Corann of the Velvet Woods." He paused a moment before saying, "Fourteenth of his line."

Isolde hissed under her breath but continued to avoid Corann's searching eye. Faolan raised one eyebrow but refrained from comment.

"Present, Queen Saraid of Appletree, seventh of her line." A middle-aged woman spoke next, her gown the red of a crisp summer's apple. Her coronet continued the apple theme with large rubies and emeralds.

"Present, King Gavin of Whitecliff, twenty-sixth of his line." King Gavin was a slight man, young but with a sharp gaze. His clothing was adorned with feathers of white and gray, and his crown mimicked the look of feathers in silver.

"And present, Queen Kaie of Southlands, thirtieth of her line," said a small but powerful-looking woman in a burgundy gown heavily embroidered with motifs of flowers.

When Queen Kaie had introduced herself, Faolan gestured to Gwen and the others.

"You will notice our guests to conclave. They are here at my invitation, as they have information vital to the current issue." Gwen's eyes flickered to Corann, whose brows contracted in confusion, then back to Faolan as he continued. "Isolde of the Velvet Woods, you may recall. Our other guests are Aidan of Silverwood and Gwendolyn of the Velvet Woods, both marked, but half-human."

There was hushed murmuring at this pronouncement. Gwen flushed and held Aidan's hand tighter as curious eyes raked over them. Faolan raised his voice.

"That brings me to the reason I called you here. Many of you may have noticed portals to the human world opening with greater and greater frequency, where there should be none. If they have escaped your notice, the unreasonable weather and shaking of the earth cannot have failed to alert you to the problem." Faolan looked around at the rulers, many of whom were nodding. "I have examined the disturbances at length, most of which are staying open as in the days of old. We have also had word from Loniel, the wild man of the woods." He briefly glanced at Isolde. "The worlds are tearing themselves apart, and it will only grow worse unless we stop it."

"What caused this?" cried Queen Brenna, the diamonds sewn on her sapphire-blue dress twinkling in the dawn light.

"All the evidence points toward a disturbance originating in the Velvet Woods," Faolan said with a forbidding heaviness. All eyes glanced between Corann and Isolde. "The previous queen, Isolde," Gwen saw Isolde swallow at this, though she kept her face emotionless. "Had a powerful spell placed on the Velvet Woods to heal it from a previous miscalculation. A replacement defense system was not devised in time, and her people grew impatient. Impatient enough for King Corann, here," he waved at Corann, who paled. "To rise up and take the throne from Isolde."

There were gasps from the crowd. Corann tightened his jaw.

"Is there any relation?" asked King Weylin.

"Not close enough," said Faolan. "The instability of the restoration spell is disrupting our worlds, and the overthrow of the rightful ruler of the Velvet Woods is not allowing the realm to recover. This may have still not resulted in disaster, but for one small detail—the restoration spell, instead of being performed by a full-strength Breenan, was instead done by Aidan and

Gwendolyn, two half-humans. Perhaps two performing the spell strengthened it, perhaps the spell is now trying to bring the two worlds together again by dint of being cast by those from both worlds." Faolan sighed. "And now, it falls on us to decide how to repair our world before it is utterly destroyed."

A silence fell on the assembly, and Gwen's stomach twisted. Was all this really because she and Aidan did the spell? She cast her mind back to that day in the magical garden on Isle Caengal.

"Isolde," said Faolan. "Do you have anything you wish to add? Anything that might shed light on our predicament?"

Isolde stepped forward and tilted her head in acknowledgement.

"Thank you, King Faolan. The usurper took my throne three days ago, no more. In that time, our world has begun to descend into chaos."

Gwen frowned. She was pretty sure the portals had started opening before that. She saw Faolan's brow contract slightly at this proclamation, but he let Isolde continue uninterrupted.

"The usurper sought to depose me to bring about a new defense system. I was already considering my options and if he had been patient, none of this would have come to pass," Isolde said. She still avoided meeting Corann's increasingly agitated gaze. "I concede, I might have removed the restoration spell sooner in favor of a more permanent solution, but I had the situation in hand. Now, however, the only way forward is for the true heir to assume the throne. Only then will chaos cease, and tranquility descend once more upon our realms."

"Who is the true heir?" asked Queen Ula. "And why did the heir not move to stop the coup?"

"My daughter Gwendolyn is the true heir," Isolde said calmly.

Corann stepped forward, his anger finally propelling him to speak.

"And what madness compelled you to choose Gwendolyn? She knows little of the Velvet Woods, and nothing of ruling. She's half-human." A few murmurs rippled through the hall, and Gwen's hand tightened in Aidan's. "I had no desire to rule. I only wished to save your life, the life you would not acknowledge was in danger from the fading spell. How can you not see that?" He breathed heavily while he stared at Isolde, who finally met his gaze. He pointed at Gwen, who flinched. "And to pass the rule to her! A half-human, who has lived with the degenerate human race her whole life. She cares nothing for our land! She was the instrument of our destruction in the first place!"

Gwen's hands shook with anger and bewilderment. How could Corann say that? He had never liked her, but everything Gwen had done had been to save the realm, and Isolde too. Her core burned hot in her chest, and she let go of Aidan's hand to step forward.

"King Faolan," she said clearly. "May I speak?"

He gestured at her to continue. Corann stepped back, seething.

"Corann is wrong about many things." She was proud that her voice didn't shake, even though her heart hammered loudly in her chest. "But especially this: I do care for the Velvet Woods. I don't want to see people suffering if there is something I can do to stop it. I will take the throne if that is the only option. But if any of you knows a way to change the succession, please speak up. If I can find a new heir that will fix the madness and allow me to return to the human world, I would be over the moon." At the confused looks from the Breenan, she said hastily, "I'd be very happy."

"Is there no one else in the direct family?" asked King Gavin. The feathers on the shoulders of his cloak twitched with tension.

"Gwendolyn is my only child," said Isolde. "And I have no siblings."

Chapter 9

Gwen's head snapped to look at Isolde.

"A sibling of yours would work?"

"Well, yes, if I had any. Any further distance, and it is doubtful the room would accept them."

"What about your brother?" Gwen could hardly get breath in her lungs. Could a chance meeting with her long-lost uncle be her salvation?

"What brother?" Isolde looked puzzled. Gwen sighed as understanding hit her.

"Your half-human brother. The one you've never met. The one your mother had—for a reason." Gwen stared at Isolde, willing her to get the hint. The last thing Gwen wanted to do was to give the other Breenan rulers any ideas. Isolde's eyes opened wide.

"But how could we find him? I don't even know his name. He's likely in the human world somewhere."

"We met him!" Gwen bounced on her toes, barely able to contain herself. "His name is Finn Sayward. He grew up here in the Otherworld, with the forest people. He said your mother visited him occasionally, in secret."

Isolde's face darkened.

"She kept him here?" Emotions flashed across her face as she digested the hypocrisy of her mother. Gwen briefly wondered what her own life might have been like if she had grown up in the Otherworld.

"Yes. And he visited the human world sometimes. Then his Breenan mother died, his anchor, and stranded him in the human world. It was only by chance that we found him. I sent him back here because he was desperate to find his wife and daughter." Gwen couldn't help but put a slight emphasis on this last word. Isolde's face twitched.

"And where does he live, when he is in our world?" asked Faolan.

"He said he lives in the Forbidden Lands."

There was a collective gasp. Gwen glanced at Aidan, who shrugged. Why the reaction? Gwen plowed ahead.

"It's perfect." Gwen found herself addressing Faolan, one of the few not muttering to his fellows. He gazed at her with consideration. "We can find him, you can put someone on the throne who knows the Breenan world, the chaos stops, and I'm off the hook."

"Why would he go to the Forbidden Lands?" asked Queen Kaie. "What possible reason would he have? Presumably he had no need, if his parents were Queen Vanora and a human."

"I can think of a few reasons," said Faolan. "All of which would convince him to stay in the Forbidden Lands. I don't consider it worth the effort to contact him."

"I could go and ask!" Gwen said with a raised voice. "Give me a couple of days. I can find out for sure, at least."

Faolan shook his head.

"It's not worth the risk. You are key to stopping the chaos currently besieging our worlds. You must be ready to assume the throne." His face softened momentarily. "I am sorry for your predicament, but this must be the way."

Gwen's head spun with a storm of emotions. There was hope, buoyant as a helium balloon, filling her up to bursting at the thought of Finn taking the throne instead of her. Rage at Faolan's stubborn inflexibility threatened to overwhelm her. Who was he to dictate her life? Why must she pander to his whims? Why was her life in his hands?

"This is insane," Aidan whispered to her. "We have to find your uncle. We'll sneak away and find him. There's no way I'm letting an opportunity like this slip away. I won't stop fighting until you are back in the human world for good."

Gwen squeezed his hand in response, overcome by his support. Of course, they would find Finn. They could leave here any time they wanted, through the portals. Faolan couldn't keep them. Gwen still meant to fix the realms, of course, but she couldn't rest until she had exhausted every possibility that she wouldn't have to become queen. Anxiety now threatened to take over as she considered how to find her missing uncle.

Before she could gather her thoughts, Corann stepped forward once more. His angular face was furious.

"There is no need for a new ruler in the Velvet Woods," he said with cold precision. "Gwendolyn is a half-human with no knowledge of our ways. As well, her magical abilities are a fraction of what we all possess, not to mention her complete lack of magical training. Even if she

141

is the chosen heir, will the room of enchantments accept a half-breed as its leader? Should we? Could she even handle the power that is necessary to fully control the realm?"

Quiet muttering followed Corann's speech, and many brows were furrowed. Corann pressed his advantage.

"Even if Gwendolyn were to find this mythical uncle of hers, would he be any better as ruler? He may have been brought up in our world, but by the forest people, and do not forget that he is also half-human." Corann leaned forward slightly, his weight resting on the balls of his feet. "And why is he living in the Forbidden Lands? Why was he so keen to return? Why else except that he has a tribeless wife?" The crowd gasped. "And what of his child, the product of a tribeless one and a half-human? What sort of abomination would we be inviting into our realm?" Corann's voice rose. "I will not stand idly by while my home is torn apart by incompetence and volatile magics. I trace my ancestry to Donovan, Isolde's great-great-grandfather, and the room of enchantments is beginning to respond to my attempts at mastery."

Gwen glanced at Faolan, who stared at Corann with skepticism. Other rulers did not share his doubt—King Weylin nodded, and Queen Kaie whispered rapidly to a companion. Corann was not done his monologue, and his fist pounded his palm.

"I vow to fight for the realm, to save the people of the Velvet Woods from terrible rulers. I took over to save the life of Isolde, but I continue my rule to save the lives of my people. Every Breenan life is precious. It is only a matter of time before the room of enchantments yields to me. Then, this chaos will cease, and a new peace will reign over the Velvet Woods."

Corann stopped then, breathing heavily. He glanced at each leader in turn. He must have seen something hopeful in a few faces, because he straightened and faced Faolan.

"I presume you mean to supplant me, King Faolan?"

"I do," Faolan said calmly. Corann bowed stiffly.

"Then there is nothing more to be said. I will take my leave and prepare my defenses."

Faolan addressed the other leaders.

"You have a choice, my fellow rulers. Fight with me to place the rightful heir on the throne of the Velvet Woods and stop the destruction of the worlds, or support Corann and his dubious claim."

"I am with you, King Faolan," said Queen Brenna.

"As am I," said King Gavin. "I trust your wisdom."

"I am with King Corann," said King Weylin. Corann looked triumphant. "I have no desire to place so much power in the hands of those who may not be able to wield it. And the volatility of the tribeless..." he trailed off.

"I agree," said Queen Kaie. "It is too risky. The room of enchantments must be made to work. I will back King Corann."

Queen Ula indicated her wish to follow Faolan. Queen Saraid pursed her lips.

"I see no reason to interfere. Appletree will abstain from battle."

"That is your prerogative." Faolan said. "The realms of Wintertree, Longshore, Whitecliff, and Riverside will mobilize our forces and march to the Velvet Woods. Velvet Woods, Midvale, and Southlands, I suggest you

143

prepare your defenses. I am sorry for this conflict—it is the first schism of the nine realms in four centuries. Nevertheless, I see no other way forward. You may show yourselves out. As soon as you leave the borders of Wintertree, we are at war."

Gwen shivered at the heavy finality of Faolan's pronouncement. Corann turned on his heel and strode toward the double doors, followed by his retinue. The other two rulers followed in his wake, Queen Kaie looking nervous and aggrieved, King Weylin resigned. Gwen leaned against Aidan.

"So, are you ready for a battle?" she whispered to him.

"No bloody way," he whispered back. "We're finding your sodding uncle and leaving the Otherworld behind in our dust."

She squeezed his hand, and Faolan spoke again.

"We will have a brief pause, then reconvene to discuss battle strategies."

Discussion broke out among the parties. Isolde brushed past Gwen and ran on light feet to the doors.

***

Isolde ran past the grim-faced Breenan of Midvale and the anxiously chattering Breenan of Southlands. She ignored completely the inhabitants of her own realm, who stared at her with wide eyes, and wrapped her fingers around Corann's forearm. She pulled him to the side and turned him to face her. He looked at her with shock. One of his retinue stepped over.

"My lord?"

144

Corann put up his hand.

"I will meet you in the stables."

The man nodded and left. The members of the other realms peered at them with curiosity as they passed. Isolde waited until they were out of earshot before she spoke.

"How can you be so blind?" she hissed. Corann flinched at the venom in Isolde's voice, but held his ground. Isolde continued. "Your usurpation is causing chaos. Your betrayal is destroying our world."

"The destruction started long ago, when you refused to act," Corann said with heat. "And how can you be so ungrateful? I did this for you."

"For me?" Isolde laughed in disbelief. "I assure you, you have given me far better gifts in the past."

"Your magic was leaving you. Couldn't you feel yourself weakening? It might have killed you, that slow draw of power. Perhaps you don't understand how terrible it was for me to watch your last dying days in the summer. To watch you fading away, leaving me, and knowing I could do nothing to save you. I couldn't see you suffer again, and this time I could do something about it."

Isolde stared at him for a moment, then shook her head.

"Still, you betrayed me. Why did you not speak to me of this earlier?"

Corann threw up his hands.

"I did! Countless times I tried to discuss changing the defense of the realm, and countless times you rebuffed me."

"You have a chance to put it right." Isolde put her hands together in a curious gesture of supplication. "Give the throne to Gwendolyn. She is the rightful heir. Save our people from the needless battles that will come."

"Gwendolyn?" Corann spat out. "I would rather see a forest person on the throne. She knows nothing of the Velvet Woods, and cares less. How could you be so reckless as to make her your heir?"

"You have always been hostile to Gwendolyn."

Corann pushed out his hands in an angry, dismissive gesture, then turned and stormed off.

"Corann!" Isolde called out, but he did not look back. Isolde pressed her fist tightly to her mouth for a long moment before she slowly turned back to the great hall.

***

The room buzzed with murmured conversation. Aidan turned to Gwen.

"A solution is in our grasp, and of course Faolan says no. Who is he to tell you that? You know what? Never mind about your uncle—let's leave and forget this ever happened. They have lots of magic here—they can figure it out. And Faolan can't reach you in Canada."

Gwen was about to remind Aidan about the destruction of both worlds and Faolan's worried face, when the ground trembled. Then it shook. A groaning roar sounded from deep below their feet. People screamed. Gwen clutched Aidan's arm until the shaking stopped.

"Fine," Aidan said unsteadily. "Fine, we won't leave. But we are going to find Finn, and he will take the throne. Even if I have to make him."

"What if you can't?" Gwen had a vision of Aidan dueling magically with Finn and winced.

"He'll come."

"But what if he won't?"

Aidan grabbed Gwen's hands.

"Then we'll both move to the Velvet Woods. Perhaps I'll finally learn how to dance."

It was a feeble joke at a terrible time, but Gwen smiled weakly.

"That won't be possible," said Isolde from behind them. Gwen whirled around.

"Why not?" What was getting in their way now?

"There is a spell on the Velvet Woods to prevent the ruling family of Wintertree from living there. It is a broad-reaching spell, however, and Aidan's blood relation to Faolan's heirs would include him in the spell."

"Why? Why would there be a spell—" Gwen shook her head. "Just take it off."

"No one can do that. It is in place for a hundred years," said Isolde with a hint of apology. "It was a preventative measure, a disincentive for Faolan to invade."

"Aidan's been to the Velvet Woods," said Gwen in triumph. "It must not work on him."

"It's a subtle spell. He could live there for a time. After weeks, he would feel a longing to leave. Eventually, he would fall ill."

Gwen was aghast. Why was the universe conspiring against them?

"Then—I'll live in the human world," said Aidan wildly. "Go through a portal every day."

"Only until our anchors die," said Gwen. "Hopefully it'd be a long time, but it's not forever."

"Fine. Breenan world, but right on the border."

"And, what? We'd live long-distance?" Gwen's breath caught in her throat. "Always?"

Gwen and Aidan stared at each other. Aidan's eyes were filled with desperation. Then, a steely resolve hardened his features.

"Then it's back to plan A," he said.

Chapter 10

"Come on," said Gwen finally. "I need some air. Let's see if we can find the history garden."

No one stopped them as they strolled out of the great hall and wandered down corridors in the direction Gwen remembered from her brief visit through Faolan's room of enchantments.

Eventually, they found a door at the end of a hall that had a carved insignia of flowers and leaves. Gwen pointed at a pattern she recognized.

"Look, there's the shape for 'garden.'"

"I'll take your word on that." Aidan peered at it. "Good memory. Perhaps that ridiculous flower-writing can be learned, after all."

"I hope so," Gwen muttered, but quietly enough that Aidan could pretend not to hear her, although his shoulders tightened as he pushed the door open.

The garden was vast, and the stone walls which encircled it barely contained the multitude of plants. Most looked bare and trim in the winter cold, although a few evergreens were bright and cheery. The glossy green leaves and red berries of a nearby holly peeked out shyly from a dusting of snow that also crunched beneath their feet.

"This is the library, is it?" asked Aidan. "Bit chilly for my liking."

"Hello, my little birds," said a voice behind them. Gwen jumped and whirled around. Loniel was perched on a low wall that surrounded a raised bed. One foot dangled carelessly while the other rested on the top of the wall. His golden eyes gazed at them calmly.

"Loniel," Gwen breathed. "What are you doing here?"

"Speaking to you, of course. How goes the conclave? What news?"

"Faolan and some others are attacking Corann in the Velvet Woods. They're going to make me queen." Gwen dropped her voice and looked around before continuing. "Unless I can get to my uncle first."

"Uncle?" A look of confusion was swiftly followed by comprehension on Loniel's face. "He has been found. I thought him lost to the human world."

"You knew?" Gwen said with a gasp. "You could have said something."

"And at what meeting between us would that have been relevant information?" Loniel said with a raised eyebrow. "Do you know where Finn Sayward resides currently?"

"Yes. He's in the Forbidden Lands."

"Faolan has said we're not allowed to look for him, that it's too risky for Gwen," added Aidan. "But we'll go anyway. We must find him. He's the only one who can take Gwen's place on the throne."

"And what world do you wish to live in, little bird?"

This was directed at Gwen.

"Me?" said Gwen in surprise. "The human world, of course. It's my home. It's where I belong, where my friends and family are, where my life is."

"And you have a chance to return there to live?"

"If my uncle agrees to be king, yes."

"Then I will support you in this. I don't want to see anyone in a world they don't wish to be in." Loniel hopped lightly down from the wall and padded through the snow toward Gwen. She willed herself not to step back. Loniel, although seemingly always on her side, had a dangerous otherworldly aura that emanated from him like a subconscious warning.

"The Forbidden Lands are to the west," he said. "They are surrounded by treacherous mountains and a deep lake. I would guide you there myself, but I find my hands full with escorting wayward humans back through portals."

"That's nice of you," said Gwen.

"You know my thoughts on being in the wrong world. But I won't deny I play my little tricks on them first." He gave her an impish grin and Aidan huffed quietly.

Loniel reached out with a finger and traced a glowing green line in midair. Gwen's eyes widened as the shape of a valley surrounded by a jagged mountain range materialized before them. Loniel pointed at the center of the valley and a gently pulsing dot appeared.

"There is a settlement here, or was the last time I passed through. It is likely Finn resides there. You will cross the lake and land here." Another glowing dot on the outside of the mountains. "You will take your watercraft through the tunnels. They will lead you to the river that

151

flows through the Forbidden Lands. And I suggest you avoid the caves of Naer." He circled a region of caves on the left of the tunnel complex. "It's rife with beithirs."

"Great. Beithirs," said Aidan, looking queasy. "Do I want to know what they are?"

"Giant venomous snakes," replied Loniel mildly. Aidan shuddered. Gwen changed the subject.

"Can you tell us more about the tribeless ones? Who are they, actually?"

"To answer that, you must first understand the nature of magic in the Breenan people. Through long separation, there are two flavors of magic: that of the Ardra, the ruling class, and that of the forest people, known as such although they do not all reside in the forest. The Ardra possess quick, showy magic, strong yet temporary in nature."

"Are we Ardra?" said Gwen.

"Precisely. The forest people have a slower, more permanent magic, which allows them to nurture their crops and persuade the deer to run a different path." Loniel sighed a world-weary sigh. "Tribeless ones, as they are known, are simply those born to parents of different peoples. Should an Ardra woman produce a child from one of the forest people, the child might grow up unmindful until their marking ceremony. But a different mark would await them on the Sacred Mountain, and the raw, volatile magic they possess would be unleashed. Occasionally, a child born this way might receive a true elder mark, which is why some risk the ceremony, but all too often they do not."

"Don't the forest people get marked?" asked Aidan.

"No. And unmarked, a tribeless one will never manifest the wild magic that everyone fears."

"Are they dangerous? The tribeless ones, I mean?" Gwen wondered if they should be nervous of traveling to the Forbidden Lands on that account.

"Not with their magic contained in the Forbidden Lands. As for their temperament, confined in a small valley for their whole lives, never once venturing past their borders? I cannot conjecture."

"You know so much," said Gwen. "Why don't you come inside to conclave? You'd really help, I'm sure."

"I avoid entangling myself in Breenan skirmishes, if I can. Besides, I have lost humans to find. Good luck on your quest, little bird. I hope you find what you search for."

"Thanks, Loniel," said Gwen. Loniel simply raised a hand in farewell. A strong wind hit their faces with a flurry of snow. By the time Gwen blinked the snow out of her eyes, Loniel had gone.

"He knows how to make a dramatic exit, that one," said Aidan with a roll of his eyes.

"He showed us where to go, though."

"And no riddling this time—that's when you know things are serious."

Gwen shivered.

"Come on, let's get inside. I'm freezing."

***

The delegates and their retinues were milling about when Gwen and Aidan returned to the great hall. Some looked curiously at them, and others looked askance at their windswept hair and the dusting of snow on their shoulders. Gwen couldn't help admiring the clothes of the Breenan, now that she passed them up close. They were dressed in their finest, with diamonds, velvets, sumptuous furs, gold and silver, precious jewels, and brilliant feathers.

Isolde stood silently in her place and stared at the far wall. No one attempted to engage her in conversation. No one wanted to be tainted with whatever had caused her to be dispelled from her throne.

Bran and Kelan approached them through the throngs.

"Father's sent us," Bran explained at Gwen's curious look. "No need for you to attend the rest of the discussions. It'll just be boring tactics. We're to keep you company."

"Okay," said Gwen. They didn't speak until the hubbub in the great hall quieted with the closure of the doors behind them. Then Aidan spoke.

"We're not staying. I don't care what your father wants. We're going to the Forbidden Lands to find Gwen's uncle."

Bran shot Kelan a look as if to say, *I told you so*, then replied to Aidan.

"I thought as much. When do we leave?"

Gwen's eyebrows rose. Bran and Kelan wanted to come?

"You're coming? What will your father say?"

"He always forgives me." Bran waved his hand. "And it's for a good cause. I know you don't want to be queen, Gwen, and you're my friend who needs help. I can make

154

Father see reason."

"And I'll go along to keep Bran from getting into too much trouble, so I'll be forgiven by default," added Kelan. "Hopefully."

"Well, thanks." Gwen almost felt teary. It was good to have people on her side.

"Although I don't know why you don't want to be queen, Gwen," said Bran. "It's great being royalty. There are loads of perks."

"Don't be dafter than you must, Bran," said Kelan. "There's a lot of responsibility being a ruler. And the weight of the connection."

"Do you suppose Father was light-hearted before he became king?" Bran said before he and Kelan started to laugh. Even Gwen and Aidan cracked smiles.

When Bran had caught his breath, he asked, "So, when do we leave?"

Gwen glanced around. No one was in sight.

"Right now."

***

Once the double doors had closed shut behind Gwen and the others, Faolan snapped his fingers. Sparks flew, and four servants entered through the doors.

"Table," he said curtly, and the servants hurried away, only to return a moment later with a wide table which they placed in the center of the room. Faolan strode forward and beckoned to Isolde.

"We shall need a map of the Velvet Woods. As detailed as you can manage. I'd like all water sources, hills and valleys, power centers, and anything that we need to avoid or that Corann can use against us."

Isolde nodded and lifted her hands. The surface of the table wavered, then rippled. Translucent sections of the table rose in tiny hills, and the surface dimpled in an approximation of dense forests.

Then the image wavered and flickered. Isolde's look of concentration dissolved into wide-eyed anxiety.

"I can't—I don't have enough power," she muttered to Faolan, then flushed with shame. Faolan's lips thinned, but he placed a hand on Isolde's shoulder and closed his eyes.

Isolde's shoulders snapped back, and her arms straightened. The image on the table firmed and solidified. Isolde continued to build detail on the map. Hills rose, and distinct gullies and valleys dug into their sides. Fluttering blue lines bisected the table and pooled in deep sapphire lakes in miniature. Dots of undulating colors materialized at random on the map, densest at the center where a tiny castle grew. Red stars appeared in a few locations before Isolde put down her hands. Faolan took his hand away and opened his eyes. He walked around and examined the map.

"Yes, that will do nicely. And the stars?"

"They represent pitfalls or other places to avoid. I can give details of each." Isolde tossed her head. "A queen knows her realm, after all."

"A queen no longer," Faolan said. "You would do well to remember that the battle we plan is due directly to your inaction in the face of peril to your realm. Your sole purpose here is to provide us with information to help our plan of attack, nothing more."

Isolde lowered her eyes and took one step away from

the table. Faolan waved an invitation to the remaining rulers.

"Shall we begin?"

"Let's finish this as quickly as possible," said King Gavin of Whitecliff. "I'd like to be back in my realm within days, if we can manage it. No need to drag it out longer than that."

"I agree," said Queen Ula of Longshore. "We have the greater numbers, and Corann does not control the realm. It should be simple. There are plentiful rivers in the Velvet Woods, I see, so my fighters will have ample water with which to work. Station them at the river crossings, and I guarantee Corann's forces will think twice about approaching."

"An opposing army should never be underestimated," said Faolan, but he looked at ease. "My fighters and their spell stones can be positioned anywhere, so let us place the fighters who have location requirements first."

"My war singers require more open spaces and visibility, unfortunately lacking in this realm," said King Gavin as he peered at the map.

"There are viewpoints here and here, as well as open meadowlands over there," said Isolde, pointing.

"My fighters are more flexible," said Queen Brenna of Riverside. She gave a wicked smile. "Hallucinations can be caused in any environment."

Faolan pondered the map.

"Unfortunately, the fighters of King Weylin of Midvale and Queen Kaie of Southlands have no restrictions. The Midvale fighters control animals, which can be sent anywhere. And the Southlands fighters deal in flower magic—choking vines, venomous spitting flowers—which can be grown from any root. It's more difficult in winter, I have heard, but certainly can be done. And the Velvet Woods fighters have the whole forest at their disposal—every tree, acorn, and root."

There was a brief silence while they contemplated the shimmering map. Isolde glanced at Faolan.

"And when we capture Corann, what then?" she asked in an offhand tone. Faolan looked at her sharply, undeceived by her attempt at nonchalance.

"We will do whatever we must. Certainly, if he does not surrender quickly, we will show no mercy. I am tempted to make an example of him to warn other would-be usurpers, but we shall decide at the time."

Isolde looked disquieted. Faolan narrowed his eyes.

"Does my answer affect your willingness to help? Tell me now, for I would rather attack with less information than proceed with a traitor in our midst."

"No," said Isolde quickly. "The portals must be closed, and Gwendolyn must take the throne. We are of one mind in that."

"Good." Faolan pointed at a narrow valley on the map.

"Queen Ula, what can your people do about this trap?"

***

After a furious canter through snowy hills, a short train ride that garnered wide eyes from Kelan, and a bus trip which made Bran sigh with happiness, Gwen led their foursome to her aunt's cottage. Her father dashed out of Ada's front door the minute Gwen put her hand on the gate.

"You're back. How did you get back? What's the news?" He looked around at the others, and his eyes fell on Kelan. "And who's this?"

"Bran's brother, Kelan," Gwen said hurriedly. "We caught the train. We're on a time crunch, so long story short: I have a long-lost uncle that we need to convince to take the throne. He lives in the Forbidden Lands, so we're headed there now."

Alan gave her a swift, crushing hug.

"That's wonderful news, Gwennie." He held her at arm's length. "But why the time crunch?"

"Because the worlds are falling apart," said Gwen.

"And because Faolan didn't agree to this excursion. We left in secret and need to get Gwen back before Faolan throws a fit and decides to glue the tiara to Gwen's head," Aidan said. He added as an afterthought to Bran and Kelan, "No offense meant."

Bran grinned.

"Father's often declaring ultimatums. We know better than anyone."

Kelan nodded in agreement.

"Then we'd better get moving," said Alan. "Hop in the car, everyone. I'll grab my keys and coat. Where are the Forbidden Lands?"

"They're not far," said Kelan. "We're close to the castle of the Velvet Woods, right? The only entrance to the Forbidden Lands is over Luan Lake, which is a short morning's ride to the north east. Father mentioned it once."

Alan looked bewildered. Aidan came to his rescue.

"I'm certain it's Grafham Water. It's a forty-minute drive."

While Alan rushed to the house, Bran looked eagerly around.

"Where's the car, Gwen?"

Gwen bit back a smile and pointed to a rental car parked on the street. Bran ran to it and tugged at the handle futilely. Kelan followed and watched Bran's antics with interest. He ran a hand over the car's hood.

"Fascinating," he murmured. "How does it work?"

"Petrol, pistons, and tiny explosions," said Aidan. At Gwen's raised eyebrow, he shrugged sheepishly. "I was never interested in cars. That's the best explanation I have."

Alan hurried down the walkway and pressed the remote to unlock the car doors. Both Bran and Kelan jumped at the loud click. A jogger ran by at that moment and stared at their Breenan clothing. Gwen was thankful she and Aidan had changed back into their winter coats—the wind whistled past her hood with great force. She hastily pushed Bran into the backseat and Kelan slid in beside him. When they were all seated, Alan slammed his door and turned the key in the ignition. Behind Gwen, the brothers jumped as one, and Aidan chuckled.

"Find us the best path, will you, Aidan?" Alan said into his rearview mirror. Aidan nodded and pulled out his phone.

"Head east for now. I'll direct you shortly."

Alan eased the car into traffic and they drove for a few moments in silence. Bran and Kelan were glued to their window and Aidan was busy with his phone. Alan glanced

160

at Gwen.

"Same procedure as before? You make a portal and call me at least once a day?"

Gwen sighed.

"That won't work in the Forbidden Lands. There's a no-magic spell over the whole thing. We'll have to make a portal before we even land our boat. I'll just try to be as quick as I can and call you once we're out."

Her father didn't directly respond to this statement, but his jaw tightened.

"What's the plan when we get to the lake?" he said instead.

"We'll have to fashion a boat somehow. Kelan has a spell to power the boat, once we have something."

"The magic won't work inside the magical boundary of the Forbidden Lands, but once we're in the caves the current should carry us," said Kelan.

"Caves?" said Alan.

"I can make a raft," said Bran. "I made one once. It held together for hours."

"Hours?" Alan took a deep breath as if mastering himself, then took the next exit off the highway.

"Where are we going?" asked Gwen in surprise.

"The nearest outdoor store. We need a boat. I'm not having you cross a freezing lake on a raft that *might* hold together. An inflatable is hardly better, but if you have magic to push it, the trip should be short, at least. And flashlights, if there are *caves*."

***

Alan pulled into the parking lot of a visitor's center, closed at this late hour, and switched off the engine. They all stared at the stormy skies and angry whitecaps that scudded across the lake. Green fields lay over the countryside to their right, and a small woodland to their left. Scrubby grasses rustled at the lakeside. The only sound was the ticking of the cooling engine and the whistling of the wind. Gwen swallowed past her suddenly dry throat. Their inflatable boat in the trunk suddenly seemed hugely inadequate.

"Please tell me you have some magic to keep you afloat," Alan said faintly. Gwen zipped up her coat with determination.

"We sure do. It'll be fine. Come on, everyone, let's fill that boat."

"Look this way, Bran." Kelan prodded Bran in the ribs. "We're here. It's your first sight of the Forbidden Lands."

"What?" said Bran. He peered through the side window. "Where are the mountains?"

"We're still in the human world. It must be different here."

Alan rubbed his face.

"Are you really crossing that stretch in an inflatable boat?" He looked to the threatening skies. "In this weather? Maybe you should wait for calmer conditions."

"I don't think we'll have any," said Gwen. "With the worlds ripping apart, the weather will only get worse."

"You'd better get that boat filled, then."

They climbed out of the car and Gwen dragged the uninflated boat out of the trunk.

"Anyone know a spell for filling this thing?" she asked.

"It might be quicker than the pump."

At Bran and Kelan's confused looks, Aidan clarified.

"Any spells to push air into something?"

"Oh, sure." Bran's expression cleared, and he put his hand over the nozzle. Within a minute, the boat was rigid and sea-worthy. Aidan hastily held down the gunwale when the wind threatened to blow the boat away.

Alan stepped out of the car.

"The weather forecast is calling for wind warnings this evening," Alan yelled over the wind. "You'd better get moving."

"Boat in the water!" Gwen shouted. She picked up a side using the built-in rope, and the others followed. They lurched through grass, down to a pebbly shore. Waves crashed on the beach, and Gwen gritted her teeth against the inevitable splash of icy-cold water soon to fill her shoes.

"It's a bit windy, but the waves aren't bad," shouted Bran. "We can get through them, no problem."

"I hope so!" Gwen yelled back. Bran and the others climbed into the boat, and Gwen turned to hug her father.

"I'll see you really soon," she said. "I'll call you when we land again. Hopefully no later than tomorrow morning. And we'll have Finn with us. Then we can have Christmas with Aunty Ada, fly back home, and forget this ever happened."

Her father didn't speak. He just hugged her fiercely and stepped back with a tight nod. Gwen waded into the roiling water—as icy as she'd feared—and climbed awkwardly into the full boat. Kelan smacked the stern twice, and they shot away from the shore.

The boat juddered in the choppy waves. Gwen held on with whitened knuckles and fingers that were already too cold.

"It's a bit brisk," Aidan shouted. Gwen snorted then coughed when spray hit her in the face.

"When should we cross over?" yelled Kelan. "The magic-dampening spell extends into the lake. We don't want to wait too long."

"No time like the present!" cried Bran. "Work your magic, Aidan!"

Aidan glanced at Gwen, who nodded. Aidan swallowed, held out one hand straight in front of him, and narrowed his eyes.

A huge portal ripped open a boat-length ahead of them. Within a moment, they were through.

Chapter 11

A wave hit them broadside and Gwen screamed. The boat teetered on the edge of tipping and they all scrambled to redistribute their weight. Another wave rocked the boat again, and cold water sprayed over the bow.

"Go back!" shrieked Gwen. "Make another portal!"

Aidan threw out his hand and they shot through another wide portal. It was calmer on the human side, but their reprieve didn't last long.

HONK.

"What's that boat doing?" Bran asked with interest. Figures on the boat waved at them.

"They must think we're in trouble!" Aidan shouted. "We can't stop. What would we tell them? We need to cross over!"

"Not yet!" Gwen cried. "It's gale-force winds over there!"

Kelan smacked the boat again and they jumped forward with renewed vigor. The boat changed course to intercept them.

"They're gaining on us," said Bran. He looked back at

his brother. "Is that all you have, Kelan?"

"This boat won't handle more," Kelan replied.

The boat was close enough now to hear shouting. Gwen clenched whitened knuckles on the rope and looked at Aidan. He threw an agonized glance at the approaching vessel, then put out his hand.

The portal yawned open, and Gwen had a sickening view of the wild water beyond before they were tossed into it. The inflatable boat slammed into the choppy water again and again. Gwen's teeth jolted together with every hit. The sleet that pummeled her face was so intense, it almost blinded her.

Aidan lost his balance and tumbled into Bran. Gwen leaned precariously toward the over weighted edge. A wave hit them broadside, and before the boat regained its balance, a log reared up. With a tremendous jolt, the light side of the boat tilted. As the boat tipped too far, Gwen saw the future before it happened. The lake rushed toward her, gray and frothing and unwelcoming. When she smacked into the icy cold water and plunged into its depths, she gasped at the shock and was rewarded with a mouthful of lake water.

Gwen's head emerged into the howling wind and she coughed and choked. The boat was mercifully right beside her, so she gripped the overturned hull with tight fingers before she looked around.

Kelan grasped the other side of the boat, wide-eyed. Aidan spluttered up from the depths and Gwen reached out her arm for him to grab. His tight grip relieved her more than she could express.

"Where's Bran?" Kelan yelled. He looked around

wildly. "Bran!'

"Bran!" Gwen screamed. The waves were so choppy that he could have been right beside them and still unseen. Sleet pelted her face and she blinked over and over. A wave hit her and she spluttered again. Then a hand appeared over a nearby crest. "Over there!" she shrieked at Kelan.

Kelan wasted no time. He swung his arm around in a wide circle and a shining silver rope appeared, swirling in midair. He let it loose to fly toward Bran.

The rope lay slack for a moment, two…

"Come on, Bran!" Kelan said with anguish.

Then the rope grew taut. It cut through the waves, and Kelan hauled with all his might. Aidan pulled himself over to the rope to help pull Bran in.

Bran appeared, soaked and with his usual cheery smile wiped away. Aidan grabbed his coat and pressed him against the hull while he recovered.

It was only then that Gwen noticed the speed they were traveling at.

"Kelan! Turn off the moving spell. We're going in the wrong direction!"

"It's not on!" he said. Gwen looked at their destination and noticed for the first time the jagged mountains that rose sheer from the water's edge. The mountains grew smaller as the overturned boat was swept back.

"It's the wind," Gwen said. "It's pushing us away from the Forbidden Lands. Quick, Kelan, put the moving spell back on!"

"I can't. Not with the boat overturned. It's meant for upright movement."

"Pass it to me, Bran." Aidan grabbed Bran's hand and pressed it to his temple. Both their eyes closed briefly, then Aidan's popped open.

"Any ideas?" Gwen asked him. Her teeth chattered.

"Hold on, hold on…" Aidan thought for a moment, his eyes flickering over the boat. Then he pulled himself around toward Gwen, passing over her with a touch she could barely feel through the cold and landing on the side opposite the mountains. He smacked the boat twice as Kelan had. "Let's hope this works," he said through blue lips.

They were approaching the opposite shore now, the lake vast before them. The boat jerked slightly then moved against the wind. But it was slow, too slow. Gwen pulled herself around to Aidan. She almost lost her grip when a wave crashed into the little boat. Aidan hauled her closer.

"Pass me the spell," she said. "We need more power."

He pressed his fingers to her temple. Gwen closed her eyes and saw a vivid vision of Aidan holding onto the boat, just as if she hadn't closed her eyes. A pulse in her core told her what to do, and she replicated the spell. The boat moved a little more swiftly across the waves. Kelan was there next, and then Bran, and Gwen and Aidan passed the spell along.

With the input of the brothers' more powerful spells, the boat flew toward the mountains at last. A wave crashed into them once more, sleet stung Gwen's eyes, and her icy feet hung like unfeeling deadweights on the ends of her legs. The mountains thrust up from the lake like the teeth of a giant, ever closer.

"There's an opening in the rocks!" Kelan yelled. "Aim

for that. It must be the entrance."

They slowly powered to a narrow fissure in the rock. Towering cliffs loomed overhead in the dusky light, their crumbling rockfaces plunging deep into turbulent water. The fissure was a black gash in gray sandstone, and water frothed at its entrance. There was a narrow ledge of flat rock at the edge of the fissure, and they headed straight for it.

They were so close, only a few boat lengths from the ledge, when a pulse of pressure passed through Gwen. By the startled expression on the others' faces, they had felt it too.

"What was that?" Gwen forced the words out of her tight jaw and chattering teeth. Kelan's face cleared with understanding.

"It's the magic-dampening spell on the Forbidden Lands. We just passed through the boundary."

"Why aren't we moving?" Aidan said.

"Magic-dampening spell," Bran said, his face tight and pale with cold. "That means magic doesn't work as well."

"Thanks for the obvious. Come on, let's kick!"

Gwen kicked her leaden legs as fast as she could, which wasn't very fast. But slowly, slowly, they approached the ledge.

"Ahh!" yelled Bran. "There are sharp rocks under here!"

The boat shuddered from impact. Gwen leaned out to have a look, and her hands slipped off the hull.

Panic instantly threatened as she slid under the water. Her legs were almost useless, they were so cold and leaden. She flailed her limbs and managed to coax her head above the waterline. The boat was too far away, the others' shouts muted in her water-filled ears. The ledge was closer, so she forced her legs into a tired shuffle. She gritted her teeth and thrashed her arms in her best impression of a breast-stroke, and slowly she moved toward the ledge. Waves washed over her head, and she gasped for breath in between crests. Finally, the ledge was in reach. She bashed against the edge a few times until strong hands pulled at her shoulders. With her last strength, she hauled herself out of the water.

She desperately wanted to lie down and sleep, but a small part of her frozen brain told her that it was a bad idea. She couldn't muster the energy to do anything but stay on her hands and knees with her head hanging between her shoulders until a hand pressed gently on her back.

"Come on, Gwen," said Aidan. "We need to get dry."

With gargantuan effort, Gwen hauled herself up using Aidan's outstretched hand. She looked around. The narrow ledge was wet from spray, and Kelan and Bran dragged the boat onto a precarious perch.

"We have to get dry," she said hoarsely. "And there's no shelter. We're going to die if we don't get dry."

"A drying spell," whispered Bran. He coughed and tried to speak louder. "That's what we need."

"But the magic-dampening spell," Kelan said. His whole body shuddered with shivers. "The spell won't be strong enough."

"So, we connect and join our magic together," said Gwen.

"C-c-connecting isn't something you do lightly," said

Kelan.

"I would connect with Corann himself if it meant getting warm," said Aidan shortly. He tried a grin. "I promise I won't tell anyone."

Kelan rolled his eyes then gripped Aidan's and Bran's hands. Gwen took their other hands.

"I'll do the spell," Kelan said. "You send power my way, all right?"

"How?" said Gwen.

"Remember the marking ceremony," said Bran. "In the willow tree, when the power passed through us all? Like that."

Gwen nodded and closed her eyes. She tried not to shake loose from the others' hands, although her body shuddered hard enough to make it difficult. A light tingling in her palms reminded her of her job, and she dug into her core and sent her power shooting through her arms.

Her back arched when she felt magic coursing through her, far more than she was used to handling. Aidan's familiar magic was there, as comfortable and thrilling as it always was, but beside it were the stronger magics of Bran and Kelan, felt even through the dampening of the Forbidden Lands' spell.

And then she forgot the strangeness of the connection with the glorious warmth that flowed over her body. Her clothes lightened as the weight of water left them, and steam clouded in front of her face. Her fingers and feet regained feeling, and there was a mixture of relief and intense pain as chilblains sizzled in her skin.

Her core flickered, then her magic pulled out of her

171

arms. The connection broke abruptly, and Gwen gasped at the suddenness. A deep weariness filled her from the cold, exertion, adrenaline, and now the warmth. With every cell in her body, Gwen wanted to cuddle under a blanket on a comfortable couch with Aidan and a mug of hot chocolate. She looked at the others, who blinked in the aftermath of the spell. Sleet still pelted down on them from the dark sky, so she pulled her hood on tightly.

"It worked," Aidan said finally. "But I could sleep for a week now."

"I think we went to the limit of your powers," said Kelan. "I forgot you have less."

"My poor half-human friends," Bran said with a fond smile. Aidan aimed a kick at him, which Bran dodged with a grin.

"Now what?" Gwen said. She looked at Kelan, and he cast his gaze into the fissure. Her eyes followed as if drawn. The sloshing water and moss-covered walls looked dank and dangerous.

"We must travel through the caves," said Kelan. "It's the only way in that I've heard of."

"That's what Loniel said, too," said Aidan. He sighed in resignation. "Back in the boat."

Bran and Aidan held the boat steady in the choppy water while Gwen clambered in and took out the oars, which had been strapped down against the sides when the boat flipped. Kelan followed and took the oars. When Bran and Aidan jumped in, he pushed against the ledge and rowed toward the fissure.

It wasn't long before the current caught them. It pulled the little boat swiftly into the roiling water and Gwen held on to the ropes tightly. Their vessel shot forward between the narrowing cliffs. Kelan grunted with effort.

"Watch out for the wall," Bran said.

Kelan merely glared at his brother in reply. They flew past dripping walls of gray stone. It was so dim at the bottom of the crevasse that not even moss clung to the sides. Gwen looked up. Far above them was a narrow strip of stormy gray sky. It grew smaller and smaller. Gwen blinked against sudden vertigo and looked forward again.

"We're almost in the caves," said Kelan. "Gwen, do you have those human lights your father found? Magic flames won't work here."

"Oh, yes." Gwen opened her backpack. Everything was soaking inside from their dip in the lake, and Gwen inwardly thanked her father for buying waterproof flashlights. She flicked them on and passed one to Aidan. He shone it forward just as the cliffs above closed to form a rapidly descending roof.

"Here we go," said Bran, with a trace of apprehension in his voice.

The light behind them grew fainter and fainter as the ceiling closed in on them. Gwen found herself huddled into the boat, as if for protection. The sides of the tunnel were worn smooth from the endless passage of water through its course. The flashlights cast a feeble pool of light forward, no more than a boat-length over the near-silent waters. Beyond was a dark question. Gwen wanted to say something, to break the terrible silence of the caves, but her throat was too dry to speak.

Kelan pulled the oars into the boat when the tunnel grew too narrow. He kept one at the ready for steering at the stern. With the narrowing of the waterway, the current pulled them even faster. Gwen's knuckles whitened on her rope.

"Do you hear that?" Aidan whispered hoarsely.

Gwen strained her ears. The quiet swishing of water against stone walls was drowned out by a new sound, that of turbulent water ahead.

"Oh no, oh no, oh no," Gwen said. "Rapids. Hold on. Where's that other paddle?"

Bran wordlessly exchanged the paddle for Gwen's flashlight and she took a stance in the bow.

"What are you doing?" Aidan asked.

"I went on a white-water rafting trip once. I think I remember what to do." Gwen didn't mention that it had been years ago, and the adult guides had done most of the paddling. She tightened her fingers and held her paddle at the ready.

The boat traveled faster and faster through the tunnel, and the sound of the rapids swelled to a roar that echoed in the dank cave. The tunnel twisted one way, then back again. White flashed under the beam of the lights.

Gwen shrieked once when the boat dropped, then she clamped her lips shut and dug her paddle in. Another drop, and the whole boat veered to the right. She paddled frantically to steer. The others shouted incoherently behind her as they dropped again. The inflatable boat shuddered but didn't puncture on the rocks scraping its hull.

Then, the light's beam illuminated calmer waters. Gwen took one deep breath in relief, but one was all she had time for. A fork in the waterway loomed ahead.

"Left, or right?" Aidan shouted to Kelan.

174

"I don't know!" Kelan yelled. Gwen looked between their choices. Both tunnels were equally dark and uninviting.

"Left!" she shouted. Someone had to decide before they slammed into the rock. She and Kelan dug their paddles deep into the swirling water and missed the divide by a handspan.

"It's a dead end," yelled Bran. "Turn around, turn around!"

The ceiling dipped down to a height much shorter than their boat. Water churned and frothed as it was sucked into the fissure.

"Turn to the right," said Kelan. He and Gwen managed to rotate the boat, but the current was stronger than they could fight against.

"Will it suck us under?" Gwen asked. She pulled the paddle with all her might, but they made no gains.

Aidan shone his flashlight over the wall of the cave.

"There are rocks here we can use as handholds. Bran, come and drag the boat with me. Gwen, get on Kelan's side and keep paddling."

Gwen flipped her paddle over as quickly as she could, but in the few brief seconds the boat slid further toward the fissure.

A hissing grew over the sound of the rapids. Gwen looked around while she paddled.

"What's that?"

Kelan threw a glance backward and his eyes widened in horror.

"I saw a forked tongue flicker out of the fissure. It was huge!"

Aidan and Gwen glanced at each other in disbelief and fear.

"Those venomous snakes Loniel warned us about?" Aidan asked.

"There are beithirs in here?" Kelan yelled in panic. "Paddle faster! They're too big to get out, but we can't get sucked in there!"

Gwen dug the paddle in again, sweating. Aidan clung to jagged rocks that poked through the softer sandstone of the tunnel. He pulled, his face contorted with the strain. Bran joined him, and the boat inched forward.

"Keep going," Aidan forced out. He found another rock and pulled harder, his feet braced against the bench.

Little by little, the boat rounded a corner. The divide was just ahead. Gwen thought her arms were about to fall off, but she didn't stop paddling until the current of the other tunnel swept them in its path. Then she collapsed onto the bench.

"I need to work out more," Aidan panted behind her. Gwen let out a breathy laugh. He shone the flashlight past the bow. "Rapids and snakes. What's next?"

"Oh no," said Bran. "I hear more rapids."

Gwen wanted to cry, but instead she braced herself in the bow and held her paddle at the ready. The roaring increased and so did their speed. The flashlight had barely caught the white froth of rapids before they were tossed down a stomach-flopping drop. Gwen's teeth clattered together on impact, and their little boat shuddered.

A rock loomed up in front of them, and Gwen and Kelan barely avoided bashing headlong into it.

"Was that another tunnel?" Aidan yelled.

"Just a rock," Gwen called out.

They swished around the rock, dropped again, and paddled until Gwen's arms threatened to fall out of their sockets. She was drenched from sweat and spray and her heart pounded in her chest as if trying to escape. They flew around a corner. Aidan's light reflected off a rock wall in front of them, and a deafening roar filled the tunnel.

"Waterfall!" Gwen screamed. "Hold on!"

She took her own advice and held onto the ropes with all her might, the paddle tucked under her clenched fists. The rock wall shot toward them, and then they angled down into darkness.

Gwen screamed, long and loud, but could barely hear herself over the thundering. Her stomach climbed up her throat as they fell. Water spray was everywhere, and Gwen wouldn't have been able to see even if they weren't plunging into absolute darkness.

It was only moments until they landed with a tremendous splash, although it felt like hours to Gwen. The thud of impact whipped her head forward on her neck and she gasped with pain. Miraculously, their little boat was still upright.

"Is everyone all right?" Kelan's shaky voice called out above the roar of the waterfall behind them.

"Peachy," said Aidan.

"Alive," said Gwen.

Bran pointed his flashlight at the waterfall behind them. The beam barely caught the bottom of the falls before the boat was whisked around another corner. The unseen top was swathed in darkness.

"Best not to know," said Aidan.

"Wait," said Gwen. She squinted and leaned out past the bow to see better. "Is there light up ahead?"

"About bloody time. I'm never going down a waterslide again," said Aidan.

The light grew steadily brighter, until they could see through the clear water to the bottom of the tunnel. They turned a corner and surged through an opening in the rock. Gwen blinked her streaming eyes in the clouded dusky evening, brighter to her than the sunniest summer's noon.

When her eyes adjusted, she opened her mouth in wonder. Before them lay a snowy valley of rolling meadows and groves of leafless trees. Forbidding, jagged peaks of severe gray stone surrounded them like a crown. They were at once oppressive and snug, as if their boat were cuddled in the arms of a giantess. No houses perched on the riverside, nor in the valley beyond.

The river widened slightly as it grew shallow enough for their boat to brush against the silty bottom. Gwen glanced at Aidan, who looked as bedraggled as she felt. He shuffled over to sit beside her on the bench.

"We made it," he whispered in her ear. "We're in the Forbidden Lands."

Gwen looked around her at the landscape. There was nothing to see except windblown hills and the winding river.

"Now what?" she whispered.

***

Corann spread his hands over the surface of a large wooden table placed in the center of the ballroom. On the table was a glowing, three-dimensional depiction of the Velvet Woods. Tiny trees waved their stick-like trunks in an unfelt breeze, a blue river glittered through the center, and small hills rose in waves across the table. Corann's courtiers ringed the edge along with the rulers and advisors from Midvale and Southlands.

"Very detailed," Queen Kaie said, clearly impressed. "You know the realm well."

"As a ruler should," said Corann. He nodded at two courtiers on his right. "Lady Fianna and Lord Kirwin filled a few holes in my knowledge. But I love this land and know it well."

"Which is one reason we supported you in your rule, my lord," said a courtier, and the others nodded. Corann bent his head in acknowledgement.

"What is over here, my lord?" asked a young courtier. He pointed at a blurry patch on the map. Corann's lips grew thin.

"Although my efforts to connect with the room of enchantments have not been entirely successful yet, I have confidence that they will soon bear fruit. Until then, we must make do with my memories of the realm instead of a magical connection to the earth below our feet."

The young courtier flushed and looked down.

"My apologies, my lord. I did not mean…"

"My best guess for Faolan's forces is that they will approach from the northeast, on the border of Wintertree," Corann said smoothly. "They will need to set up a center of command from which they will send forays to test our defenses." He turned to King Weylin. "Have our forces been organized by ability? Are they ready to move?"

"Yes," he answered. "We have arranged our fighters in groups of three when possible, with one of each of our realms' fighters in each group—Midvale's animal connections, Southlands' flower venoms, and Velvet Woods' forest control. Where shall we send them? We have forty groups ready and waiting."

"I have a mind to send them to the gap of Anyon and the river crossing at Perth." Corann snapped his fingers and small yellow stars twinkled at the far border of the map. "Is there another location that should be patrolled? Any thoughts, my advisors?"

"Perhaps the Tremaine should be fortified," said one. She sent a spark from her fingertip to land on a forested area near the border. "It is a very inviting passage, especially from the Wintertree side."

"Well said. We shall send groups to all three locations. How long until they can be in place?"

"A few hours," said King Weylin with a brisk nod. A howling wind outside surged and ended with the ballroom door swinging open with a bang. The startled courtiers stared, and Corann made a pushing gesture with his hands. The doors slowly closed against the raging storm outside. King Weylin coughed. "Perhaps a little longer."

"Indeed," said Corann. "Let us send our forces at once. There is no time for delay."

King Weylin nodded and turned away. Before he had walked three steps, a rumbling roar echoed in the vast hall. The parquet floor trembled underfoot. Dust drifted from the ceiling, and the courtiers shrieked and shouted. Corann gripped the edge of the table with whitened knuckles until the shaking calmed, then he spoke.

"Let us prepare our forces for immediate departure, on my command. There is no time to waste."

King Weylin nodded brusquely and retreated to an inner door.

"But your work with the room of enchantments," Queen Kaie said tentatively. "It is going well, is it not?"

"Yes, very well," said Corann. He stared at the glowing map on the table. "But I need time to work, and Faolan is proving a distraction. The sooner we vanquish his forces, the sooner we can restore the realm."

Queen Kaie nodded without much conviction.

"And we will defeat Faolan's forces, have no doubt." Corann reached for a carved wooden box that lay on the edge of the table. "I have a secret weapon that Faolan cannot use, and the half-blood Gwendolyn will not use." Corann turned to the courtier on his left, who was the only one who did not look perplexed by Corann's words. "Tanguy, distribute the weapons to each fighting group and explain their use. I would do it myself, but it is time to conquer the room of enchantments once and for all."

"Yes, my lord." The courtier bowed crisply and strode across the ballroom. A tiny quake caused him to stumble but he recovered quickly and continued walking. Besides a few stifled gasps, the others made no comment. Corann ignored it completely.

"As for the rest: Varney, I would like you to oversee delivery of provisions to the fighters. Queen Kaie and Lady Selma, perhaps you could continue to examine the map for potential defensive maneuvers." He made a gathering motion with his hands and the map condensed into a glowing blue ball, which he then tossed to a female courtier on the far side. "I suggest the small banquet room for your comfort."

One by one, the courtiers bowed and left the ballroom. Corann stared at the door to the room of enchantments with an expression of distaste.

As if it could sense Corann's notice, the door rattled against its latch. Corann grimaced then snapped his fingers. Sparks showered onto the table, and moments later a servant appeared with the tired-looking man and a woman, both disheveled and looking frightened.

"Here are the humans, my lord." The servant bowed and glided away. Corann sighed and gestured to the door.

"Come on. Let us conquer this room today. Time is running out."

"I—" The man swallowed and glanced at the woman, who nodded encouragement. "I have an idea about that."

"Truly?" Corann brightened. "It's about time. Come in to the room and we'll test it."

***

Gwen and the others sat in silence in the boat for a long minute. The current pushed them downstream in a meandering way. The sleet had stopped, and the wind was mostly blocked by the mountains, but Gwen was still wet from the caves and starting to shiver as the adrenaline left her body. The darkness of a winter's night was closing in, and all she wanted to do was sleep.

"I know the Breenan are good at hiding their houses, but I find it hard to believe anyone lives on the river's edge," said Aidan. "We've seen nothing."

"Should we get out and start walking?" Bran said.

Gwen shook herself and thought.

"Yes," she said slowly. "Loniel showed us a map of the Forbidden Lands, and the village is right in the center."

"We're almost there now," said Aidan. "But the river curves away from it soon. We'd better paddle to the left bank and hike in."

Gwen heaved a sigh.

"So, we keep walking. Story of my life in the Otherworld."

"Makes you wish for a horse now, doesn't it?" said Aidan.

They paddled to the shore and pulled the boat up on the muddy bank, partly frozen in the cold weather. The ground was easy to traverse, for which Gwen was very thankful. After a few minutes, Kelan paused.

"Do you hear hoofbeats?"

Gwen stopped and listened closely. Through the breeze whistling in her ear, the distinctive clip-clop of a single horse emerged. A thrill of fear traveled through her body. Friend or foe? What were the inhabitants of the Forbidden Lands really like? All Gwen knew of them was that they were magically volatile and trapped within these mountains. What sort of people would come out of that combination?

She strained her eyes through the dark to make out the solitary figure riding a wooden cart pulled by a resigned-looking horse. A lantern swayed from a pole on the cart. The figure was bundled in a thick cloak and carried a bulky bundle on its front. As the cart approached, Gwen realized that it was a young woman with a sleeping baby slung against her chest.

"What do we say?" Gwen hissed.

"Anything," Aidan answered. He looked pale but determined. "We have to find Finn. Nothing else matters." Before Gwen could reply, he stepped forward and gave the woman a wave. "Hello! Can you help us? We're looking for someone."

The woman stopped the horse and considered their group with curiosity.

"It's not a pleasant day to be searching. Have you come here from a marking ceremony? I didn't realize any of the realms marked in the winter." Her eyes raked over their faces and came to rest on Kelan's, for he was clearly a few years too old to have recently received his coming-of-age tattoo at the Sacred Mountain.

"No, we are not tribeless ones," said Aidan. The woman's eyes narrowed in suspicion, so he continued hastily. "We're looking for Finn Sayward. Do you know where he lives?"

At Finn's name, the woman's expression cleared.

"Finn! Of course, our long-lost Finn. He only came back a few days ago. We're so happy to see him, Nialla most of all, his wife of course. We had such a feast yesterday! I'm returning to the village from dropping off some celebrants who live further afield and came in for the party."

Aidan glanced at Gwen, his face alive with hope. Gwen clutched his hand and spoke to the woman.

"Please, can you tell us where to find him? It's urgent."

"Of course." She waved at the cart. "I'm going back to the village now. Climb in and I will take you there."

Gwen could hardly believe that their luck had finally turned. They stammered their thanks and piled into the cart, where they even found blankets to wrap themselves in.

Bran perched near the woman to chat, who introduced herself as Mabina. Gwen lay against Aidan in the back and let her weariness take over. She was almost fully warm for the first time in hours. Her eyelids dropped.

***

Faolan paced the tent, deep in thought. It was a large pavilion, lavishly hung with furs for insulation and containing orange magical fires in hanging lanterns for warmth against the raging storm outside. The sides of the tent flapped tightly but were firmly tethered to the ground and let no errant winds inside.

The floor was spread with a thickly woven rug, upon which lay the three-dimensional map of the Velvet Woods. Isolde and Queen Ula of Longshore leaned over a section of the map.

"Send warning to this fighting group." Isolde pointed to an orange dot that inched imperceptibly along the narrow blue line of a river. "The Beast of Sand and Mist has its lair on the western bank. It is docile unless otherwise instructed, but certainly Corann will have it on alert."

Queen Ula nodded and touched a green stone to the dot.

"That will alert all three fighters in the group to danger directly ahead, thanks to the connection with their battle belts. A sensation of heat will warn them to the direction of the danger."

"Good," Isolde murmured. She continued to scan the map for other pitfalls.

"Are the selected groups nearing the Guennola Falls yet?" Faolan asked without looking at the map. Queen Ula replied.

"Presently. They are moving slowly due to the infestation of kelpies in that stretch of river."

"The kelpies will not attack unless Corann subverts the room of enchantments for his own purposes," said Isolde. With a sidelong glance at Faolan, she added, "I have been assured that is nearly impossible."

"Let us hope so," said Faolan. He stiffened when King Gavin of Whitecliff entered the tent in a flurry of snow. His cheeks were red with the cold.

"King Faolan, Queen Ula, I have stationed my war singers along the canyon cliffs, out of sight." He swirled his index finger in his other palm and a dozen golden stars twinkled into existence. He blew them gently and they drifted into position on the map. "And a few at the Glenway bridge. They will attack at the first sign of Corann's forces."

"Excellent, King Gavin." Faolan nodded with a satisfied smile. "Your singers are a formidable force to be reckoned with. I still recall the avalanche at the battle of Greenhall against the Northern Kingdoms."

King Gavin's face cracked in a grin.

"What a battle that was! The Northerners routed, of course." King Gavin rubbed his hands together. "Queen Brenna has almost completed her preparations, from what I understand. Some of her traps, well, they're so ingenious they might have been human-designed."

186

"It's possible," said Faolan. "Riverside guards its secrets jealously, and it would not surprise me if Queen Brenna had ancient plans deep in her vaults, to pull out at the opportune moment."

"Two groups down!" Queen Ula shouted. Faolan and King Gavin leaned over the map and Queen Ula pointed at the tiny wisps of smoke where two lights used to be. "At the Orin cave."

Isolde's eyes raked feverishly over the map. Faolan rounded on her.

"You assured us Corann had no knowledge of that hidden cavern."

"I had no idea, I swear," cried Isolde.

"Are you on our side or Corann's, Isolde? Answer me truthfully. I have no use for traitors."

"Your side, I swear!" Isolde jabbed her finger at a nearby location on the map. "But if he knows of the cavern, he must surely be aware of the eastern exit. Warn the group stationed there."

Faolan nodded at Queen Ula, who placed a polished violet stone on the glowing dot Isolde had indicated. Immediately, the dot crawled into the cavern. Faolan strode to one wall of the tent covered in a featureless drape of ivy. He touched the vines and they writhed to form a few intricate knots, loops, and bunches of leaves.

"Two groups down," Faolan said with a heavy sigh. A dot at the edge of a mountain flared once, twice, three times.

"Three of the Velvet Woods fighters down!" Queen Ula said with relief. Faolan put his hand on the branch and once more recorded the casualties.

"Corann will have much to answer for," he said. "This entirely unnecessary war is already costly, in time and magic, not to mention the injuries sustained by our fighters. I am tempted to take his head as payment."

"I would not gainsay you," said King Gavin. When they turned to read the tally vines together, Isolde's face twisted with dismay. A momentary lapse, then her expression smoothed, and she spoke calmly.

"One of our fighting groups is too near the Cardew pits. If they wish to avoid an unpleasant end, they must walk on the ridge only."

Queen Ula moved to alert the fighters with her colored stones. Isolde scanned the board. Only her tight lips betrayed her emotions.

***

Tristan lay flat on the snow-free ground under a dense, leafless elder bush, a short knife dipped in a dark substance in one hand and a sack filled with lumpy objects in the other. His chestnut-brown hair was dusted with snow. Rhiannon shifted beside him.

"Where are they?" she whispered over the howling of the wind. "I heard footsteps ages ago. They can't have left already."

"There!" Another female fighter with them hissed. "Beside the oak. Three of them."

Tristan silently picked out three spheres of polished wood from the sack, each no larger than a child's fist and glowing red. Tristan whispered inaudibly, and the spheres hovered in midair, then whizzed through the whirling

188

snow toward their opponents.

But before the spheres could reach them, the other fighters stepped behind the slender oak and disappeared. The spheres whistled harmlessly by and planted themselves in a snowbank. Muffled thumps and tiny wisps of smoke emerged from the holes. Tristan heaved a sigh.

"I only have so many immobilization spell stones. What a waste."

"Did you see where they went, Bretta?" said Rhiannon. She squinted at the empty trees in front of them.

"Must have crept behind some bushes," said Bretta. "Come on, let's follow them."

Rhiannon narrowed her eyes but did not contradict the other woman. A small earth tremor gave them pause. Once the world had stopped shaking, Tristan sat up and tied his sack to his belt.

"I want a clean shot this time."

The bush behind them exploded in a flurry of shouts and sparks. More alarming was the snarling and growling that followed.

Tristan, Rhiannon, and Bretta scrambled out of the bush and adopted fighting stances. Tristan held out his knife and rummaged in his sack for more spell stones; Bretta held an arrow nocked and pulled in a taut bow, the tip of the arrow glowing with violet fire; Rhiannon's hands were empty but held out in front of her in readiness, sparks dancing between fingertips.

The three fighters they had spotted before ran around the bush. Two huge wolves accompanied them, their silver coats rippling as they leaped forward.

Tristan yelled and threw a glowing red sphere at the

nearest wolf. The animal paused in mid-stride, mouth agape in a frozen snarl. Bretta let her arrow loose, but narrowly missed the opponent with a green cloak, who dodged the arrow and then threw a knife at her. The knife flipped through the air, trailing a glowing blue net behind it, which fell over Bretta. She shouted and twisted within her bonds, to no avail. The attacker ran to the left and disappeared.

Rhiannon threw balls of fire from her palms at her opponent, who deflected them with a magical shield. A wolf lunged, and their opponent threw a fireball at the same time. Rhiannon fell to the snow to avoid the fire. Tristan sliced madly at the wolf until it snarled and leaped away.

A sudden stillness, and the clearing was empty.

"Where did they go?" panted Tristan. "Curse the Midvale Breenan—beast-taming skills give them a numbers advantage, not to mention the fangs."

"At least they can only command one at a time," said Rhiannon as Tristan pulled her to her feet. "But why did they leave?" She bent down to untangle Bretta from her net.

"So we can surprise you," shouted a smug voice. Rhiannon had hardly turned around before the attackers were on them. Fire blazed and snarls filled the air again. The attackers yelled as Tristan's knife and Rhiannon's flames found their marks, but Tristan cursed loudly when a wolf sank its teeth into his leg. Rhiannon pelted it with three rapid-fire spell stones, each hitting the animal's fur with a blaze of fire until it bounded away with a yip and ran off with its tail low.

"Take that, mongrel!" Tristan yelled, then looked around. "Where did they go? Again?"

"And how?" Rhiannon muttered. "Come on, we need to move, we're too vulnerable here. Can you stand? Good." She ran over to Bretta and ripped away the remains of the net. Bretta sat up and rubbed welts where the net had burned her skin.

"There's something strange going on," said Rhiannon. She began to jog forward, but a knife whistled by her ear from the left. She ducked, but a moment later another knife flew in from the right. Both times, the grinning face of the Breenan man with the green cloak danced from behind the knife, yet no one ran in front of them.

"How is he in two places at once?" Rhiannon gasped. They darted into dense trees to their left.

"No magic I've ever heard of," said Tristan. "How many are there?"

"Only three that I've seen," said Bretta. She whirled around to check behind them. "It feels like a dozen. How can they move without our noticing?"

Rhiannon did a double-take at the sight behind a nearby tree. A portal shimmered there. It exposed a water-logged field of grass in the human world beyond, at odds with the snow-laden storm of their world.

"They're using portals," Rhiannon breathed. Another glimmer directed her eye to a different portal beyond. "Why are there so many here?"

An attacker leaped at them with a yell. Sparks and flames flew, but within moments the three had subdued the one. Tristan put a knee on his chest and gripped his wrists. Bretta sat on his legs. Rhiannon bent her face into his.

"What's the game here?" she hissed. "Are you using the portals? Why are there so many?"

"I won't tell you anything," he spat. Tristan pressed a knee more firmly into the man's chest. He wheezed, "All right, all right. We were given amulets to make portals, to confuse you and gain the advantage."

"And where is this amulet?" Rhiannon said with exaggerated patience.

"Necklace."

Rhiannon ran her hands along his neck until she pulled out a leather strap with a flat bead threaded on it. Inset into clear resin was a picture of a laughing man on one side and a dark-haired woman on the other. A tiny segment of black hair lay embedded on the edge.

"Here." Rhiannon pulled the leather strap over his head and brandished it at Tristan and Bretta. "They've been making portals to get around us." She made a sound of disgust. "As if we don't have enough portals popping open everywhere."

"Anything else you want to know from this one? His fellows don't seem eager to rescue him." Tristan nodded at their captive, whose eyes flickered between them with fear. Rhiannon shook her head.

"That's enough for now. We'll take him to the king."

Their captive opened his mouth to protest, but Tristan swiftly bent down and pressed his forehead against the other's. Immediately, the captive's eyes rolled back in his head and he fell limp. Tristan hoisted himself up.

"We'll hover him for transporting. Let's get back to the king." He rubbed his hands together. "Perhaps they'll have a cup of warm wine for us."

"To dull your senses and magical abilities? Not likely."
Rhiannon held out her hands, and the unconscious captive's body lifted into midair. Tristan sighed and sheathed his knife.

"I can dream."

***

Gwen was jolted to terrified consciousness. She sat up with a gasp.

"Apologies," said Mabina. "The road is rough this time of year."

"Where are we?" said Gwen. Aidan groaned sleepily beside her.

"We're almost at the village," Mabina said. "You weren't asleep for long. It's not a large valley." A note of discontent crept into her otherwise cheerful voice.

"Is it difficult, living here?" asked Gwen. She was curious on her own account, but she also wanted to know more in case it helped her to convince Finn. The woman shrugged.

"Does it matter? Ever since my failed marking, I can't live anywhere else. Crops don't grow as well here, not without forest magic, but we make do."

"Was it awful, trying to get away from the marking ceremony?" asked Bran. "Did they hunt you down?"

Mabina laughed.

"No, nothing of the sort. I don't know how those rumors started. When I didn't come down the mountain—I was frightened beyond belief and didn't know what to do—they came and brought my things, then one of them escorted me to the Forbidden Lands. I never saw my family again." She paused for a moment, and Gwen pondered the sorrow of her words. "But it was for the best. The ceremony had awakened latent magical abilities in me. On the journey here, my magic became harder and harder to control. I almost capsized the boat on the crossing. This was the only place for me."

"But how can you stand living without magic?" Bran said. "I don't even know how I would cope."

"It feels like a part of me is tied in chains." Mabina stared forward for a moment, then she laughed lightly. "I don't know why I told you that. I do love this valley. It's beautiful, and we can live safely. My eldest son—he wouldn't be able to survive outside of these mountains. Some of the tribeless do try to leave when they are restless for more, but it never ends well. We are safe here. For better or for worse, this is my home."

"Was your son born here?" asked Gwen.

"Yes. And with two tribeless parents, it was inevitable that he would have difficulties. His magic is scarcely controllable, even here."

"There should be different levels of dampening for every person," Aidan said thoughtfully. Mabina looked surprised.

"I suppose that would make sense. My son certainly needs more." She peered forward, then her face opened in a joyful smile. "And there he is. Culain!" she shouted in the direction of a small boy who ran down a hill on their path.

"Mam!" The boy shouted back with a happy grin. He was no more than five, with sandy hair and gangly limbs.

A man crested the hill—Culain's father, by the similarities in facial features—and waved to the cart.

Then Culain stumbled. His arms flailed wildly. His feet desperately stomped to gain purchase on the slippery ground until, suddenly, they trod in midair. Culain's eyes were wide with shock as he climbed up into the air, unsupported.

Then he fell. He tumbled to the ground with his limbs askew and started to cry. Mabina clambered down from the cart as fast as she could with the baby on her chest and ran to pick up her son. He quietened in her arms and she brought him back to the cart with her husband close behind.

"You see?" Mabina said when she was back in the cart. "Even the dampening sometimes isn't enough for him. I can't imagine what would happen outside of the Forbidden Lands."

"And who are your passengers?" her husband said. He took the reins from his wife and clucked at the horse. It trundled forward once more.

"Fearghus, this is Gwen, Aidan, Bran, and Kelan. They're from outside. Gwen is looking for our own Finn."

"He's my uncle," Gwen said.

"Really?" Fearghus turned to look at Gwen. "Is this a family greeting, or do you have business with him?"

"Business, I suppose," said Gwen. She sat up straighter. There was no reason not to tell these people the truth. "It's a long story, but the essence is that I am the heir to the throne of the Velvet Woods. A usurper has the throne currently, and portals to the human world are ripping the land apart because of it. An appropriate heir must rule to fix the destruction. I will do it if I must, but I don't belong here—I'm half-human." Mabina glanced at her in surprise, but she plowed on. "But Finn could rule. I've come to ask him to take my place."

"I forgot Finn was the son of a queen," Mabina said. "Our past lives are simply irrelevant here."

"I am sorry to crush your hopes," said Fearghus. "But Finn would never leave his family. Not now that he's finally been reunited. He will stay in the Forbidden Lands."

Chapter 12

There was silence in the cart. Even the sleet had turned to quiet snow that whipped less fiercely across their faces than before. Finally, Aidan spoke.

"Is there no way for you to leave here?"

Mabina shook her head.

"None at all. Some have tried, of course. It never ends well."

"But what if there was a way?" Aidan pressed. "If you could live safely, somewhere else, would you?"

Mabina and Fearghus looked at each other.

"In a heartbeat," said Mabina. "I adore the trees and glades of the forests. The Velvet Woods was my home, you know. Long ago."

"And young Culain has never seen the world beyond these mountains," said Fearghus. "I wish I could show him more."

"And he could meet our families. His grandparents, cousins, aunts, uncles. He could see my childhood home."

"We could find a lake to settle near," said Fearghus wistfully. "Build a cottage on the shore." Mabina nodded with a faraway look. Fearghus sighed. "But it's an impossible dream."

Aidan lapsed into silence, but he looked thoughtful. Gwen prodded him with her elbow.

"What are you thinking?" she whispered.

"There has to be some way to allow these people to leave. We simply have to think of the solution." He stared into the snowy night, his eyes narrowed in thought. Gwen looked past him when she heard a friendly shout.

"Mabina, Fearghus. You're back!"

Low houses emerged in the dim light, tucked into the sloping ground. Their grass roofs covered with snow and gray stone walls blended into the landscape, except for gentle streams of smoke that drifted from short chimneys. At the sound of horse hooves, doors opened and spilled light onto the accumulating snow. Cheery faces greeted them.

"Mabina, you made it!"

"Who are your passengers?"

"Come in out of the cold."

"We're driving to the far end of the village," said Mabina loudly. "Gwen and her friends have come to find her uncle, our own Finn." There were exclamations of interest. "She is supposed to rule the Velvet Woods but hopes Finn will take her place."

Chatter burst out with renewed vigor as people relayed the news to their neighbors who hadn't heard. The village wasn't large, but by the time they reached the last house, there was a substantial crowd following their cart.

"Luckily this isn't a stealth mission," Aidan murmured to Gwen. She released a breathy laugh, and a cloud

198

appeared in the cold air.

"What do you think he'll say?" she whispered back. Aidan shrugged tightly, his face grim.

"Hopefully the right thing."

Culain slipped down from the cart at a word from his mother and ran to the last house in the village. It was small but snug, with a welcoming flicker of firelight creeping between gaps in the shutters. Culain knocked loudly, then scampered back to Mabina. The door opened to reveal Finn. He looked confused to see the whole village at his door.

"Are we having another party?" he said. Then he spotted Gwen and Aidan and his eyes widened. "Niece! What are you doing here? Wait, I'll come out."

He disappeared for a moment and returned wearing a thick cloak. A woman with long braided hair followed holding a girl by the hand. The girl stared at Gwen when Finn walked forward to greet her.

Gwen climbed stiffly down from the cart. Finn gripped both her hands in his and brought them to his forehead.

"Greetings, Gwen. It's wonderful to see you again." He moved to Aidan and greeted him familiarly with one hand on either side of his head. Aidan did likewise, and they briefly touched foreheads.

"Gwen, Aidan," Finn said with a happy smile. "Meet my wife Nialla and my daughter Ione." He ushered them forward and Nialla nodded her head with a smile.

"It is a pleasure to meet a relation of my dear Finn. Have you had a long journey?"

"All the way from the human world, my love," said Finn. "These are the two who brought me back.

Remember?"

"Of course," said Nialla warmly. "My deepest thanks to you both."

"But what brings you here?" asked Finn. He looked around at the crowd of his curious neighbors. "And with an entourage?"

"It's a long story," said Gwen. "But the short version is this: Isolde was deposed. A usurper sits on the throne of the Velvet Woods, and due to a mistake made by Isolde, the worlds have become unstable and are ripping apart. It's chaos. It will all stop once I'm queen." Gwen took a deep breath and gazed into Finn's concerned eyes. "But I don't belong here. The only other person who can fix this—is you. You could be king instead." Gwen bit her lip and waited for Finn's reaction.

It was not long in coming. Finn seemed to understand what she would ask before all the words had left her mouth and he shook his head sadly but firmly.

"Do not ask this of me, niece. Please believe me when I say I understand your anguish—I spent years in a world I didn't want to live in—but I cannot help you. I only just returned to my wife and daughter." He pulled them both under each arm. Ione smiled up at him shyly. "I cannot—will not—leave them again."

Gwen's shoulders slumped, and she fought back tears. She had expected this answer from Finn, but it put the final nail in the coffin of her life as she knew it. Visions of an unknown future in a Breenan world filled Gwen's mind, and she recoiled with dismay. Finn looked at her face and tried to soften the blow.

"Nialla is tribeless, as you know. She and Ione need the

magic dampening of this place to avoid their magic going wild. Especially since Ione has episodes of stronger magic than even the dampening spell can cover, there is no way they could step foot out of the Forbidden Lands. It pushes down magic into a manageable size. Without it, neither tribeless ones nor those they are near would be safe."

"What if you commute?" Aidan said. His voice rose in volume. The villagers leaned in with interest, and through her fog of disappointment Gwen wondered if this was the most entertainment they had seen for some time. "It's not that far. You could spend a week there, a week here."

"The rule of a realm only works if the ruler stays in contact with the land of the realm," said Finn. He sounded as if he were quoting. Then he sighed. "A ruler can leave their realm for a few days at most. The journey from the Velvet Woods takes the better part of a day, even with the fastest conveyance possible. How could I be the husband and father I want to be, especially after my absence? No, I'm afraid there is no way."

Aidan's hands balled into fists and his face grew red. He opened his mouth to reply, but Bran grabbed his shoulder.

"Come on, cousin," he said lightly. "A short walk will do us wonders."

Gwen hurried after them. Her stomach cramped with dread at her future. She looked back once: the villagers clustered together in conversation, oblivious to the gently falling snow; and Finn, quietly staring after her with a frown.

**

Bran pushed Aidan behind a cottage, out of earshot of the villagers. Kelan joined them with Gwen.

"That was quick thinking, Bran," Kelan said. "We didn't come here for a fight, and we were vastly outnumbered."

"I could have taken my share," said Bran.

"Without magic?"

"Oh."

Aidan's ragged breathing interrupted them. He leaned his forearms against the cottage and pressed his head into the wood to control himself, but his breath came faster and faster.

Gwen couldn't hold back her tears any longer. They spilled over her cheeks as a flood of fear and disappointment welled up inside her. She hugged herself tightly to hold herself together. Her core flickered with her uncontrollable emotions, although the magic-dampening spell of the Forbidden Lands kept her magic at bay. She wished Aidan would hug her—she had never felt more alone. Kelan and Bran looked at each other, unsure what to do.

Finally, the sound of Gwen's sobs broke through to Aidan. He turned his anguished face to Gwen, then threw himself toward her. They clutched each other fiercely.

"This can't be happening," Aidan muttered into her hair. Gwen felt, rather than saw, Bran and Kelan back away a short distance to give them privacy. "What can we do?"

"There's nothing to do," Gwen choked out. She took a deep, shuddering breath and tried to compose herself.

"This is it. I'll be queen and live in the Otherworld. Forever."

The enormity of that statement hit Gwen like a punch in the stomach. She clawed the emotions that followed back inside, glad for once of her ability to control herself. She had a feeling she would need it in her new future. She pulled away from Aidan.

"You should live in the human world. Keep doing your music. Find another—" She stumbled briefly. "Another girl to love. You deserve the best, so keep searching. We just—we aren't meant to be."

"No!" Aidan burst out. He gripped her shoulders. "I refuse to accept that. This is not how this ends, how we end. Do you hear me?" He shook her as if trying to rattle sense into her.

Tears sprang unbidden to Gwen's eyes once more at the strength of Aidan's faith in the two of them, but she didn't see how they could wriggle out of this one.

"What can we do?" Gwen whispered. "I won't run away to Vancouver. Even if it means…"

"I know." Aidan took his hands off her and ran them through his hair, making the snow-dusted copper stand on end. "Let's just think for a minute. We thought our way out of the restoration spell garden in the summer, when you were about to die. We can do this." He waved Bran and Kelan forward.

"Where do we start?" Gwen couldn't see how to fix any of this, but she was willing to listen, for Aidan's sake.

"Let's break it down. The only obstacle for Finn becoming king is that his family can't come."

"The only obstacle we know."

"We can confirm that with him."

"And really," said Bran. "Who wouldn't want to be in a palace instead of in this isolated village?"

"Fair point," said Aidan. "All right, how can we get him to come? We need Nialla and Ione with him. Can we put this magic-dampening spell on the castle?"

"No," said Kelan. "For a few reasons. First, we don't know the spell. It was done centuries ago, and who knows if records of it still exist. Second, we don't know how the magic of the tribeless ones works. Third, the functioning of the realm is dependent on the connection with the room of enchantments, which presumably would be severed by the spell."

"What about on a house near the castle?" said Aidan. "Nialla and Ione could live there, and Finn could visit."

"That would be cruel, forcing house arrest," said Gwen, but she was interested despite herself. Could a solution be hidden in the fog of details? "Is there some way to make the spell portable? So it hovers over a single person and follows them around, like an umbrella that shields them from magic?"

"Shields others from their magic, you mean," said Kelan.

"An umbrella would be cumbersome all the time," Bran mused. "How would you hunt?"

Gwen punched his shoulder.

"It's metaphorical. Keep up, Bran." Gwen was energized with a manic hope. She stared at Aidan, trying to will the answer out of thin air, then turned to Kelan. "Can you affix a spell to a person, a long-term spell?"

Kelan twisted his mouth in thought.

204

"Not that I can think of. Any spell cast directly on a person is generally superficial and temporary. You need something unchanging to hold the magic."

"Like a tracker ring," added Bran.

Gwen breathed faster. She stared at Kelan's wrist, encircled by his leather wristband for headaches. He caught her eye and looked confused at the attention.

"Kelan," she said with forced calm. "Tell me everything you know about how your healing bracelet works."

Chapter 13

Kelan still looked confused at the apparent change of topic, but he answered readily enough.

"It's simple, really. The spell is cast for each particular malady. It's not a cure—it acts rather to dull symptoms, to keep them behind a gate, of sorts. I'm prone to headaches, so the spell is tuned to reduce them."

"Do you know the spell?" Gwen asked breathlessly.

"Sure, it's one of the first spells we learn in our advanced training."

Gwen looked at Aidan with shining eyes. He smiled widely, the first real smile she'd seen on him in ages.

"What do you think?" Gwen whispered. "Can we hope?"

"Absolutely," Aidan said with confidence. "This is our chance."

"Can we really solve a centuries-old issue? Why hasn't it been done before?"

"What are you talking about?" Bran asked. "How can you fix the tribeless ones?"

Aidan looked at Gwen, and she laughed.

"Point taken," she said. "Let's find Finn—he'll get it."

Gwen rushed back to the cottage, the others close behind. The villagers had raised awnings and tents in front of Finn's house during their brief departure, and someone had brought out a table with a huge pot on it, which was gently steaming. Bright lanterns swung in the breeze from the tent poles.

"Oh good, a party," said Bran.

"I guess not much happens here, if they take our arrival as an excuse for a party in this weather," said Kelan.

Finn was chatting to Fearghus when Gwen skidded to a stop in the snow at his feet.

"Finn," she said breathlessly. "We have an idea. You need Nialla and Ione to come with you to the Velvet Woods, right?" Finn barely had time to nod before she continued. "What if we made a portable version of the dampening spell? We could base it off the spell of a healing bracelet."

"And we could adapt it to be stronger for those who need it," Aidan added.

Finn frowned, but in thought instead of disagreement.

"It's an interesting idea. I admit, I hadn't considered the healing bracelet angle. We don't know the dampening spell, though."

"You've lived too long with the Breenan," said Aidan. "You haven't learned how to exercise your creative side. I'll bet we can figure it out. Gwen and I make up new spells all the time."

"What about the tribeless magic?" asked Kelan. "How can you make a spell for something you know nothing about?"

Finn gazed at Kelan in thought.

"I've gathered some knowledge, after living among the tribeless for years and talking to those who know more. The magic of the tribeless ones appears to be a mix of Ardra and forest people magic. It's not unlike the magic of a realm's ruler—an Ardra deeply connected to the land, with the ability to make long-lasting changes—but on a much smaller scale, of course. Their magic can come out in flashy, quick spells, such as those of the Ardra, but they seem to be stronger and more permanent, like those of the forest people. Hence their destructiveness. On Nialla's boat crossing, the water sloshed around for a week after she was safely ensconced in the Forbidden Lands."

"If you know all that, why can't the tribeless ones figure out how to use it?" asked Gwen.

"It's not that simple. How can they learn? No one knows enough to help. The forest people have no difficulty, as their magic is dormant until they need to access it. The Ardra attend training to corral their abilities. Most of the tribeless ones have been through the Ardra training, and it certainly did not give them the skills to harness their powers."

"It's a roadblock," Aidan conceded. "But I think we know enough to try."

"Please, Finn," said Gwen. "Can you help us try? If we can't figure it out, nothing needs to change here, and I'll go be queen. But if we can make a dampening bracelet, would you consider being king?"

Finn stared at her for a long moment, then he looked to his wife, who had drifted to his side during their conversation. Nialla nodded.

"Yes," he said finally. "I will consider it."

Gwen gripped Aidan's hand and he squeezed tightly back.

"Wait," said Fearghus. "Are you saying that there might be a way for us tribeless ones to leave the Forbidden Lands?"

The villagers, already hushed to hear Gwen speak, ceased their murmuring. Ione took Finn's hand.

"Is it true, Papa? Could I see the other lands like you do?"

Nialla looked annoyed.

"Keep your voices down. It's not right to spread false hope. People are content here, mostly. If you give them hope only to snatch it away, that's cruel."

"But there is hope," said Finn softly. He stroked his daughter's hair. "Nothing more, but nothing less."

"How can I help?" said Fearghus. "Anything at all."

Gwen and Aidan glanced at each other. Gwen bit her lip in thought.

"We'll need a way to get outside the boundary, to test the spell," she said.

"A quiet place to think," said Aidan. "Preferably warm."

"And a bracelet," added Finn unexpectedly. "Forged metal, something strong yet comfortable enough to wear always. We'll need to affix the spell to an object."

"All right," said Fearghus. "I will make it happen."

"And an escape from the Forbidden Lands for Gwen," said Kelan. "We need to take her back to our father. She isn't needed here anymore." To Bran he said, "You know Father will kill us if she's not there for the occupation.

You take her back—Father will forgive you much more easily."

Bran laughed.

"I suppose he will. You should stay here—they'll need more power for their spell." He smiled at Gwen. "Our poor halflings."

Gwen wrinkled her nose at him, then turned to Aidan while Kelan wandered toward the awning with the steaming pot.

"Don't you need me? Can you figure it out on your own?"

"I've been self-taught since I first realized I had magic. I can do this. I'll bounce ideas off Finn—hopefully he's lived in our world long enough for some creativity to rub off on him."

Finn chuckled.

"I'll do my best. I was a choreographer, remember? You may stay the night in our cottage, of course, and Gwen and Bran can leave at first light. Come in when you're ready."

He moved off. Nialla lingered for a moment.

"Please don't fail. You have brought a disruption that I fear we won't recover from if you don't succeed. Longing for something that can never be is a poison."

"I'll do everything in my power to make this a reality," said Aidan. "My future is also dependent on success."

Nialla nodded and followed Finn and her daughter inside. The remaining villagers, those who had not rushed off with Fearghus, were talking and gesturing under the awnings, their drinks largely forgotten. Kelan strolled back with a drink in his hand.

"You could have brought one for me," said Bran.

"You have legs," said Kelan amiably. He took a sip then said, "No one in the realms will like this."

"What do you mean?" asked Gwen.

"Tribeless ones living among us? It won't be easy to get past the prejudice and fear. We're brought up with stories of the Forbidden Lands. Monsters and wild men and the like."

"I always loved the Tale of the Tribeless Tunnel," said Bran. "Terrifying at night before bed."

"Most know the tales as folklore to frighten children," said Kelan. "Warn them from seeking out the Forbidden Lands, from getting too close to the forest folk, but dig deep enough and even marked adults have those prejudices. Even if you can find a way for the tribeless to leave the Forbidden Lands, it will be difficult for them to gain acceptance."

"But they're just regular Breenan," said Gwen in exasperation. "Once they meet them, it will be fine."

Kelan shrugged.

"Hopefully."

"Well," said Bran. "I think they're great. Look how nice they are! I'll bet they make delicious drinks, too, if someone had bothered to get me one." Kelan took an ostentatious slurp and Bran shook his head. "Besides, people can change. I used to think humans were stupid and stinky, and now look who my friends are!"

"Thanks, Bran," Aidan said. "No offense meant, I'm sure."

Gwen yawned with jaw-cracking ferocity.

"I need to lie down before I fall down. Come on, let's

get inside."

The cottage was small, but a fire burned brightly in the hearth set into the stone wall, and the floorboards were covered with woven mats in welcoming reds and oranges. A ladder led to a dark loft above. Nialla waved them in.

"If you're hungry, I have some fish stew. It's plain, but it will fill you."

"Thank you," said Gwen. She was almost too tired to eat, but the bowl Nialla handed her smelled too good to resist. She couldn't remember the last time she had eaten. A pre-dawn breakfast at Winterwood, perhaps?

There weren't enough stools for everyone, so Gwen and the others sat cross-legged on the floor. No one spoke much. There was too much to talk about, and not enough familiarity between them. Gwen didn't know if she could string her rambling thoughts together into coherent sentences—her mind wandered in its sleepiness.

Soon, their bowls were empty. Finn banked the fire and Ione shyly presented them with blankets.

"You'll have to sleep on the floor, I'm afraid," said Finn. "The loft is small enough for the three of us. But the fire should keep you warm, at least."

"Thanks for putting us up, Finn," said Gwen. "The floor is great."

The little family disappeared up the ladder. Aidan and Kelan spread out their blankets, and Gwen lay down.

"Wow, that's hard," she whispered. She didn't want their hosts to hear her, but it had to be said. Bran stretched out as if he lay on a luxurious down mattress.

"I've slept on harder. We pack light during patrol."

"I would have thought you'd be soft, being a prince and

212

all," Aidan said. A gentle snore was his only reply. Aidan looked at Kelan, dumbfounded. "He's asleep already?"

Kelan laughed.

"He can sleep anywhere. As can I, in fact. Good night." And with that, he closed his eyes.

Aidan lay down beside Gwen and pulled the blankets over them.

"Are you warm enough, Gwen?"

She snuggled into his side in response.

"Now I am."

He kissed the top of her head. They lay in silence with only the red glow of the banked fire for company, until the soft breathing of Kelan's sleep drifted past them.

"Do you really think you can make this work?" she whispered in his ear. He squeezed tighter.

"Yes. It's our only chance. I won't rest until I find a way."

Gwen pulled back to see his earnest green eyes, dark in the dim light.

"Don't be silly. You can't think properly without pacing yourself. Sleep, eat, then solve the riddle."

He just squeezed her tighter in answer.

"I don't like leaving you in the Otherworld," Gwen said. "How can I contact you, especially if tracker rings don't work with the magic-dampening spell?"

"I don't suppose my mobile works here." Aidan reached into his backpack and turned on his phone, kept dry in a plastic bag. The screen showed no signal. He put it away with an expression of resignation. "We'll have to rely on optimism."

Gwen didn't like that at all but couldn't see any

alternative. She nestled in closer, then stiffened.

"Aidan. Kelan said the healing bracelet was like a gate, blocking the pain. What if our dampening bracelet worked the same way? Keep the magic behind a gate, and they can open and close it when they want to access their power."

"And that's how they can train," said Aidan with suppressed excitement. "Letting more and more out at a time, until they can control it at will."

"Yes, and you can have different sized 'gates' for different amounts of magic. Like that Culain boy, he'll need more."

Aidan sighed.

"That's figured out. Now, to find the right series of spells for all those specifications."

She poked him.

"Let's not think about it anymore. Tell me something normal. What do you do on Christmas?"

Aidan rubbed his cheek against the top of her head.

"It's pretty quiet. Mum and I open gifts, drink eggnog. Aunty Lucy comes over about mid-day, and we finish making dinner together. What about you?"

"Something like that. It's usually Dad and me. Sometimes we visit my cousins in Campbell River, or sometimes Ellie's family has us over. It's nice."

They lay in silence for a moment.

"You know what would be nicer?" said Aidan at last.

"What?"

"Spending Christmas with you."

Gwen pressed her face into his chest.

"Yeah, that would be nice."

**

Gwen woke before dawn, her body stiff from the hard floor. Kelan was rolling up his blanket and Bran stretched beside him. Finn was building the fire and Nialla cut bread on the table.

"Good morning, sleepy," Bran said when he spotted her open eyes. "Ready for a boating adventure?"

"Adventure is the polite way of saying it. How are we getting out of here, anyway? I'm not paddling up that waterfall." Gwen stood with a groan and shook her arms to work out the kinks.

"Finn says that if you follow the river, it will pass through another tunnel through the mountains," said Kelan.

"Oh, great," Gwen said.

"But this tunnel is wide and calm, and much shorter." Kelan smiled. "You'll be fine."

"I hope you're right. We could use a break," Gwen muttered.

Kelan and Bran moved away briefly to say their farewells, and Gwen threw her arms around Aidan.

"Be careful traveling the river with Finn, when you figure this out. Tunnels are still tunnels, no matter how calm."

"You too," he said, and then his lips pressed against hers, fiercely, urgently, as if it were their last. Gwen melted into him, twining her fingers in his hair and pushing her body against his. She didn't care who was watching—they needed this moment, right now.

But a moment was all they had. Bran approached.

"Sorry to interrupt, but we should leave soon, Gwen."

"Nialla," said Finn. "Would you take Gwen and Bran to the river? I will begin our work with Aidan."

"Of course," said Nialla. She put slices of bread into Gwen's and Bran's hands. "Here, eat this on the way."

Gwen nodded quickly and gave Aidan one last kiss.

"You can do it," she said to him. "I know you can."

He didn't say anything. He just nodded and watched Gwen as she walked out the door with Bran and Nialla.

***

Nialla led Gwen and Bran through muddy grasslands edging the river. Their inflatable boat was pulled up in the grass, with the oars neatly shipped.

"It's still here," said Bran.

"And it still has air," said Gwen. She gave the boat a grateful pat.

"Follow the river. It will lead you through a tunnel, wide and calm. Past that, I do not know. Finn tells me you can easily paddle to the shore and disembark."

Gwen turned to look at the mountain range downstream.

"Are you ready, Bran?"

"Always." Bran grinned at her and she smiled weakly back.

"Then let's take it to the tunnel."

"I think the snow will hold off for a while," said Bran after they had dragged the boat to the river. His eyes squinted against the breeze as he gazed up at the sky. "See, Gwen, you always need me along. I bring good luck."

Gwen laughed aloud at this.

"Yes, that capsize we had on the way here was so lucky."

"But we made it!" Bran bowed with arms extended and a twirl of his wrists. "You're welcome."

"Best of luck," said Nialla. She rubbed her hands together. "I hope we may meet again soon, far from here."

"I hope so too," said Gwen. "I really do."

Nialla climbed up the riverbank. Gwen moved to the back of the boat.

"Come on, Bran. Let's get this over with."

They pushed hard at the boat, and it scraped against the frozen mud and slid into the water. The current pulled at the light boat. Bran waved at Gwen and she climbed in, hissing when cold water rushed into her boots. One final push, and Bran nimbly leaped in. Bran settled into position and fitted the oars into their oarlocks.

"And heave!" Bran shouted with a playful splash of the oars. "We're on our way!"

They flew down the river, Bran's strokes helping the current push them along. Within minutes, they approached the edge of the mountains. Ahead was a dark gash in a cliff wall.

"Here we go," said Gwen. "I'll turn the flashlight on."

Bran stopped rowing and they gazed forward in an attempt to pierce the utter blackness of the tunnel. Gwen's flashlight cast a feeble ray that illuminated nothing. The arch of the entrance passed overhead, and they were inside.

Gwen's eyes adjusted slowly, and she looked around at the rough walls of the tunnel. It was more of a cavern—its roof was twice as tall as Gwen, and the walls were wide enough for four boats.

"Nialla was right," said Gwen. "So far, it's a smooth ride."

"Did you doubt her? Finn must have done this a dozen times, if he was gallivanting off to the human world on a whim. Lucky man."

Bran dipped the oars in from time to time to correct their course, but for the most part he and Gwen enjoyed the calm of their journey. Soon enough, a pinpoint of light shone through the blackness, and grew until it became the exit to their tunnel. Brighter and brighter it glowed, until the river whisked them out into the light, wind, and chaos of another stormy winter's day. A pulse of pressure passed through Gwen and she gasped.

"There's the boundary," Bran said. He held up a hand and blue fire appeared. "It feels good to have my magic back."

"Row to the right shore," Gwen called out over the wind. "I'll make a portal there."

They beached the boat and jumped out, then hauled it up the bank. Gwen called her father to mind and sent her magic out of her hand. A ragged portal ripped open and she and Bran leaped through onto a paved road between soggy fields. Gwen pulled her phone out of her backpack.

"Dad really thought of everything." She unzipped the plastic bag her father had insisted on buying at the store before their voyage and pulled out her phone to call.

"Gwen!"

"Hi, Dad. We're out. Can you pick us up? We're..." She looked around for a landmark. "Somewhere to the northwest of the lake. I can see it in the distance. There's a big red-brick house not far away."

"I'll be right there."

Ten minutes later, the rental car roared up the road. Her father waved his hand wildly through the windshield before the car lurched to a stop.

"I think he might be happy to see you," Bran said with a grin. Gwen laughed in relief.

"I get that sense, too."

Alan leaped out and gripped Gwen in a breathless hug which she returned ferociously. He eventually let go and realized that their party was missing a few members.

"Where's Aidan, and Bran's brother? What happened? Where's your uncle?"

Gwen sighed.

"Finn would only come if his wife and daughter could come too, but they need the protection of the Forbidden Lands. Aidan and Kelan stayed to try to figure out a way to make a portable spell, so Finn's family can live in the Velvet Woods. I have to go back so I'm ready to take over when the army defeats Corann."

Alan's face crumpled in despair.

"Is it certain, then? You'll stay there? What are the chances of Aidan figuring this out?"

"Pretty good, I think." *I hope*, Gwen thought, then grabbed her father's hand. "We have a good idea to solve it. It's not over yet, I promise."

Alan nodded and squeezed her hand.

"All right. It's not over. What now?"

"We need to get back to Amberlaine."

Chapter 14

At first, they filled her father in on all that had happened in the Forbidden Lands. Gwen tried to downplay the dangerous crossing, near-hypothermia, and rapid-filled caves, but Bran's gleeful retelling of every peril made it difficult to keep the horror from her father's face.

Eventually, they lapsed into silence. Gwen's mind dwelled on Aidan. What was he doing now? Had they tested a solution yet? How long before he would be able to follow her? Had she set him an impossible task? She envisioned a gray-faced Aidan desperately trying spells in vain until he passed out in exhaustion. Then she imagined herself in Isolde's castle, never to see Aidan again. She shivered.

A sign for Amberlaine flashed past them on the highway, and Gwen roused herself from her depressing thoughts.

"Bran, how are we going to find your father? Where should I make a portal?"

"It'll be easy to find him in my world," Bran said with a wave of his hand. "I have a link for emergencies. We'll have to dip our heads in from time to time to get a direction."

Alan put his signal on and pulled over on the side of the highway.

"Right here?" Gwen said in surprise. There was no cover to hide her actions from passing cars.

"No one will see. I'm less concerned about someone discovering the Otherworld than getting you where you need to be."

"And there are so many open portals, one more won't matter," said Bran. Gwen grimaced.

"Not helping. Okay, Bran, let's check."

Gwen straightened her arm, but Bran grabbed her wrist to stop her.

"Not in the car, Gwen. Haven't you heard the Wayfarer's tale?" At Gwen's confused and exasperated look, he grinned. "No, I suppose not. It's a long story, but at the end the wayfarer is forced against a portal edge and his arm is sliced off."

"What? What are you saying?" Gwen glanced at her father, who looked as horrified as she felt.

"I'm saying that I don't know what will happen if you make a portal here, and then drive the car. Will bits of the car slice away? Will we be unable to move? I don't know."

"All right, enough said. We'll make a portal outside."

Gwen climbed out of the car and opened a portal just large enough to squeeze a hand through. Bran slid his fingers into the portal and held out a ring. It was a plain metal band, swirled with varying shades of gold and copper. At Gwen's quizzical look, Bran explained.

"It's a tracker ring, but for Father and all my brothers together. I can mask my signal if I don't want to be found, but it's handy for situations like this." He closed his eyes briefly, then popped them open. "Northeast."

"How far?"

"Not long on horseback."

Gwen raised an eyebrow.

"That is really not helpful. Oh well, we'll drive for a bit then check again."

They drove for ten minutes, and Gwen opened another portal.

"West, now."

It took two more attempts before Bran was certain they were within minutes of walking. Gwen kissed her father.

"I'll call you soon with updates, I promise."

"Make sure you do." Her father stroked her cheek with his thumb. "Even the radio is warning people to stay away from 'disturbances in the air,' and the earth tremors have experts flying in from other countries to confer. It's getting serious. I'll go back to the lake and wait for Aidan. He'll need a ride when he comes back with your uncle."

"Good idea," said Gwen. She turned to Bran. "Ready?"

"I'm always ready." Bran beamed at her. They got out of the car and Gwen held out her arm to summon her magic. The portal ripped open, and the snow-covered trees of the Velvet Woods beckoned.

***

A fire burned smoky and hot in the hearth of the cottage. Nialla and Ione were out collecting more wood, and Kelan rested by the fire with his feet on a bench, chewing thoughtfully on a strip of dried meat. Finn and Aidan sat at a rough-hewn table with an oil lantern between them. Finn leaned his elbows on the table with his eyes closed. Aidan feverishly scratched at a layer of sand spread over the table. He looked at his markings for a moment, then scrubbed them out with an exhalation of annoyance.

"I'm sorry we don't have paper and pen," said Finn without opening his eyes. "Not much call for it here. That sand is the best I can muster."

"It's fine," Aidan muttered. "It's only for thinking out of my head."

"Talk to me. What have you thought of so far?"

"Not much that will work," Aidan admitted. "This would be far easier if I had magical training. But if we don't know a dampening spell, surely there's an enhancing spell that we can reverse?"

"Interesting. And then combine that with the targeting nature of the healing spell. It could work."

"There are three enhancing spells," said Kelan from the fire. "The common one is the most specific, but if it doesn't work, there are others to try."

"All right," Aidan said with a glimmer of hope. "It's worth a try. Can we go out past the boundary now?"

"There is a dry tunnel not far from here," said Finn. "I found it years ago. It goes straight through the narrowest part of the mountains and out past the boundary. Fearghus was going to see if it was still clear. Why don't we walk down and check his progress?"

Aidan leaped up and knocked over the stool in his

haste.

"I'm ready. Let's try this spell."

Kelan looked sadly at the fire but stood without complaint. Finn took his cloak off a hook by the door.

"Don't forget your coat—I hear the wind picking up."

The storm hit them like a slap to the face the instant they stepped over the threshold and pelted their cheeks with sleet. In the distance, Nialla and Ione hurried toward the cottage with branches piled high in their arms. Finn waved, and they changed course to intersect them.

"Nialla," said Finn when they were in earshot. "We have an idea but need you to test it on."

Nialla looked nervous but nodded. She put her bundle of sticks on the ground and gestured at Ione to do the same.

"Go inside and keep warm, Ione. We will be as quick as we can."

Ione nodded and pulled her hood tight as she ran to the cottage door. The rest followed Finn to the edge of the valley.

Twenty minutes in the sleet had them all shivering, and they picked up pace when they saw the gaping hole of a tunnel in the steep rockface before them. The wind died once they entered, but the darkness beyond was absolute. Aidan pulled his flashlight out of his coat pocket and flicked it on.

The darkness retreated to the edge of the flickering beam, but no further. A dank smell floated past their noses, although a breeze flowed softly through the tunnel. Aidan and Kelan glanced at each other. Finn smiled.

"It's not far, I promise. Come on, the sooner we try the

spell, the sooner we can go back to the cottage and warm up."

Aidan shot Finn a sharp look.

"And get out of these mountains."

"And that too," said Finn calmly.

"Where is the boundary?" Nialla asked with trepidation while they walked cautiously over the smooth, sandy floor.

"Outside the tunnel. You won't be surprised by it, I swear. Once we're out, I will go first and feel where it is."

Another twenty minutes of careful steps following the beam of the flashlight, and a light emerged at the end. They all sped up, eager to leave the dank darkness of the tunnel.

The storm was far worse out of the protection of the mountain range. The wind blew in heavy gusts that threatened to whip away their hoods, and snow flurried in their faces until they could hardly see. Finn put out a hand to stop Nialla before she stepped out of the tunnel.

"The boundary is very close to the mountains here," he said. "Let me go first."

He walked forward for three paces, then shuddered and stopped. In the cold ground, he dug his heel in to make a mark.

"The boundary is here, love. Don't cross until we're ready."

Nialla nodded and huddled in the shelter of the tunnel entrance. Aidan almost leaped to Finn's side. Kelan followed more slowly.

"How shall we do this, exactly?" Aidan said with a frown.

"Setting up the healing bracelet is a two-person

endeavor," said Kelan. "The different parts of the spell are done at the same time."

"I'll cast the modified healing spell," said Finn. "And Aidan, you focus on the reversed-enhancing spell. Kelan, put your hands on both of us and lend us your power simultaneously. I'll do my best to bind it all together."

Kelan's nose twitched in discomfort at the idea of joining magics with a near-stranger, but he put his hands on their shoulders as requested. Finn drew out a bracelet of silver filigree, finely polished to a soft gleam. It was a bright counterpoint to the gray, forbidding clouds above.

"Don't lose that," Nialla warned from the tunnel. "It was my grandmother's."

"I'll be careful," Finn promised. "All right, Aidan, hands on the bracelet. On the count of three. One, two, three…"

Aidan squeezed his eyes shut. Kelan tilted his head back and breathed out slowly. Finn closed his eyes and grew still.

A glow emerged around Aidan's and Finn's fingers in the bracelet, sky blue and pale ivory with a deeper blue below, swirling around and over their hands in a mesmerizing kaleidoscope of colors. Nialla watched with wide, longing eyes. A brilliant flash, and the colors faded. Aidan opened his eyes.

"I think it's done."

Kelan rolled his shoulders.

"That was a power-hungry spell. I hope it works because I'll need a rest before we attempt another version."

"Let's find out," said Finn. He made his way to the

boundary. "Nialla, love, are you ready? Step out and I'll slip the bracelet on your wrist."

Nialla bit her lip.

"Why not put it on before I leave the boundary?"

"Ideally, I would like to see some of your magic's reaction to being uncontained before we dampen it. Then we can be sure it works."

Nialla nodded jerkily, took a deep breath, and stepped out.

Nothing happened for a breath, and Nialla's shoulders slumped in relief. Then her hands sparkled with golden lights. They swiftly traveled up her arms. The already stiff wind began to whirl around Nialla in a funnel.

"Finn!" Nialla screamed. She stuck out her arm. Finn jammed the bracelet on her wrist.

The whirlwind calmed, and the golden sparks died. Nialla stared at the bracelet for a moment while the wind blew her cloak around her legs. Then she looked at Finn with shining eyes.

"Can it be true?" she whispered. Aidan gripped his head with an expression of intense relief, and Kelan looked pleased. Finn touched Nialla's cheek.

"Will you be my queen?" he said quietly.

Nialla smiled and opened her mouth to speak. Instead, her happy expression faltered, and she clutched her chest. Golden light welled from between her fingers, too bright to look at. Then it pulsed. A cracking noise made them look up. Another pulse—rocks burst from the cliffs above and tumbled toward them in a rain of stone.

"Get back!" Finn yelled. He pushed Nialla, and she sprawled on the sandy floor of the tunnel. Kelan leaped nimbly past her. Aidan had stumbled to his knees and was crawling to the entrance, but Finn grabbed his arm and dragged him to safety. The rocks fell like thunder outside, then all was still.

For a long moment they sat in panting silence, the wind the loudest sound. Then Aidan kicked at the wall in his frustration.

"It should have worked! Why didn't it work? How can we do this?"

"It was only our first attempt," said Finn. "We'll simply learn from it and apply what we know to the next time." He caught sight of Nialla's silent tears and his tone changed. He pulled her into an embrace. "Don't cry, my love. We will keep trying."

"I know," she said. She sniffed and dried her eyes with the edge of her cloak. "It was just a remarkable feeling to think I might be able to leave this place…" She gave Finn a rueful smile. "I'm being silly."

"Of course not." Finn squeezed her hand. "We'll keep trying, as long as it takes. Do you hear me, Aidan? We'll keep trying."

Aidan nodded, although his expression was still despondent.

"Thank you," he whispered.

***

"Stay quiet," said Bran softly. He drew Gwen between two trees. "There will be sentries everywhere, and they won't be expecting friends. I'll send a signal."

Gwen pressed herself against the tree. Bran cupped his

hands and closed his eyes. A blue light shone through the gaps between his fingers and he opened them with a grin. Inside was a tiny bird, the size of a winter wren, but with a bright blue glow. It chirped happily and tilted its head to look up at Bran.

"Off you go," he whispered, and the bird flew away through the whirling snow in a flash of wings.

"Now what?" Gwen whispered. She looked furtively around her tree.

"Now we wait." Bran leaned against his tree and sighed. "All this fresh snow, and no brothers to throw snowballs at. What a waste."

Less than a minute passed before light footsteps crunched through snow nearby. A flash of blue, and Bran's bird landed on his shoulder. It chittered happily, then melted without a trace into Bran. Bran leaped out of their hiding place, and Gwen followed with trepidation.

Two guards stood a few paces away, dressed in Wintertree clothing with heavy fur cloaks over top. They tried to look impassive, but relief shone through their eyes at the sight of Bran.

"Prince Bran," the female guard said. "It is good to have you back. The king awaits you."

"Then we shouldn't keep him waiting any longer." Bran spread his arms. "Come, take me to him. We must keep our revered ruler happy."

Gwen snorted, and the guards fought to keep smiles off their faces.

"This way," the male guard said, and they tramped through the storm after him.

One moment, the forest was empty and covered with

untouched snow. The next step, a camp materialized, filled with tents, fighters, knives sharpening, and horses neighing.

"What just happened?" said Gwen.

"The camp? We passed through the shield barrier, that's all." Bran waved at a group of fighters idly chatting, and they waved back. "We can't have Corann finding headquarters too easily."

The central tent was much larger than the others, tall and wide enough for a crowd. The guards led them directly to the doorway, demarked by a wide square of woven tapestry with the Wintertree in brown against a white background. The guards withdrew to either side and bowed. Bran marched to the tapestry and flung it open.

"Hello, Father! I'm back."

Exclamations drifted out of the open flap. Gwen gritted her teeth and scuttled in after Bran. She wasn't looking forward to facing Faolan after their unannounced departure.

It was warm in the tent, warm enough that Gwen needed to unzip her coat immediately. Furs of all colors lined the walls as if they were snuggled in the folds of some enormous beast, and orange flames in hanging lanterns gave off welcome heat. Gwen relaxed involuntarily—she hadn't been this warm since her night at Winterwood.

Ten or so people ranged around a table with a glowing map that reminded Gwen of a hologram. Most of the figures she recognized from conclave, rulers and their advisors, and Isolde was there as well, looking inscrutably at Gwen. Faolan stepped forward, lines of anger on his face.

"Bran. Running away without a word, at this critical juncture, off to the human world or worse. You could have been trapped, you could have died, you could have lost our one chance to repair the damaged portals." He waved at Gwen. "What do you have to say, Bran?"

Bran bowed.

"I'm sorry, Father, if I caused you distress, it was not my intention," he said formally. Then in his usual voice he said, "But I had to help my friends. And I wasn't alone, Kelan came too. And look, both Gwen and I are back in one piece, and in time too. So, no harm done."

Faolan stared at his son for a long moment. A muscle in his cheek twitched. Then he sighed and rounded on Gwen.

"And you. How could you desert your post at this hour? This entire plan hinges on you."

Gwen stood up straighter. She was tired of being pushed around by Faolan. It was time to show him how things really stood.

"I did what I needed to do, what you should have 'allowed' me to do anyway. And I don't—owe—you—anything." She smacked her fist into her palm to emphasize each word. "I could have gone back to my home in the human world, far away from any destruction that might happen, and happily carried on with my life. But I came back. I said I would rule if I have to, and I will. But I had to make sure it was the only option. So, let's have less blame and finger-wagging. I am not inferior because I am partly human, and I am not a child to be ordered about. I am the future queen of the Velvet Woods, and you will treat me accordingly."

231

Faolan gazed at her for a long moment. Gwen kept her chin high and maintained eye contact. Finally, Faolan nodded.

"Very well." A slight pause, and then, "And was your mission successful?"

Gwen sighed.

"I don't know yet. My uncle won't come without his family, and they can't leave the Forbidden Lands. Aidan and Kelan have stayed to devise a way to make the magic-dampening spell portable." Gwen straightened her shoulders. "But until then, I am here."

Faolan did not hide his doubt at the likelihood of Aidan solving the centuries-old conundrum, but he said nothing, for which Gwen was grateful. He merely nodded once more, then turned to Bran.

"How does the battle progress?" Bran asked. He leaned over the map.

"Well, but Corann is proving to be a tricky opponent. He knows the lay of the land and is keeping Isolde on her toes trying to second-guess him. However, our army has many different strengths and we are using every one of the magics at our disposal."

"Can I help somehow?" Gwen asked tentatively. "It is the battle for my throne, after all."

"Absolutely not," said Faolan. Then he collected himself and said with more composure, "You are very precious to our cause, and I do not want to risk further harm to you. As well, you have no formal battle training. I recommend that you take some rest, so you are ready for your eventual coronation."

A rumbling groan accompanied a shuddering of the

ground. Gwen clutched the edge of the table and stared with wide eyes at the lanterns, which swung wildly and cast crazy shadows on the furs lining the tent.

Pale faces glanced at each other, and even Bran looked shaken. Faolan cleared his throat.

"Please stay close and out of the fighters' way, Gwendolyn. We will need you immediately upon our success, but our forces needs focus." He waved an attendant forward. "Guard, please escort Gwendolyn to a sleeping tent."

Gwen felt the weight of her adventures press down on her like a lead coat, and she gratefully followed the guard outside. Howling winds took her breath away and she scuttled hastily after the guard.

He held the tent flaps open for her on a small pavilion close to the main tent. By the dim lantern light, two pallets emerged from the gloom, both spread with thick furs. Gwen almost moaned with longing at the sight of a bed. The hard floor of Finn's cottage had not allowed for much sleeping, and she was tired despite the early hour.

"There is a chamber pot there." The guard pointed to the corner. "And if you wish to leave the tent, please summon me with this." He put a polished purple stone the size of Gwen's thumb on the floor by the pallet. "Simply touch it with your magic." He bowed and left the tent.

Gwen kicked off her boots and burrowed into the cold furs, coat and all. Her eyes closed immediately. She gradually grew warmer and warmer. Just before she drifted off to sleep, she thought of Aidan. She pictured his concentrated face, frantically trying to find a solution, and she squeezed her eyes tightly shut.

"Please, please, please let it work," she whispered.

***

Gwen woke with a start. In her sleep-fogged mind, it felt like a herd of cows was stampeding on the roof. Then her eyes opened. Above her, the tent swayed wildly, and her pallet shuddered. She sat bolt upright, heart racing, all sleepiness forgotten.

"Another earthquake," she whispered to herself. As she said it, the rumbling and shaking died. The commotion outside, however, did not.

Gwen shoved her feet into her boots and flung her hood over her head. Her eyes caught the purple stone despite the dark, and she grabbed it. She pushed her magic hastily into the stone, which glowed before she tossed it back on the ground.

Moments later, her guard appeared.

"Come on," said Gwen. "I want to see what's going on."

"Mainly a change of fighters," said the guard as he followed her out of the tent. "But their reports are not encouraging. The other side is crafty indeed."

"Indeed," Gwen muttered. She pulled her hood on more tightly against the driving snow. Breenan were everywhere in the darkness, rushing about and shouting, wrapped in furs or woolen capes or long coats of oiled canvas. A woman stumbled by, holding her bleeding arm, and another escorted her into a nearby tent. Gwen's heart dropped. Was this what a winning battle camp looked like, with desperation written on every face?

Then across the clearing, Gwen spied two familiar faces. She raced their way.

"Rhiannon! Tristan!" she called out. Aidan's half-siblings' heads spun in her direction. Tristan's dirt-streaked face opened in a broad grin, and Rhiannon smiled despite the blood on her lip.

"Gwen! You're here." Tristan grabbed her in a quick hug. Rhiannon winced when Gwen embraced her next.

"Sorry," said Gwen, pulling back. "Are you okay? What's happening out there?"

"A bruised rib, perhaps?" said Rhiannon. "And a bloody lip. Otherwise, I'm fine. But it's not great out there."

"Corann's throwing everything he has at us," said Tristan. "And it's working. Something changed a few hours ago, and every land-based power that attacks us is far stronger than it was."

"And don't forget the portals." Rhiannon took a breath to speak and grimaced at the pain. "Corann's fighters can make portals. They've been flitting in and out of the human world to disorient us and make sneak attacks."

"What?" Gwen was dumbfounded. "How do they manage that?"

"I don't know how it works. Some sort of amulet. All I know is that we're fighting opponents who have a huge advantage," Tristan said.

Gwen bit her lip in thought.

"I wonder if I could help…" she started, then someone squeezed her around the shoulders.

"Hello, cousins," said Bran, cheery as ever. He was wearing a sheathed knife on a belt. "You look a little worse for wear."

"Bran," Gwen said. "The other side is using portals."

"So I've heard."

"What if I helped? I can make portals too. Maybe I could look through and watch where they're going, so our fighters aren't surprised."

Tristan looked thoughtful, but Rhiannon frowned.

"Should we make more portals? I heard that Corann's unwarranted portal-making is accelerating the bad weather. Certainly, there have been more tremors since he started his campaign."

"Only one way to find out," said Bran. He steered Gwen toward the main pavilion. "Let's go ask the king."

The first thing Gwen saw when she ducked through the pavilion's opening was Isolde, white-faced, frantically scanning the three-dimensional map on the ground. It was liberally sprinkled with red and gold stars. The figure of Faolan caught her eye next, and he looked almost as strained as Isolde.

"What's happening?" said Gwen without preamble. Faolan glanced at her.

"Corann is using portals, and excessively. He has given all his fighters a charm to create the portals. I don't know how it works."

"May I see?" said Gwen. Faolan handed over a leather loop with a large flat bead on it. Isolde watched her warily as she examined it. There were pictures of both Isolde and Alan on the faces of the bead, and along one side was a tiny piece of black hair. Gwen's lips tightened.

"I see." Gwen did not elaborate, and Faolan, after a brief look at her, did not ask further.

"In addition, Corann has managed to subjugate the realm's room of enchantments, at least partially," he said. "This affords him an advantage that we are hard pressed to best."

Up close, Faolan looked exhausted. A tingle of hope ignited in Gwen's chest.

"Can Corann be king if he can connect with the room?"

"No," Faolan said shortly. Gwen's hope extinguished in an instant. "We should have seen an immediate improvement in weather, for a start, but it has only grown worse. He cannot be our answer, unfortunately. However he managed to coerce the room to do his bidding, it is not a solution."

Gwen sighed.

"Of course not. I have an idea, though. Since Corann's fighters are using portals to sneak up on our side, can I help? I could make portals to see where the others are in the human world and alert our fighters…" Gwen trailed off when Faolan shook his head.

"We cannot risk injury to you, our only hope of mitigating this disaster. You must be kept safe at all costs."

King Gavin nodded, but Queen Brenna frowned.

"Knowing the other fighters' movements before they happen here would be invaluable. Surely we can secure her person with adequate guards?"

"I agree that she should not be sent off in the main fray as part of a trio of general fighters," said Queen Ula. "She is our reason for war, after all. But what of our plans for Einion canyon? Perhaps we could install her in a place where she could see the entire valley, while still remaining

237

secure." She turned to Isolde. "Is there such a place?"

Isolde nodded slowly.

"Yes, there is."

"And would a contingent of at least four fighters be able to join her for protection?" asked King Gavin.

"Yes."

"You wish to do this?" Faolan said to Gwen. "Join the battle?"

"Of course not," said Gwen. "I don't want to be in a battle. My father will be appalled, that's for sure." Faolan's eyebrow twitched. "But we need to win, and if this is how I can help, then I'm ready."

"Spoken like a true queen," said Faolan softly. "You are certainly proving your suitability for that tiara I gave you." He turned and addressed the other rulers. "Is it decided? Gwendolyn will join the battle at Einion canyon?"

The others assented, and Gwen took a deep breath. How had she found herself going to war?

Chapter 15

Bran led Gwen out of the tent after the rulers had pelted her with advice.

"Watch behind boulders and hills, they've been scuttling out from them and startling our fighters."

"The river Kennocha winds through there. Any sign of watercraft on the human side, you tell someone."

"Don't let them dominate the ford."

"Whew," said Gwen to Bran once the tapestry closed behind them. "There's no way I will remember all that. What if I forget and mess everything up? Lives are at stake."

"You'll be fine," Bran said. "Your fighters will be doing most of the watching, I don't doubt."

"That's true." Gwen felt a little better. It wasn't entirely up to her—she was simply the portal maker.

"I wish I could see it," said Bran with a faraway look. "I love portals."

"You won't be there?" Gwen hadn't even considered that Bran leaving her side was an option. Ice filled her stomach.

"I'll be one of the fighters you'll be watching," said Bran. "If you can spot me, that is. I'm excellent at camouflage." He caught sight of her downcast face. "But don't worry, I'm sure you'll be in good hands."

Gwen felt a prickling at the nape of her neck, then a gentle tug on her core. She gasped and clutched her chest.

"What is it?" asked Bran. "Are you all right?"

"It's weird. Like I'm being drawn in this direction." She pointed and started to walk that way, almost involuntarily. Bran followed her with curiosity written all over his face.

"It could be a trap by the other side. But they haven't been close enough to you to cast a spell, that we know of. Not since conclave, anyway."

"Should I stop?" Gwen felt a strange mix of panic and calm. "I don't know if I can stop."

"We're almost at the boundary. Let's take a few steps out before I break the compulsion."

"You can do that?" Gwen said, aggrieved.

"Probably. Likely. Oh, look, we've crossed."

"Bran!" Gwen said in exasperation.

The bustle and clatter of a camp full of fighters cut off suddenly and left only the howling of the wind. Gwen's eyes darted from tree to shadowed tree and her unease grew with every reluctant step she took.

A dark movement at the edge of her vision brought her to high alert. She jumped, and her heart thrashed about in her chest. Then she squinted through the snow.

"Loniel?"

The wild man smiled at her, his silver fur cloak wrapped tightly around him against the cold. His cheeks were painted with broad stripes of red.

"Hello, little bird."

"What are you doing here?"

"The portals are increasing in number, hour by hour. Too many humans have stumbled through. A few makes for a pleasant diversion, but now—you know my feelings on living in your own world." He raised a hand and Gwen glanced at it curiously before he dropped it. "I preferred the world the way it was, so we have come to lend our numbers to your cause."

"Who's 'we?'"

"Gwen?" Bran tugged on her sleeve. "You know these people, right? They're friendly?"

Gwen whirled around. In a semi-circle around them stood a crowd of Breenan, dressed in a motley assortment of leathers and furs, although a few had capes of feathers. The women had red swirls on their faces, and the men had stripes to match Loniel's. It gave them a primitive, wild look that did not inspire comfort. Gwen recognized some faces from that wild night in May, dancing with Aidan at Loniel's bonfire. She blushed at the memory.

"Mostly, I think," Gwen answered. Loniel laughed lightly.

"For today. Bring us your father, young princeling of Wintertree. We wish to fight your foes."

"Go on, Bran. Run and find him. I'll be fine here."

Bran gave her one last inquiring look. At her nod of reassurance, he bolted in the direction of the invisible camp. Loniel looked Gwen up and down.

"Your clothes do not look warm enough for a winter battle." He glanced at his followers. Three women came

241

forward with serene smiles and patted Gwen on her shoulders, her cheeks, her back.

"Different trousers," said one.

"Furs. Mink, for certain."

They walked around her. Gwen's breathing quickened, especially when more Breenan gathered close, many with scraps of material in their hands. The women accepted each piece one by one and gracefully transferred it to Gwen's body, where it stuck and molded to the shape of her clothing. Piece by piece, the women transformed her cold jeans and winter raincoat into fur-lined suede leggings and a thick coat of soft and intensely warm fur. It remained patchwork until the women stepped away and Loniel placed his hands on her head. A faint prickling sensation and a green glow ran down the length of Gwen's body, then Loniel stepped back. He looked pleased.

"There we are. We can't have the heir freeze to death before her coronation."

Gwen examined her new coat, which was made of a seamless blend of furs.

"Thank you," she said. She ran her hand down one soft sleeve. "It's so warm."

Six figures emerged from thin air, Faolan striding at the forefront with Bran, Isolde, and the other rulers close at his heels. Loniel waited for them with an enigmatic smile on his face, and his followers arranged themselves behind him. Faolan stopped a few paces away.

"Loniel of the Green Woods," Faolan said. His voice was restrained, possibly a little wary. "My son tells me you and your people wish to fight."

Loniel gave one slow nod. Faolan waited a moment for

him to speak, but when Loniel showed no signs of breaking the silence, Faolan continued.

"You are most welcome. The battle is not progressing as successfully as I had hoped, and I will not turn away an offer of help."

"It is unlike Wintertree to underestimate an opponent," said Loniel mildly. Faolan grimaced.

"Too true. Corann has somehow forced the room of enchantments to do his bidding, although as it has not healed the portals, it must not be a true connection."

"Ah," said Loniel softly. He looked at Gwen. "A true connection to the very earth under our feet is needed."

Was Loniel trying to tell her something? Gwen stared at his golden eyes but couldn't fathom any meaning from his words. Neither could Faolan, because he said with even more restraint, "Yes, that is the purpose of our battle—to connect Gwen to the realm." Bran caught Gwen's eye and they both smothered grins. If anyone less important than Loniel had said those words, Faolan would not have hesitated to show his impatience.

"Where shall we position ourselves?" Loniel said more matter-of-factly. "I do not wish to interrupt any maneuvers of your people. And it is best to give us our space—once we engage, it is difficult for us to differentiate friend from foe."

Faolan looked askance at Loniel's followers but did not ask more.

"We are planning a push in the Einion Canyon at dawn." Faolan turned to Isolde. "Where would you recommend?"

Isolde thought for a moment.

"The meadow at the sharpest turn of the river Kennocha," she said finally. "It's flat and open. They will be forced through there, most of them. And they will expect covert attacks, not—your style of battle."

"Good. I know it well. We will wait there for the opportune moment."

Loniel gestured to his followers. Without a backward glance, they all disappeared noiselessly into the trees.

Faolan shook his head in wonderment.

"We are fortunate that Loniel had decided to join our cause. The records state that the last time the Gwerud's followers went to war was very long ago indeed. Whether it will be enough to turn the tide is anyone's guess."

"Is it that bad?" Gwen asked with a sinking heart.

"It takes a great force to overcome the natural defenses of a realm if the ruler has access to their realm's room of enchantments. We have the strength of five realms' fighters, but the other side has three realms and the connection. But perhaps with the wild man, and your eyes in the human world, we may yet defeat them." Faolan beckoned to the others. "Come, my lords, my ladies. Let us complete our battle plans in the warmth."

Bran and Gwen followed the others through the snowy woods until they passed through the boundary. The dull roar of the preparing fighters—sharpening knives, talking, stomping feet to keep warm—assaulted Gwen's ears after the relative quiet of the stormy forest. Bran waved at a nearby group.

"There is your guard. They're all great fighters, you'll be well protected."

"Wait a minute," Gwen said, panicked. "You're leaving

now?" Her father, then Aidan, and now Bran—everyone was leaving her. She had a horrible vision of herself, standing in a black dress, in the center of the parquet floor of Isolde's ballroom, alone. She shivered despite her warm furs.

"I have to go with my patrol group," said Bran. He checked his knife before he looked at Gwen's face. "I'll see you soon, I'm sure. And look who will be with you."

"Hello, Gwen," said Rhiannon. Tristan grinned from behind her. "We'll be right beside you all the way."

Gwen sighed in relief.

"Thanks. That's good to know. Bye, Bran. And good luck."

Bran patted her on the shoulder and trotted away. His sheathed knife and a leather bag bounced from his belt. Gwen turned to the others.

"When do we leave?"

"We're waiting for the command," said Tristan. "Stay on your toes."

"I need a couple of minutes. Where can I make a small portal?"

Rhiannon pointed at a nearby copse of trees.

"Make it against a tree, so no one walks into it accidentally."

Gwen hurried over and concentrated on her father on the way. It was a matter of seconds to pull out the magic. A small, ragged portal ripped quietly open. She pulled her phone out of the pocket of her now-suede pants, stuck her head out of the hole, and called her father.

"Gwen?" Alan said urgently.

"Hi, Dad." It was good to hear his familiar voice amid

245

the strangeness of a battle camp. "Everything is fine here. I'm just calling to check in. Any word from Aidan?"

"No. I've stationed myself in a bed and breakfast nearby, but no call yet."

"I'm sure they'll be out soon," said Gwen, even though her father's words hit her like a punch to the stomach.

"What's happening on your end?"

"A big battle is coming up." At Alan's sharp intake of breath, she added hastily, "I'll just be watching." It was sort of true.

"Good."

Rhiannon waved at her from the tent.

"I'd better go. I love you, Dad."

"I love you, Gwennie. Stay safe."

***

They marched in the predawn light that managed to filter through oppressive gray clouds that hung above the snow-covered forest canopy. Gwen and her fighters walked in single file, with Rhiannon at the end erasing their footprints in the snow with magic. Gwen tried her best to match the near-silent footfalls of the others, but the snow squeaked and crunched underfoot. No one spoke a word over the whistling wind through the empty woods.

After a half-hour of walking, just when Gwen was starting to wonder for how long they were planning to move, the terrain grew rough. They climbed up and down hills, but their altitude steadily increased. The trees shrunk and became twisted and gnarled from a lack of soil and greater exposure to the elements.

Before they reached the crest of the next knoll, their leader, Bretta, held up a hand and they all slowed. She crept over the hill and melted into the trees, where she stood motionless for several long moments. Gwen had stopped holding her breath and was starting to fidget when Bretta beckoned.

They resumed their climb over the crest, but slowly and with great stealth. Bretta shimmied into a dense cluster of hornbeam shrubs to their left. Before Gwen followed, she paused at the view.

A steep valley spread before them. The sides were carpeted with thick evergreen forest, but the valley alternated between stands of deciduous groves and stretches of snowy meadows, bisected by a wide, meandering river. Even from her height, Gwen could see ice that clung to the edges of the water.

Tristan chivvied her forward, and she stumbled into the bushes. There was a clearing inside, enlarged by Bretta and Rhiannon as they encouraged growth of the hornbeam into a roomier shape for their covert operation. Branches swayed above them, but inside their snug enclosure they were protected from the wind. Gwen kneeled down on the dirt with relief.

"Before we modify the vegetation much more," said Rhiannon. "Make sure this is a good spot for viewing in the human world."

Gwen nodded and opened a portal in the direction of the river. A pile of rocky debris met her eyes.

"Let me try over here." Gwen moved to the far left to avoid the human-world rocks. Now, a valley spread before her, but quite different to the Breenan side. Trees were

247

scarce and fallow fields predominated, well cropped by grazing sheep. A small village lay on the riverside with a paved road running east, deserted at this time of the day.

"Here. This is good." Gwen drew back and the Breenan clustered around the portal. Gwen considered the terrain—what else did they want to see?—and made another portal in a different direction.

"Anywhere else?" asked Gwen to Bretta. She shook her head.

"That ought to do it. All right, I need a pair of eyes on each portal, and one on the valley. Shore up the bushes while you're there so we can't be seen. Devin, set up the map."

The Breenan moved into position. Gwen looked at Bretta.

"What about me?"

"Look through the portals if you wish, and make sure we are interpreting the human side correctly. Otherwise, stay still and quiet and we'll do our best to pull you through this in one piece."

Tristan caught her eye and gave her a lop-sided smile. Gwen shrugged and turned to watch Devin spread a roll of leather on the ground and place a set of colored stones in a pattern on the center. He saw her looking and waved at the stones.

"They've been spelled to create the map only if set in a certain way on this particular piece of leather. In case it falls into the wrong hands." He placed the last stone in the center and a glow resolved into a three-dimensional depiction of the valley below. Golden dots were sprinkled liberally across the eastern end of the valley. Gwen peered closer.

"Is this us?" She pointed at a dot high on a tiny brown hill. Devin nodded. Gwen gazed at the map for a moment longer then shuffled to Tristan, who stared out of a small opening in the branches. She gazed at the unmoving scenery, dimly lit by the hidden sun.

"According to our map," she whispered to Tristan. "There are dozens of our fighting groups spread across the valley. Where are they all?"

"Don't worry, they're there," he said quietly. "You wouldn't see us, either, if you were looking."

"What's the plan, anyway? Why are we all focused on this valley? Why would Corann's forces necessarily come here?"

"We've seeded the idea in some of his released fighters. The story is that we are planning a concerted attack on the castle via this valley as a last effort to win the war."

"That's kind of true. Where's the strategy?"

"They think we'll be marching, not preparing to spring an ambush. The hope is to take them unawares."

"Makes sense, I guess." Gwen sat more comfortably on the cold earth and spread her gloved hands behind her in support. "What will this battle look like? Nobody has guns or swords."

"I don't know what guns are, but hardly anyone bothers with an ungainly sword, not anymore. Knives are much defter. Arrows are decent for long distance, but I don't favor them because it isn't often you can see your opponent until they're too close for arrows."

"What do you mean?" Gwen had been picturing medieval warfare with lines of armored cavalry, swords drawn, advancing on one another. Of course, no one looked like that here, and there were hardly any horses, but she had supposed it would be similar. "What does a battle look like?"

"Fighters are mostly hidden. The element of surprise is crucial, which is why the other side's use of portals is so damaging."

"It sounds horribly tense."

"That's the fun." Tristan grinned. "But knives and arrows are only part of the story. Magic weapons are key to any battle."

"Like what?"

"General spells are helpful, like ones to trip opponents, throw rocks, or cause general mayhem. But where magic really excels is in the secret spells of each realm, those that have been developed to enhance the strengths of their people. Wintertree, for example, has perfected the spell stone, small nodules of wood polished with a spell of attack, like immobilization, confusion, disarming. They will trigger when thrown with good aim and better concentration."

"So much for secret weapons," said Rhiannon from her post at a portal, but she was smiling.

"Do they work as well for you if you're only half-Wintertree?" Gwen asked.

"It's more a function of training than predilection, thankfully. As much as we like to emphasize what realm we're from, we're really not all that different."

"What are we looking for?" said Gwen, bringing them back to her original question. "If all fighters are lurking in the shadows?"

"Hidden is the goal, but when the spells start flying, you'll see the skirmishes." Tristan stretched his arms above his head and winced when his hands touched branches above. "There'll be plenty of sparks when things heat up."

"But for now, we wait," said Rhiannon.

***

Bran braced himself in the crook of a tree, its branches leafless but plentiful. With his gray pants, silver-brown fur cloak, and a hood to hide his distinctive hair, any observer would be hard-pressed to find Bran. He remained motionless, and only his eyes flickered, watchful.

Crevan was nearby, as was a Riverside fighter of their group, but they remained hidden even to Bran. His fingers twitched in readiness. Fighting was fun—waiting was the hard part.

A cawing arose from a nearby tree, and three crows flew in a burst of black wings above the canopy. Bran tensed, and his fingers crept to his belt. One hand grasped a slingshot and the other reached into a small bag to extract a spell stone.

The copper and gold tracker ring on his finger grew warm in a succession of pulses. Bran nodded to himself. Crevan had seen their opponents but guessed that Bran would have the better shot. Bran placed a spell stone in his sling and crooked his arm in readiness.

Noiselessly, three fighters emerged through the snowy woods. One wore a heavy wool coat with flowers embroidered on the bottom edge. Another wore a thick fur cloak, black and coarse, and the last a lighter brown fur coat with a green hood.

Bran waited until the three figures were only a few trees away. Then he pulled the sling taut and released.

The spell stone struck the green-hooded fighter from the Velvet Woods on the shoulder. She spun in a circle from the blow, her hand clutched over the injury. Then she froze mid-spin and toppled to the ground, motionless.

The others dove into the trees while the spell stone was still whistling through the air. Bran grinned, until a rustling noise made him turn his head. A vine crawled toward him, growing lush green leaves and fat flower buds as it approached, incongruously fertile in the barrenness of the wintery wood. Bran's smile became uncertain, and he shrank away from the advancing foliage. A bud near him opened swiftly, lushly.

Bran sprang to a lower branch before the flower spat a shining jet of magical venom in his direction. The vine followed him with unnatural rapidity, and two more buds prepared to open.

Bran leaped out of the tree. Behind him, the flowers puffed clouds of glittery pollen. He rolled away and ran to avoid the dust.

Crevan dropped to the ground beside him.

"To the river," he hissed. "We want them to follow us there."

A snarl overtook Crevan's final words. The brothers spun. A wolf bared its teeth and advanced with deliberate steps. Bran drew his dagger and held it ready. Crevan looked around while they backed away, until he spotted a shadowy figure with a shaggy fur coat lurking behind a nearby tree.

"Ha! Take that!" Bran shouted as he lunged at the wolf. It released a blood-curdling growl. Crevan whipped his slingshot out of his belt, loaded a spell stone, and fired.

The wolf's expression changed from predatory to confused. A yelp revealed the Midvale fighter's position.

"What did you do?" he yelled.

"Lessened your connection to the animal," Crevan shouted back. "Now what do you have for us?"

Their attacker retreated without another word. The wolf whined.

"Bah! Away!" Bran gestured at the confused animal, and it ran away with its tail tucked under its belly. Bran laughed in delight.

"Nicely done, Crevan!"

A figure dropped from a nearby tree. Her woolen coat was gray to blend into the forest, but the lining flashed a deep blue.

"Where did they go?" the Riverside fighter said without preamble.

"I'm not sure," said Crevan. "Let's go to the river, draw them there. I'm not comfortable with our location now exposed."

"Good idea." She nodded. "The Longshore fighters are stationed nearby."

"Exactly. Come, the spell stone on the Midvale fighter won't last forever." Crevan spied Bran examining the massive pawprint of the wolf with interest. "Come on, Bran. Father would never forgive me if you were captured on my watch."

"Probably not," said Bran cheerfully as they jogged

through the woods.

"Quiet," the Riverside fighter whispered. "We're here."

The three slowed and crept behind boulders and a fallen tree. Beyond lay a wide expanse of river, its edges lined with ice but its center flowing dark and fast. No Breenan were in sight, until Bran pointed to a flash of embroidered woolen coat. The Riverside fighter nodded and held up her hand. A moment passed, and then…

"Argh! Get them off!" The Southlands fighter stumbled out from her tree and batted at the air around her head. Crevan leaped to restrain her.

"What does she see?" asked Bran.

"A swarm of wasps," said the Riverside fighter smugly. "A hallucination, of course."

"Well done." Bran nodded with approval.

With a shout, the Midvale fighter ran from the trees. He had no wolf, but his dagger was sharp, and its edge was rimmed with a viscous liquid.

"Crevan!" Bran yelled. He ran out to intercept the fighter. "Behind you!"

Another three fighters burst from bushes and dropped from trees, their clothing clearly marking them as from enemy realms. Their Riverside ally jumped to Bran's side while he fended off the Midvale fighter with his dagger.

"Retreat to the river," Crevan yelled. He threw a spell stone at an oncoming fighter, who ducked to avoid it.

The Riverside fighter tripped over a rapidly growing root, and a branch narrowly avoided crashing on her head. Her Velvet Woods attacker laughed. The Riverside fighter threw up her hand and her opponent shrieked and clutched his uninjured leg in pain.

"I don't have many more hallucinations," she said to Crevan. She looked pale. "They take a lot of power."

"Keep going to the river," he said.

The ground below their retreating feet shivered as dandelions burst forth. Heat from the enchanted flowers rapidly melted the snow. Bran danced with agitation when the heat traveled through the soles of his boots.

"We're almost there," shouted Crevan. He flung a spell stone at the nearest attacker, who fell over, stunned.

WHOOSH.

A huge wave rose up from the river. It carried slabs of ice in its watery darkness. Bran and the others dove out of the way, and their advancing enemies fell under the onslaught of icy water. One fighter was sucked into the river and clung to a chunk of ice. The others were knocked to the ground in a stupor.

Crevan and the Riverside fighter ran to tie up their waterlogged opponents. Bran scanned the trees until he spotted the silvery canvas cloak of a Longshore fighter. He grinned and waved his thanks, and the fighter waved back.

Bran whipped his head around at a cry in the distance. Crevan put a hand on his belt.

"There are more, over there." He paled as he understood the information from the pulsing warmth of his belt. "A lot more."

Bran looked uncharacteristically grim. He gripped his dagger more securely and took a deep breath.

"Then we'd better go help."

***

Gwen's tense anxiety gradually faded into utter boredom. Dawn grew to day, and nothing stirred in the valley below except flocks of crows and the ever-present wind. Occasional earth tremors shook their hiding place, but after an hour even these failed to break the monotony.

Until Tristan stiffened. Three crows rose from a tree on the far end of the valley. Instead of resettling on a nearby branch, they flew rapidly away, cawing wildly. At the same time, one of the golden dots on the map pulsed and flickered.

"We're under attack," said Devin.

"Eyes on the valley, here and through the portals," Bretta ordered. "It has begun."

A howl pierced the stillness, a solitary sound that tore right to Gwen's heart and sent a shiver down her spine that had nothing to do with the icy weather.

"What was that?" she hissed to Tristan. He kept his eyes scanning the valley but answered her.

"The Midvale realm can control animals. Looks like they've found a wolf."

"What?"

Tristan smiled without humor.

"It's a formidable power, to be sure. Each person can only control one animal at a time, thankfully, but that still results in a doubling of their forces, if managed right."

"Three more groups under attack," called out Devin at the map. "Look to the curve in the river."

"Still too far to see through the portals." Rhiannon ground her teeth in frustration. "I can see the attackers, but not clearly enough to tell where they'll be next."

Gwen shuffled over to the portal and peered through.

The wind whipped through brown grasses across the hillside. Cars drove on the road that followed the river's curves, their drivers oblivious to the figures materializing and disappearing on the hill above them.

Another sound started on the dying echoes of the wolf's howl, and Gwen scuttled back to Tristan's viewing hole. From far above them rose a chorus of voices, unlike any Gwen had heard before. High, and pure as the tone of a bell, the notes of a song without melody fell over the valley with eerie grace. Gwen found her mouth agape and was relieved that Tristan looked as awed as she felt.

"The war song of the Whitecliff realm," he whispered. "I've never heard it before. Watch the wind."

No sooner had Tristan spoken than three whirlwinds appeared over the valley, visible only from the swirling snow caught in their vortices. They spun faster and grew smaller until each was a narrow cone over the trees. Then, one by one, figures were tossed high in the air and flung into the trees. The song faded until only echoes remained, and the winds resumed their normal bluster.

"Wow," said Gwen breathlessly. "What was that? Who—"

"The other side will have some broken bones after that," said Tristan. "Out of commission for a while. The war song of Whitecliff is powerful indeed."

"Just broken bones?"

"Likely. No one aims to kill here—life is too precious for that. Disabling, capturing, injuries, those are all fair game." Tristan grimaced. "Not that broken limbs are fun, but better than dead."

"Then why don't they just sing and take out all of the

enemy?" said Gwen. She swallowed—those figures were people, people who were likely terribly injured now—but the worlds were at stake, and they couldn't afford to lose. She clenched her fists to steady herself.

"A few reasons. They need to pinpoint the exact location, and our people also need to move out of the way. And it takes a tremendous burst of power, so I've heard. I wouldn't doubt that all three of those singers are unconscious right now. There are only so many skilled enough in war song to pull off feats such as that."

"More attacks," said Devin. He leaned over the map. "Closer now. On the south bank."

"They just emerged into the human world," Rhiannon called out. "I think I can give useful directions now. Bring that map closer."

Devin hastily dragged the leather over to Rhiannon. She briefly studied it, looked through the portal, then brought her glowing fingertip to the map. It traced a path that approximated the running Breenan in the human world. Gwen kneeled behind Rhiannon, careful not to get in her way. Three Breenan sprinted across the grasslands, far above the snug cottages in the village below. They stopped abruptly, and one held out his hand.

"They're going to cross over!" Gwen cried. Rhiannon jabbed at the map. A golden dot that had been following Rhiannon's finger now pulsed with light.

"What does that mean?" Gwen asked.

"They're fighting," said Rhiannon. "But they weren't taken by surprise this time, thanks to us."

Through the bushes, sparks and flashes of light burst above the tree line at the spot marked on the map. Gwen held her breath.

Then the trees went dark. Gwen glanced at the map. The once-flickering dot now gleamed golden and steady once more. Rhiannon sighed in relief.

"They did it."

"There's more!" called Bretta at the other portal. She gestured at the map wildly and Devin pushed it between her and Rhiannon. She jabbed her finger at the map and a different golden dot followed the trace. Howls drifted across the valley and Gwen shivered.

Trees below them began to sway, unconnected to the howling winds. Tristan leaned forward.

"Were you wondering what spells the Velvet Woods can cast, Gwen? Look at those trees."

"What are they doing?" Gwen gasped. The trees looked alive, sentient, flailing wildly at something near their trunks.

"Doing their best to attack our people. Corann definitely has the room of enchantments figured out, enough for a battle, anyway."

Rhiannon and Bretta feverishly traced path after path as Breenan appeared in the human world and dashed across the hillside. Gwen peeked in. A few humans stood at their doorsteps and watched the antics above with folded arms and open mouths.

The eerie singing started again, and some trace of the sound must have made its way to the human world, because a few of the watchers crossed themselves and retreated into their houses.

Drums started, a powerful bass that forced Gwen's heart to beat in time. Rolling shudders traveled up and down Gwen's back at the combination of song and deep drum. Then a shrieking cry started, and a crowd of people in the Otherworld burst out of the tree line to cross a small meadow beside the river Kennocha. They looked mad, tearing their clothes and screaming war cries in a wild frenzy. Even from this distance, Gwen recognized the foremost figure as Loniel.

Gwen had thought the meadow empty, but that was far from the truth. Her untrained eyes had not spotted the Breenan slide behind tree and bush, but now that a frenzied horde descended upon them, all thought of hiding was gone. They sprinted before Loniel and his people, fleeing the crazed crowd. An earth tremor caused some to stumble, but Loniel's bonfire folk leaped on, undeterred.

Loniel raised his hands and grasses grew around the legs of the fleeing Breenan. They tripped and flailed, but the sparse trees growing in the meadow bent to attack the bonfire folk.

"They're everywhere!" Rhiannon shouted. "In the human world. All running toward the same place."

She and Bretta frantically traced paths with multiple fingers. Golden dots followed.

"Everyone's coming to the meadow!" Gwen said. Breenan were popping out of portals all around the grassy space in the Otherworld. There were so many portals that the air surrounding was a patchwork of human and Otherworld.

There was no pretense of hiding any longer. The Breenan on their side burst out of the woods with flinging spell stones and hands held high to cast spells. A song began again to the counterpoint of drums, and the already wild wind became focused once more. Wolves howled, and Gwen clutched Tristan's arm in fear as massive animals leaped into the fray. Flowers burst open, incongruous in the snow, and spat venom. The river rose in angry tendrils and flung itself toward the fighters. Lights flashed, and sparks flew.

Then the trees came alive. Grasping and reaching, branches flailed and dropped. Whole trunks uprooted themselves and toppled toward grappling Breenan. Screams of fear trailed up to their hidden lookout.

"Corann's too powerful." Tristan pressed his fingers to Gwen's temples and she received a flash of memory— Tristan, much younger, in a grove of trees among other students—and a pulse of knowledge in her core. "Gwen, take over Bretta's place. Bretta, come here. I have to go help."

"Tristan! Your orders are to stay here." Bretta's brow furrowed.

"I can't stand by and watch this." Tristan crashed through the bush without another word and was gone.

Gwen scuttled over the root-strewn dirt to the portal, shaking. Now what? Was everyone really relying on her?

"Gloves off, Gwen." Rhiannon was pale but composed. "The spell won't work through leather."

Gwen slipped her gloves off sweaty palms and twisted to place them behind her on the ground. Perhaps she was still shaky from Tristan's departure, or perhaps the earth shook again, but she lost her balance. Her unsupported upper body tilted in place. Both hands splayed onto the bare earth to break her fall.

And Gwen's world stopped.

Chapter 16

Sound lost all meaning. Time slowed. Everything centered within Gwen, between Gwen's core and her hands in the frozen earth. There was something in the ground. It knew she was there, somehow, a deep knowledge that had little to do with sentience. Whatever was in the ground knew her the way a mother knows the shape and solid weight of her child in her arms. The magic in Gwen's core reached out instinctively. It passed through her arms into the soil, and was met by a great welling of magic, deep and huge. Gwen felt a fierce gladness at the connection, as if she had finally found what she hadn't known she had been looking for. She was vaguely aware of her body glowing with a pure white light and her hair floating, drifting as if gravity no longer existed. She let out a long breath.

"Gwen?" Rhiannon whispered, her voice unusually timid and sounding very far away. "What's happening? Are you all right?"

"I don't know," Gwen said, her voice soft and wandering. Everything was unreal to her right now, everything except the connection.

"The trees have stopped attacking," said Bretta. She peered out to the meadow. "Everyone looks confused." She turned to look at Gwen with wide eyes. "You're the true heir. Did you just connect with the realm?"

"Is that was happened?" Gwen smiled serenely. "Neat."

Rhiannon and Bretta glanced at each other with concern, but Gwen had other things to think about. Something was interrupting her connection with the earth below. She could feel its insidious power, wrenching parts of the realm away from her knowledge. The earth magic didn't like it, she could tell, but couldn't seem to resist. Gwen explored with her mind, sending her thoughts out of her hands down through the ground, following the magic as it flowed everywhere.

She passed roots of trees, slow and green, and the pink wriggling magic of cold worms in the soil. The glow of a Breenan on the surface interested her for a moment, but she sensed it was a friend and so she moved on. Other Breenan glows passed overhead, some different, antagonistic, and she sent flares of annoyance skyward.

"What's happening to them?" Bretta said. "Something is pushing all the enemy fighters down to the ground."

"Gwen? Are you doing that?" Rhiannon kneeled in front of Gwen. "Do you have control over this?"

"Mmm, I think so," Gwen said slowly. Part of her spoke with Rhiannon, and the other part flowed through the earth under the battle. "They shouldn't be here. The magic doesn't like it."

"It's chaos down there," said Bretta. "No one knows what's happening, but they can tell it's against the other side. Corann's people are fighting hard now, desperately, really."

"Can you help our fighters?" Rhiannon asked Gwen gently.

"I'll try."

Gwen wasn't sure what to do, not really, but she wasn't anxious about it. She would simply try things until she got it right. She and the realm had only just truly met, after all, and they were still getting acquainted. She found a friendly glow, and then another, and she sent some magic up in their direction.

Then she felt the grasping, foreign power again, tugging more insistently at the magic, wresting parts of it away from her. Gwen's serenity was interrupted by indignation: how dare it? She pushed back, but the power was slippery, and Gwen didn't know enough about the magic yet to successfully repel the power. The magic funneled into the foreign power, despite her best efforts to hold on.

"It's Corann," she whispered to herself. "He shouldn't be here."

"The fighting is moving," said Bretta suddenly. "It's as if they know where we are now. We have to move."

"Not yet," said Gwen. She pushed hard at the power. Was she making headway? Gwen wasn't sure.

"Grab the map," Rhiannon told Devin. She flung a bag over her shoulders and reached for Gwen. "Come on, Gwen, we have to go."

"No…"

"Yes, they're coming—"

"Who are they?" Bretta's eyes were fixed on a new

group of fighters who ran down the hillside toward the melee. "Whose side are they on?"

Gwen reached out into the magic and felt the glows of the newcomers, bright and powerful. The magic flowed gladly under their pounding feet, and she released some to hurry their running strides.

"Ours. Definitely ours."

The new fighters brought their hands up as they approached the battle and let loose a volley of spells that lit the dim meadow with a rainbow of colors. Opponents fell unconscious left and right, and still the spells came. There were no spell stones, no songs, no venomous flowers. Simple, powerful spells poured forth from the hands of the newcomers, and few could withstand the onslaught.

"Who are they?" Rhiannon whispered. "I've never seen general spells with so much power."

With every opponent that was knocked to the ground, Gwen felt the foreign power grow angrier, but also clearer. Distance and direction of the power's source emerged from a fog.

"I know where he is," she said quietly. Rhiannon and Bretta weren't listening.

"Corann's forces are in a rout! Who are these people? This is incredible!"

An earth tremor shook them, and the wind picked up. The realm groaned under the strain of the quake. More lights flashed in the valley below.

"I know where Corann is," said Gwen, louder. "He's at the castle."

"At the castle?" Rhiannon finally answered.

"We need to go," said Gwen calmly. Another tremor, longer and stronger this time, swayed the branches around them. Gwen felt a squeeze in her core as the realm twisted and wrenched. "There's not much time. I need to take control of the realm away from Corann now."

"I suppose—everyone is in a rout—it might be safe." Rhiannon looked doubtful.

"Now," Gwen said firmly.

Rhiannon drew out some stones and touched them with a glowing finger in a pattern.

"I told the king where we're going."

Gwen lifted her hands with reluctance but found herself still pleasantly connected to the magic of the realm. It wasn't as immediate and clear, but it was there.

"Let's go," she said.

***

An attendant leaped up from where she sat before a row of colored stones. Faolan glanced at her, while the other rulers talked and gestured at the foliage-covered wall of the tent.

"My lord," she said. "A message from the fighting group with the heir. Gwendolyn has sensed that Corann is at the castle, and she and her group are going there now."

Faolan turned to the other rulers.

"It is time," he barked. "The battle has turned, and the heir approaches her room of enchantments. Come, let us clear the way for her coronation. Corann must be removed."

He swept out of the tent, and the others followed.

Outside, a row of horses waited in the snow. Their hot breath formed clouds that were whisked away in the wind. Faolan vaulted onto a chestnut-brown horse and cantered away without waiting. Queen Brenna was next, her blue cape a swirl behind her as she leaped into her saddle. Isolde mounted a nearby horse with less enthusiasm and followed the rulers through the snowstorm. A crowd of waiting fighters trailed behind.

When they reached the castle after a swift ride, Faolan and the other rulers dismounted and strode up the steps of the castle. Isolde's lips trembled as she looked up at the ruins of her former home, and she followed the fighters inside with halting footsteps.

From the ballroom came shouts of fighters and flashes of magical light, but the few guards that were left in the castle quickly fell captive to the greater numbers. Isolde hung back near a shadowy pillar while the rulers marched toward a carved wooden door behind the dais. Faolan flung it open.

Inside the room of enchantments, Corann kneeled on the center of the daisy. Three frightened-looking people in simple wool cloaks were clustered around him. The glow of magic faded when Corann looked up at the intruders.

"It's over, Corann," said Faolan with a heavy finality. "Your forces have been overcome. Surrender."

Corann's eyes blazed for a moment, then dimmed. He hung his head.

"So be it."

Isolde looked away. Her eyes blinked rapidly.

***

Gwen took the lead, to the immense surprise of Rhiannon. Gwen could feel exactly where the castle was, the room of enchantments within it, and Corann, and it was simple to follow the pull. Tree roots and stones were no impediment to her feet, made nimble with the knowledge of their placement. She loped ahead, tireless and steady despite the swirling snow, the warmth of the realm's magic residing deep in her core.

"Come on," she called to the others. "Keep up!"

From Rhiannon's stupefied expression, she had not expected this burst of energy and skill from Gwen. Gwen chuckled to herself. The last time she had traveled with Rhiannon, she could barely ride a horse. Now she felt like she could do anything. It probably wasn't true, but it was a euphoric feeling nonetheless.

Gwen didn't know how long they ran for. All she knew was the feeling of her destination getting closer and closer. The room of enchantments called to her, like a lighthouse to a searching boat at night. At one point, she felt a pulse in the magic, and the sensation of the foreign power retreating made her smile in satisfaction. The ground trembled, and she ran faster.

"We're almost there," she called to the others. Grunts of acknowledgement greeted her words—no one had breath to spare for talking.

They stumbled upon a well-trod path and ran through a clearing where the trees were singed as from a fire. Gwen nodded to herself—this was where she had first discovered her magic and made a portal, so many months ago. They rounded a corner and the castle rose before them, imposing amid the trees. The crenelated turrets were rounded and crumbling, and torn pennants whipped on their poles in a frenzy. A bevy of horses huddled in a cluster beside the stone wall with steaming breath. Heedless of danger, Gwen sprinted up the stone steps to the open ballroom doors. She ignored Rhiannon's shouts and ran inside.

There was a crowd of people in the ballroom, including Faolan and the other rulers. The scent of drying furs and leathers permeated the air. Corann was on his knees against a pillar on the ballroom floor, ropes wrapped around his wrists and ankles. He saw Gwen first, and his look was of loss and resignation, with only a hint of hate left for her. Faolan turned at the sound of Gwen's footsteps, and his face registered relief. The building shook and groaned, but Gwen anticipated it and kept her footing while dust rained down on her party. Faolan noted her sure-footedness and nodded.

"Gwendolyn. Well met. I see you have somehow begun the process of connection for your coronation. It was you who changed the course of the battle, for which we are grateful."

Gwen frowned.

"It wasn't entirely me. That last group of fighters, they really made the difference."

Faint confusion crossed Faolan's face.

"We still aren't sure who they are. Nevertheless, if they present themselves, they will have our thanks. But we must set that matter aside. Time is running out, and you must assume your position as queen of the Velvet Woods."

Gwen closed her eyes. Here it was, the moment she'd been expecting and dreading since Isolde had turned up on her great-aunt's doorstep. Was it only four days ago? Gwen felt a lifetime older. She thought of her life, and mentally said goodbye to everything: her new apartment, her studies, her favorite coffee shop, the dance class with her best friend Ellie, Sunday dinners with her father, Aidan… but at that thought, she closed off the memories. It was time to say goodbye. There was no point dwelling on them. She couldn't dwell on them without bursting into an endless ocean of tears, so she didn't let herself feel. This decision was not for her, it was to save untold people, Breenan and human both, whose lives would be destroyed if the realms ripped.

She had a sudden insight into her request to Isolde back in May, when she had asked for the locket that brought in humans to power the realm. What it must have taken Isolde to give her the necklace, to do something that would hurt the realm—Gwen now understood the enormity of her demand.

It didn't matter what Gwen wanted. This was the right thing to do. The pure fire of that thought, while it didn't warm her the way her memories did, gave her enough resolve to open her eyes.

"I'm ready."

Faolan's eyes held a hint of compassion, but he waved forward two attendants. One hung a green velvet cape from her shoulders, its edges finished with gold braid. The other held out Gwen's tiara on a pillow. Faolan took it and placed it on Gwen's head.

"I have heard it is customary for human rulers to make vows and proclamations upon their coronation," he said quietly. "Those are unnecessary here. Once you have fully bound with your realm, you will know what is best for it and for your people. The vow you make is an unspoken one, but no less powerful. But you understand that already, don't you?"

Gwen nodded. She could feel the magic of the realm under her feet, in the air around her, and deep in her core. Her eyes moved from Faolan's to the door of the room of enchantments, behind the dais in the corner. Its carved wooden door beckoned her. She walked toward it with measured steps.

"Niece! Have you changed your mind?"

Chapter 17

It took a full astonished heartbeat for Gwen to understand the meaning of those words. When the truth dawned on her, she spun around.

Finn and Aidan stood at the front of a crowd of people. Kelan and Nialla were there, along with Fearghus, Mabina, and others from the Forbidden Lands. On every tribeless wrist was a copper bracelet. Gwen's hand flew to her mouth and her knees wobbled. Then she ran to Aidan and flung herself in his waiting arms. He squeezed her until she could scarcely breathe. She lifted her face to see Finn's beaming one.

"Shall I go back, Gwen? Would you like to be queen?"

"No!" she blurted out, then let out a hysterical giggle. "No, you're just in time."

Gwen couldn't help herself—she pressed her lips to Aidan's and he eagerly responded. An earth tremor made him sway.

"Gwendolyn." Faolan's voice was sharp. "We have very little time. You must enter the room."

She disentangled herself from Aidan.

"King Faolan, meet Finn, my uncle and the future king of the Velvet Woods."

The other rulers gasped and muttered. Faolan fixed Finn with a beady eye.

"It was you," he said slowly. "You and your followers turned the tide of the battle."

"It was," Finn said calmly. "I brought my friends and countrymen with me. They are all people of great power and greater hearts. They are the tribeless ones."

Silence and wide eyes followed this proclamation. Finn stood quiet and self-assured. Gwen was impressed with his poise and could see him clearly as a king.

"We found a solution for the tribeless ones," she said into the silence. She looked to Aidan for confirmation.

"Bracelets with the magic-dampening spell on them," said Aidan. "And tuned to the strength needed for each wearer. It's permanent and portable."

"There is no need for the Forbidden Lands now," said Gwen. "And Finn can rule with his tribeless wife and daughter by his side."

"And when I am king," Finn said. "All tribeless ones will be welcome in my realm."

Queen Ula stepped forward.

"May I see your charm?"

Nialla held out her arm. Queen Ula touched the bracelet for a few moments.

"Ingenious," she said. "Astounding."

"But we can't have tribeless ones running around uncontained!" said King Gavin. "They're far too dangerous. Wild and out of control."

"Only without this spell!" Gwen said with heat.

273

"It might work," said Queen Ula. "It might."

"Are you willing to stake the safety of your people on it?" said King Gavin.

"And how did they manage to fight—and win—the battle today?" demanded Gwen. "If they're so uncontrollable, how did they harness their power to take down our enemies? And now they stand here, calmly waiting for you to accept them. They have as much right to be here as you do, and even if I were taking the throne, you can bet they would be as welcome in my realm as they will be in Finn's!"

She breathed hard. Queen Ula faced King Gavin.

"It really will work, King Gavin. I've never seen its like. The bracelets will work."

King Gavin threw up his hands. Faolan stepped over to Nialla and touched the bracelet.

"I believe they will. Well, it is your realm to rule as you will. You may have an uphill battle for acceptance of the tribeless ones, but you are free to try if you wish. Now, Gwendolyn, I must give you the spell to transfer heirship." He placed his fingertips firmly on Gwen's temples, and the warmth in Gwen's core was accompanied by a vision of a much younger Faolan with a be-crowned older woman who might have been his mother.

"Now, go," Faolan said as another tremor shook the floor under their feet. "End this once and for all."

"Wait," said Isolde. She hurried to Finn with a coronet in her hands. It was a golden circlet of overlapping leaves with ruby berries sprinkled throughout. "A crown for my brother-king." She smiled. "Welcome to the family."

Finn nodded his thanks, and he and Gwen strode to the

274

room of enchantments. The door swung open of its own accord when they approached, and the light from twelve white-flamed lanterns glowed over the threshold. Gwen took a deep breath and walked inside.

***

As soon as Gwen stepped into the room, she felt that same sense of blissful connection she had felt when her hands had touched the ground of the Velvet Woods. She smiled in recognition, and her eyes closed. Now that Corann's coercive presence was gone, her consciousness could stretch to every part of the realm. Every tree, every sleeping squirrel, every forest family snug in their cottage, every living thing announced its presence with a soft glow to the magic of the realm. It was intoxicating. The magic welcomed her, folding her essence into itself until she wasn't sure where she ended, and it began.

She opened her eyes. Finn gazed at her with a curious expression on his face.

"You feel the connection, don't you?" he said. "My mother spoke of it. Are you sure you want to give it up?"

Gwen thought for a moment. She considered the draw of the realm and the feeling of belonging. Then she thought of Aidan. It wasn't a long moment.

"Yes, I'm sure." She took a deep breath and released it slowly, then addressed the room. "I'm sorry, realm, but I have to go. I'm leaving you in good hands, though. This is my uncle Finn. You'll meet him in a minute." She turned to Finn. "Are you ready?"

He nodded with determination.

"Yes. You may begin."

Gwen closed her eyes and brought out the magic from her core in the way Faolan had taught her. The lanterns dimmed, and a warmth flowed over her. The deeper magic of the realm felt confused, searching. Gwen touched her palm to Finn's forehead, who closed his eyes. The magic found him, poured into him through Gwen, and her back arched as it flowed past her and into Finn, who glowed with a brilliant white light. Yipping and howling, growling and chirping, animal noises of all kinds filled the air. The carved animals on the walls jumped and ran, suddenly alive with the magic flowing through Gwen to Finn. Eventually, the sensation of connection grew less and less, until the last speck of the magic passed out of Gwen and she fell to her knees, empty, drained. The animals froze in their carvings. Finn's glow faded, and he took a shuddering breath.

"It's done." He scrubbed his face and let out a low whistle. "This is life-changing, isn't it?"

He held out a hand to Gwen, who hauled herself up from the floor. She was shaky and felt a profound sense of loss, but also very free. She had been so distracted by the heady connection to all life that she hadn't truly noticed the weight of responsibility for everything. Now that it was gone, she felt lighter than air.

"Are you okay?" she asked Finn.

"I think so. And yourself?"

"Never better." Gwen smiled widely and untied the velvet cape from her neck to drape over Finn's shoulders. It looked good on him. She plucked the tiara off her head and admired it for a moment. The blue sapphires and emeralds winked in the lanterns' light. Gwen held it out to Finn.

"Here. Your daughter will need it one day."

Finn smiled at Gwen.

"I never expected to see this day. Me, a king, and my wife and daughter able to live freely... thank you, Gwen."

"Thanks for giving me a chance. And for the gift of choosing my own path." Gwen gave him a swift, spontaneous hug. "Come on, let's greet your new subjects."

Gwen let Finn exit first, and applause and cheering greeted him. It started with the tribeless ones, Nialla and Ione at the forefront, but quickly spread to the others present. Even a few of Corann's advisors tried hard to not look interested. Finn raised his hand in acknowledgement. When the applause died down, he spoke.

"Thank you, all, for your efforts to install a true heir on the throne of the Velvet Woods. I will endeavor to treat my people justly, to defend them when needed, and to protect the realm: stone, animal, and tree."

Another round of cheering burst out. Gwen took the pause to open a small portal. Would it close? She waited, breath held, until it shrank to a pinpoint and vanished. She sighed with relief, and suddenly the weight of her tiredness descended on her. She looked past the crowd to the open doorway, through which a gentle snow was falling, devoid of harsh winds and uninterrupted by earthquakes.

Faolan approached Finn, with the other rulers close behind.

"Welcome to the alliance of the nine realms, King Finn. Our first order of business is to decide the fate of our

277

prisoners." Faolan waved at Corann and the other two rulers. "The fighters are being held outside, the ones we managed to catch. As well, there are five strangely dressed humans whom we have captured. As the leader of the wronged party, and a member of the alliance, your opinion is desired."

Finn nodded.

"Thank you, King Faolan. I would suggest a release of the other rulers and their fighters. No good will come of a fractured alliance, and I'm sure they had their reasons. Of course, they will need to pledge their acceptance of my rule."

"Of course," said Faolan.

"And those of the Velvet Woods, those who are willing to live under my rule may go free. Those who are not willing may live in the Forbidden Lands."

Faolan's mouth twitched with the hint of a smile.

"As for the humans, I will send them to their home shortly," Finn said.

Faolan turned to the other rulers.

"Are there any objections to King Finn's suggested course of action?"

Heads shook. King Gavin stepped forward.

"I'll keep my eye on King Weylin, make sure he stays in line."

"Excellent." Faolan clapped his hands. "We should move while we still have light, but you all are summoned in a week's time to Wintertree, since conclave ended so abruptly. Saving the worlds is something worth celebrating."

Nialla slipped her hand into Finn's with a happy smile.

He stiffened, and his gazed turned inward. Then he beckoned to Gwen. She hurried over.

"Gwen. When Nialla took my hand, I felt the realm respond. Do you remember when I said that the tribeless ones' magic was like that of a ruler's?"

"Ardra and forest people. One temporary, the other permanent," said Gwen. "What are you saying?"

"The realm. Do you think…"

Gwen lifted her eyebrows.

"You could use their magic to power the realm's defenses?" She looked at Nialla with consideration. "Take her into the room and see what happens."

Finn pulled Nialla eagerly toward the carved door. She followed him into the room of enchantments with a bewildered look on her face. Faolan stepped closer.

"What is happening?"

"Finn thinks he might have a way to power the defenses. The realm is somehow connecting to the tribeless ones. Perhaps because they have powerful Ardra magic that is more permanently connected to the forest? Finn said it was like a ruler's magic."

Faolan looked thoughtful. Finn burst out of the room of enchantments, beaming. He hurried over, Nialla still in tow.

"She is connected! Only a little, and nowhere near the connection I have, but I felt the realm grow stronger with her presence."

Faolan gave him a slight smile.

"Then you have the solution to the question of your defenses. Connect the tribeless ones who are willing, send them to live as stewards throughout the realm, and your realm will prosper with its new power."

"Tribeless ones! My neighbors and my friends!" Finn shouted out. "Anyone who wishes to be a steward of the forest will be connected to the realm and strengthen the defenses of your new home. Who will come forward?"

A great cheer arose from the gathered crowd, and a press of people surged forward.

***

Isolde slid quietly to Corann's side in his place beside a wide pillar. He had no guards, as his ropes were strong and infused with protection against magic. Corann looked up at her with bitterness.

"Are you happy now?"

"No," said Isolde softly. "Nothing about this makes me happy. How did we come to this?" She waved at Corann's ropes, the occupied ballroom, the dust on the floor and the tapestries askew on the walls. Corann hung his head.

"I don't know. Everything went too far, out of control. I only wanted you to be safe." He looked up at her with eyes that pleaded for understanding. "I couldn't bear to see you sick again."

Isolde placed a hand on Corann's cheek, and he leaned into it.

"Thank you for loving me that much. But next time, speak to me first. I promise I will try to listen."

Corann looked confused.

"Next time?"

Isolde glanced around, but all eyes were fixed on the new king and had no attention to spare for the kneeling prisoner. Isolde slipped a little knife from a small sheath on her belt and neatly sliced Corann's bonds. She slid a blackened steel tracker ring on his finger, the exact shade of her raven hair.

"When I am with the crowd once more, take your chance," she whispered in his ear, then kissed him lightly on the lips and glided away.

Corann waited until Isolde blended into the crowd. Then he melted into the shadows against the wall and slid to the doors.

Once outside, he took a deep breath, then ran lightly down the steps. No one was in sight, and he kept running through the white forest. His light steps left footprints beside clusters of early snowdrops that pushed through the snow.

From the distance drifted the sound of crackling wood and the murmur of happy voices. Drums began to pound with an insistent throb. Corann paused, undecided. Then he directed his feet toward the promise of the bonfire.

***

Gwen ran to Aidan's side while Finn spoke with the tribeless ones. He welcomed her with a fierce hug.

"We did it."

"We did it." Gwen laughed. "It's still sinking in. Finn is king, and I can go home. How did you manage with the bracelets?"

"Yes, I want to hear this," said Bran, who had sidled over to them. "Tell us the whole tale."

"There's not much to tell, really. We tried different

281

versions of the healing spell and binding spell, with some spells in reverse, and worked backward to reinvent the dampening spell. We must have walked through the tunnels a dozen times to get past the boundary and test the bracelet. There were dry tunnels, by the way, the Ardra only send new tribeless ones through the lake because they don't know any better. Eventually we set up camp at the tunnel entrance." Aidan squeezed Gwen's shoulders. "But we did it. Nialla was overwhelmed, I think. We all ran back to the village and she and Finn started banging on doors and spreading the news. Within an hour, Fearghus had given us enough bracelets for everyone and we cast the spell on them all."

"How did you get everyone to the Velvet Woods so quickly?" asked Gwen.

"Once we'd walked through the tunnels, your Dad had the great idea to rent a couple of big vans. We drove them all to Amberlaine, and I made a portal. It wasn't hard to find the battle—we weren't far away—and we came in with guns blazing, so to speak."

"You weren't fighting, were you?" said Gwen with a frown.

"They made me hang in the back, but I brought down one fighter," Aidan said with pride. "But I mostly let the tribeless ones take over. They were ferocious, mainly because they're so glad to use magic again."

"I wish I'd been there to see," said Bran wistfully.

"You were in the battle," said Gwen in surprise.

"Well, yes, but Aidan tells a good tale of the journey." Bran looked over at Faolan, who was gesturing to his people to prepare to leave. "Will I see you soon?" he asked. Gwen and Aidan glanced at each other.

"We're leaving," said Gwen. "Going back to Vancouver, I mean. I don't know when we'll be back."

"And we can't rely on the portals always opening," Aidan added. "If one of our anchors dies, we can't pass through. We're reliant on them. Think of Finn."

Bran deflated. Gwen didn't think she had ever seen him so sad. Gwen bit her lip, then looked at Aidan and touched her necklace. Aidan looked surprised, then he laughed aloud.

"If you want."

"Bran, I'm going to give you the locket, but you have to promise to use it carefully." Gwen pulled the necklace off her neck.

Bran looked dumbfounded. Then his face split open in a wide smile.

"Truly?"

"Let's make it a little safer," said Aidan. He plucked a few hairs out of his head and folded them into the locket. "You know my father Declan, and here, let me show you my mum." Aidan touched Bran's temple with one hand.

"Cool trick," said Gwen, impressed.

"Nice, right?" said Aidan. "I gave Bran a mental image. Hopefully, it will stick. Anyway, now if something happens to one anchor, he'll still be able to get home."

Gwen whirled toward Bran.

"And for goodness' sake, don't tell your father I gave you this. He would hunt me down, human world or not."

"Are you kidding? This is a secret, for certain. He gave all the other amulets to Loniel, apparently. Loniel wanted to burn them in his bonfire. What a waste. This is

283

incredible! I can visit the human world!"

"And who knows, we might meet again. Perhaps one day I'll open a consulting firm in the Otherworld," said Aidan, laughing. "Ingenuity for hire. What do you think?"

Gwen bumped his shoulder with hers.

"I think you're crazy."

Kelan and Finn approached them.

"Bran, Kelan," said Finn. "I'm eager to include the tribeless ones in my realm, but I'm not naïve. I know there will be resistance, despite their new role as stewards of the realm. Would you be willing to work with me on improving relations between tribeless ones and other Breenan, both here and in other realms?"

Kelan nodded, and Bran quickly followed.

"We would be honored," said Kelan. "If Father agrees, of course. He is our king, after all."

"I passed the idea by him," said Finn with a smile. "He approved."

Gwen sighed a happy sigh. Corann was finally dealt with, the realm and its people were safe again, and she was going home. She looked over to the pillar where Corann was. Only a bundle of ropes remained.

"Finn!" she yelled. "Corann's gone!"

Everyone spun around at Gwen's words, but Corann was no longer in the ballroom. The other rulers showed some consternation, but Finn shrugged.

"He's no longer a threat. Let him run—we have what we need here."

"If that is your decision, then I will abide by it," said Faolan. He strode forward to speak quietly to Finn, and Gwen had to strain her ears to hear. "Corann confessed that he took control of the realm by harnessing the power of a group of forest people, in conjunction with his own magic. The combination of magics seemed enough to wrest control, enough for a battle, at any rate. I recommend you keep that information to yourself, however. We do not want to give unscrupulous subjects the power of usurpation." In a louder voice he said, "I will take my leave. Farewell, King Finn, and I will anticipate your arrival next week."

They joined foreheads in the customary Breenan greeting, and Finn said farewell to the other rulers. Bran folded Gwen in a hug, then touched foreheads with Aidan. Kelan did the same.

"Goodbye, my friends," said Bran. His voice caught. "I wish things were a little different."

"Bye, Bran." Gwen's eyes misted. She blinked quickly and pasted on a smile. "Thanks for always being there for us."

He and Kelan followed their father out the door, and Aidan gave her a one-armed hug.

"You never know," he said. "Perhaps one day."

Finn waved at a figure across the room. Isolde looked surprised but glided over.

"Isolde, my sister," said Finn. "Thank you for joining us."

Isolde bowed her head in acknowledgement.

"I have found some humans locked in the castle," She waved at the side of the ballroom, where a man and a woman stood shivering. "You may wish to return them to their home."

Finn nodded with approval.

"Excellent." He glanced briefly at Gwen. "I have a request for you, Isolde. As many have pointed out, I have little experience with ruling. I would be grateful if you would reside in the castle with me and act as my advisor. Your understanding of the realm and its people would be invaluable to my rule."

Isolde's eyes softened with pleasure and relief, although she did her best to hide it.

"Thank you, brother. I would be honored—" Isolde swallowed, then smiled. "To serve you." She curtsied deeply, and Gwen was gratified by Isolde's humility. In a more familiar tone, Isolde said, "The best guestroom will be ample for me, thank you." She turned to Gwen and cautiously took Gwen's hand in both of hers. Gwen didn't resist. "Farewell, Gwendolyn. Whatever our differences, I am always grateful that I had the chance to know you, a little."

Gwen didn't know what to say to this, so she just smiled and squeezed Isolde's hand in return. Isolde gazed into her eyes, nodded once, then gracefully moved away. Gwen shook her head.

"How do you think it'll turn out having her as your advisor?" she asked Finn. He shrugged.

"It's a big castle, and she is family, after all. But if she starts giving me too much unsolicited advice, we'll have words." He grinned, and Gwen laughed. Then she sobered.

"What about the humans Faolan mentioned?"

"Ah, yes. And those that Isolde found. Shall we go see about sending them home?"

Finn beckoned the humans over, and they approached warily. Outside and around the corner of the castle, a group of five figures in orange hazmat suits peered through face shields. Gwen hid a smile behind her hand.

"Friends," Finn said. He approached the group with welcoming arms. "Are you lost? Where do you come from?"

The figures milled about and muttered among themselves. One stepped forward and cleared his throat.

"We're from a place called Great Britain, Earth," he said, his words clearly pronounced as if Finn didn't speak English well. Gwen tried to keep her face expressionless, although it was increasingly difficult to not laugh.

"And I imagine you would like to go back there now. Your way through has closed, but my niece here can make you another one. Gwen? Would you do the honors?"

"Of course," she said, and held out her arm. A wide portal ripped open to expose a soggy field with a hedgerow nearby. The man and woman from the castle sprinted toward the portal and disappeared without a word. When the other figures didn't move, she said, "You'd better hurry. It will close in a few seconds."

Four of the figures immediately scrambled to be the first through the portal. The leader paused briefly before them.

"We have so many questions," he said. "What is—"

"Quick!" Gwen said. "It's closing!"

The man threw an agonized glance around the forest, then leaped after his colleagues. The portal healed shut. Aidan chuckled.

"They'll be wondering forever."

Gwen laughed too.

"Poor guys. Well, we need to go, I'm sure my dad is

anxiously waiting."

"Of course," said Finn. "Thanks will never be enough, but you have mine all the same, both of you."

"You too," Gwen said. "Thanks for everything."

They walked down the path until the castle was out of sight. Gwen was startled to hear a bird trilling in the distance. The sun peeked out from the clouds and a gentle dripping sound filled the air.

"A bit early for spring, isn't it?" said Aidan, but his face turned to the sun with an expression of satisfaction.

"A little reprieve." Gwen slipped her hand into Aidan's. "And a promise."

"Do you think we'll ever come back?"

"Who knows? I have no idea what the future will hold, and that's an amazing feeling. All I know is that it doesn't involve being a queen in the Otherworld."

"Or dancing forever."

Gwen laughed, then squeezed Aidan's hand.

"All I know is that it's with you."

He took her face in his other hand and kissed her deeply but slowly, leisurely, as if they had all the time in the world. And Gwen realized that they did.

She pulled away and kissed him lightly on the nose.

"Let's go before we get stuck here again."

Aidan nodded fervently.

"Let's go home."

Gwen raised her hand and opened a portal large enough for the two of them to walk through hand in hand, and they left the Otherworld. The portal wavered for a few moments, then shivered and mended itself. It grew smaller and smaller until at last the window to the human world disappeared.

The portal was closed.

Dear reader,

I hope you enjoyed reading *Realm of the Forgotten*. We've traveled a long way with Gwen and her friends since *Mark of the Breenan*, and it's been a ride I've enjoyed sharing with you.

I have a favor to ask of you. If you're so inclined, I'd love a review of *Realm of the Forgotten*, or any of the books in the Breenan series. If you loved it, if you hated it, if you're somewhere in the middle—I want to know what you think. I write because it is a joy to explore Gwen's world, but I also write for lovers of the fantastical. Reviews are difficult to come by, and you have the power to make or break a book. You can find my book list if you search for my name on Amazon and on Goodreads.

If you enjoyed Gwen's adventures in the Otherworld, you may enjoy my other series. Check out my webpage or sign up for my newsletter at emmashelford.com where you can receive news of upcoming releases and sneak peeks.

Happy reading!
Emma Shelford

Titles by Emma Shelford

Breenan Series
Mark of the Breenan
Garden of Last Hope
Realm of the Forgotten

Musings of Merlin Series
Ignition
Winded

Acknowledgements

My editors were exemplary as usual, and deserve all the applause: Gillian Brownlee, Wendy and Chris Callendar, Jude Powell, and Kathryn Humphries. Christien Gilston scored again with his beautiful book cover design. My husband, Steven Shelford, supports me always, in so many ways. And to Oliver Shelford, for bringing me joy and for teaching me the meaning of the word efficiency.

About the Author

Emma Shelford is the author of fantasy novels for adults and young adults, including the Breenan Series and the Musings of Merlin Series. She adores fantasy and history, which makes writing these series such a joy. She lives in Victoria, BC with her husband and young son.

28231661R00176

Printed in Poland
by Amazon Fulfillment
Poland Sp. z o.o., Wrocław